STELLA

STELLA

Eric
Morecambe
with Gary Morecambe

SEVERN HOUSE PUBLISHERS

This first world edition published 1986 by
SEVERN HOUSE PUBLISHERS LTD of
4 Brook Street, London W1Y 1AA

British Library Cataloguing in Publication Data
Morecambe, Eric
Stella.
I. Title
823'.914 [F]   PR6063.067/
ISBN 0-7278-1391-9

Printed in Great Britain
at the University Printing House, Oxford

Dedication

This book is dedicated to the memory of my father-in-law, Major Derek Allen, who in the short time I knew him managed to teach me the many benefits of self-confidence.

Also to the doctors and staff at Harefield Hospital to whom my family are ever indebted for the five extra years of life they gave to my father.

And my thanks to Susan Mott who so patiently and efficiently typed out the final draft copy of *Stella* for me.

G. M. 1986

Introduction

It must have been about two days after my father's untimely death that I ventured into his upstairs office.

It had taken some courage to do this, because this book-laden room was his shrine, and almost every previous time that I had entered it I had discovered his hunched figure poised over his portable typewriter, the whole room engulfed with smoke from his meerschaum pipe.

The acrid smell of stale tobacco still lingered, and would continue to for weeks to come. The silent typewriter was still sitting in the position it had been when my father had last sat in front of it. I would have paid no more attention, had it not been for the sheet of paper that caught my eye.

Headed STELLA, P.61, there were only about eight typed lines on the sheet. I cannot wholly recall what they said, but it was enough to remind me that my father had been deeply involved in what would have been his second novel.

Intrigued, I began a search for notes, pages, anything that had been destined for the novel. It was remarkable just how much turned up considering that he had never before kept many notes. But then, as we discovered shortly after his death, it was as though he knew that something was going to happen to him, because he had tidied up most aspects of his life from taxation to photo albums.

Anyway, by the end of that day spent searching, I had gathered nearly two thirds of the manuscript—some completed, some merely in note form.

I asked my mother how she would feel about me taking on the project of finishing the novel. 'It's a good idea,' she said. 'He had spent much of his time on it. It would be nice to see it finished.' And so my first draft of STELLA went into production.

He had often talked to me about STELLA, quoting lines from it, showing me the latest passage he was working on, and explaining that the background would be very similar to his own. I would smile and listen attentively, glad to see the pleasure it was giving him, but totally unaware that day I would desperately be racking my brain for those little snippets of information he had casually given to me.

Stella's background is very similar to his own. She even plays in the streets he played in when he was a boy. In fact, the pattern of Stella's career is not so different from his own, though I'm sure he won far more talent competitions than poor Stella is allowed to win in this story.

While the characters are not based on particular individuals, there is a sense of recognition about them. They suit the story so well, one can't help but assume that they closely resemble many of the people my father had to contend with on his way to the top.

Perhaps it was because most of the work I did on this book was carried out at the same desk in the same favourite office of my father's that I felt he was ever-present, and always there to give me a guiding hand. And during the more hilarious pieces I worked on I am convinced I could hear him chuckling over my shoulder at his own lines. So, in a strange way I feel we worked at the book together and not independently.

The office has altered very little during the last two years and I still often use it, convinced it is a source of great inspiration to me.

My father's notes on Stella are now blended with mine in brown and blue card-board folders that line a shelf of the study. They represent the months of pleasure I derived from putting the novel together. I hope you derive as much pleasure from reading it.

Gary Morecambe
1986

Chapter 1

Stella stood in the wings. Her eyes were unblinking, her vision not focusing, her mind remembering the past and not caring too much about the future.

Somehow she had managed to reach the theatre through her haze of confusion, to change into the right clothes and prepare to face an ecstatic audience.

But she hadn't felt it had been she who had done these things: it wasn't she who was the star of the show and who was supposed to now be enthralling and entertaining some of her vast following who had paid to see her that night. She remembered the letter. She would always remember that letter until the day she died. She shuddered: death wasn't a subject she wanted to think about.

She gave an ironic laugh that more resembled a cough, and thought of her sister.

Fifteen years ago she couldn't have begun to guess at what life held for her – the tears, the joy, and the horror.

It had started as a dream, and as if by magic had been transformed into reality.

Like the letter, she would always remember the last fifteen years of her life most vividly . . .

The change in what could only be described as a typical, unexceptional, northern upbringing of the early part of the twentieth century began in Lancaster in 1924. During that year, Stella Ravenscroft grew into a sprightly ten-year-old and her sister, Sadie, into a more subdued eight-year-old. They were inseparable chums, though Stella made sure her sister knew who was boss, and it was something Sadie would never be allowed to forget.

It was a bleak January that had hailed the beginning to that year, the city being buried beneath an unmoving thin white carpet of crisp snow. Returning home from school one evening during that month, Sadie revealed that she had heard that Tommy Moran – Stella's childhood sweetheart – had kissed Molly Chadwick.

'Whereabouts did she kiss him?' demanded Stella.

'On the mouth,' innocently replied her sister.

'No. I mean *where*? You know – *where*?'

'Oh. Outside the tobacconist's on't corner of Penny Street.'

She threatened to give her sister a Chinese burn if she didn't expand on her story of the event. As she roughly grabbed her wrists Sadie blurted, 'Winnie Robinson told me.'

'When?'

'This morning.'

'Tommy kissed Molly this morning, eh?'

'No,' she said. 'Winnie *told* me this morning.' Then she added, 'And you know that Winnie never tells lies.'

Stella released her prisoner, if only for the time being.

The familiar greyness of Corkell's Yard loomed up before them as it always did when they neared Penny Street. It was an unremarkable collection of grim-looking buildings, and if you closed your eyes there wasn't a single definite feature that would come to mind. Yet the two whitewashed cottages and one wooden shack that held a bench lav was home.

They pulled up short of the yard so Stella could give the tobacconist's some scornful glances. Sadie asked her in a whisper, 'Are you never going to forgive Tommy, now he is not pure?'

'Them's private matters,' she replied brusquely, 'and certainly not for the ears of younger sisters.'

Sadie was well acquainted with Stella's manner and just mouthed an 'Oh', before digging into her pocket to pull out a boiled sweet she had been saving.

She dropped it into the snow and Stella gave a short,

2

derisive laugh. Unabashed, she bent down, picked it up, and popped it into her mouth.

Stella winced with mock revulsion, and said, 'I'm going to tell our Mam. It's disgusting, is that.' She didn't add that she was jealous she hadn't a boiled sweet to eat.

'Tell-tale tit, yer tongue be split,' retorted her sister, and at once took flight in the direction of Corkell's Yard and the safety of home. Stella was a fast runner, and in spite of Sadie's lead they entered the tiny house together.

In the downstairs room there was a gas light, and an oil lamp on the window ledge but it was rarely lit, and now was no exception. Next to it a candle lay horizontal on a chipped green saucer, where it had fallen the previous night and hadn't been uprighted again. Both box-like bedrooms upstairs had a candle of their own, and the one in their parents' room had a proper candle holder.

In winter they were grateful for the cooking range as it kept the rooms warm, but in summer it kept them hot. The planked front door had a thick curtain across it on the inside, supposedly to help shield against the draughts, but it was so full of tears and holes that it had become more of a hindrance than a help.

Mrs Ravenscroft ensured that their house was kept in a sustained state of cleanliness but she didn't extend this virtue upon herself. The range was as black and shiny as a full bottle of Guinness and the windows were washed daily. Her saying was, 'Cleanliness is next to godliness, but in Corkell's Yard it's next to impossible.'

She was smiling to herself about her saying when the sound of her daughters' feet cracking against the iced cobblestones caught her attention. Instinctively she glanced across the kitchen to a battered cuckoo clock that for many years had given out the incorrect time. It was a habit of hers to check the time. She liked to note how long it had taken them to get from school back to home and, of course, always took into account the temperamental nature of the clock.

'Hello, Mam,' cried both girls.

'Wipe your feet,' came the firm response, but it was delivered in a gentle way. They both immediately back-stepped to the doormat.

3

'What's for tea, Mam?' asked Sadie, always first to make enquiries on the food situation.

'Balloons on toast,' kidded her mother with a little smile forming on her lined face.

She was a tall woman with a frail frame, and the only secret she'd ever kept was her age. She never lied about this, she merely stated that she was the same age as her sister-in-law, Mildred from Carlisle, and then lied about *her* age.

Her father was called Sven Ronnorf and was Swedish. Her mother, Daisy, was pure Lancashire. Both had been dead for some years, or at least, as Jack Ravenscroft would say, 'I hope they're dead – we buried 'em.' Ronnorf had been a stoker on a Swedish cargo vessel that used to bring wood to the Lancaster Docks. Then, in 1885, having met Daisy several times, he proposed to her, married her, and settled in Lancaster.

Lilly was very proud, if not a little touchy, about her Swedish background. Although born in Lancaster, and unable to speak more than two or three Swedish words, none of which were clean, she would proudly tell her daughters all about life in Sweden, as though she had spent most of her own life there.

Stella and Sadie couldn't wait to visit this mysterious land, having heard from their mother how they lived off giant black puddings and green shrimps.

'Go on, Mam. What's for tea?' Sadie pressed.

'I've told you once. It's balloons on toast, and you'll have to eat them quick before they fly away.'

'No, Mam, truthfully,' she pleaded. Stella always ignored all this mundane twaddle, as she called it. She knew it was all a tease and that it would conclude in them having a normal tea.

Stella peered out of the window at the house next door, hoping to catch a glimpse of Tommy Moran. Tommy was quite nice even though he was supposed to have kissed Molly Chadwick, she thought. He was certainly more likeable than his younger brother Colin. He was horrible, and his nose was always running.

'Your father will be in within the hour and it's his favourite, so I thought you could have a mug of tea and a biscuit to tide you over 'til he's here.'

'Oh, yes,' gasped Sadie, squeezing her hands together with anticipation. 'It's a fry-up, isn't it? I know that's Dad's favourite.' She licked her lips as she pictured a plate full of crispy bacon, fried bread, sausages, and fried potatoes – and, of course, a mountain of brown sauce.

Stella pulled a long face that was full of disappointment. 'And what's up with the Queen of England, then?' asked her mother. Sadie turned to see her sister still peering through the window onto the dimly lit yard.

'She's jealous 'cos Molly Chadwick kissed Tommy Moran,' she said quickly.

'I'm not,' Stella screamed back at her sister, desperately enough to make her mother realise she was.

Having committed herself to this accusation, Sadie dived back in with 'And she kissed him on the mouth.'

Stella took a swipe at Sadie but it didn't connect.

'Now that's enough, both of you,' ordered Mrs Ravenscroft, not as loudly as the girls but in an authoritative tone that demanded obedience.

'Sadie Ravenscroft, I'll thump you when Mam's not looking.'

Sadie stuck out a long pink tongue through thin, compressed lips. After returning it to its standard position, she said, 'It's true, Mam. She's in love with Tommy Moran.' She looked up at her mother, expecting to see her faint.

'I'm not, Mam, honest I'm not.' The swelling vein on Stella's forehead was joined by one on either side of her neck.

Mrs Ravenscroft could see her daughter trying to control her tears of embarrassment and quickly recalled the many events of her own awkward youth.

'Well,' she sighed, and both girls looked up to her. 'I don't see anything wrong with that. Tommy's a nice boy, and if I was a young woman again I think I might give him a kiss.'

Sadie's mouth fell open and Stella at once grew in confidence and stature. 'In any case,' said Stella, 'our Sadie's in love with Colin Moran, and he's got a runny nose.' Sadie began to boil inside. 'And his nickname's Sniffer.' And now Sadie's eyes nearly left her face with shock.

'OOH!' she swooned. 'Ooh, Mam, I'm not, I'm not. I can't stand him; he's 'orrid.' Her cheeks reddened like highly polished apples.

5

'He's a nice boy as well,' said their mother, 'so stop teasing each other.'

'You like everybody,' said Sadie in a frustrated voice.

'Quite right, too,' she replied. 'And now that's all done with we'll set the table. You do the knives and forks, Sadie, and put a big spoon out for your dad, and you, Stella love, you're in charge of plates and cups and the jug of water. I'll do the lights, so pass me a taper, there's a good girl.' She glanced at Sadie. 'Don't throw the knives and forks on the table, just place them careful like. Any fool can throw 'em down.'

The gas was lit and the fire in the hearth prodded. The green velvet tablecloth had been whisked away, folded, and pushed into the nearest drawer, and the places were set on the bare wooden surface. Hands had been scrubbed and the kettle filled and put on the range to slowly come to the boil.

A firm knock at the door signalled the arrival of the master of the house, Mr Ravenscroft – or so they had thought.

Stella opened the door to see an awkward Tommy Moran filling its entrance. 'Hello, Mrs Ravenscroft,' he said, looking beyond Stella. 'Could you give us right time?' Tommy's dark eyes fell briefly on Stella from within his round pasty face. 'Our clock's stopped,' he lied.

Stella, ever the mistress of most situations, snapped, 'Then why not go and ask Molly Chadwick?'

At this remark Sadie's heart beat faster at the prospect of war. Mrs Ravenscroft, whose sole job in life seemed to be to defuse everything, did some mental arithmetic on her own clock and said, 'Ten past five, and close the door, Tommy.' He did as he was told, with himself on the inside.

Tommy was simply 'the boy next door' and lived with his mum and dad and brother Colin. They never had two pennies to grind together because anything spare was spent at the pub. Tommy couldn't recall the last time he had seen his dad sober, and he had drunk so much through the years he had seemingly grown into a state of continuous unreality, his sense of decision and responsibility permanently blurred by a liquid mind.

Tommy felt a great difference from being in the Ravenscroft home than his own home. There was an undefinable warmth here: more comfortable chairs, a brighter glow from the gas light.

As he subconsciously took in the familiar surroundings the door burst open, striking him between the shoulder blades. It was Jack Ravenscroft, and he sent poor Tommy flying into the arms of Stella.

For the first time in his life, Tommy experienced the softness and scent of woman. Mr and Mrs Ravenscroft and Sadie were there to witness the growing up of a boy into a boy and a half.

Stella shoved him away, not because she had wanted to but because she thought it was right to. She did, however, delay this action to the last possible second. 'Hello, everybody. Sorry about your back, Tommy. Mind you, you should never stand in doorways, yer daft bugger.'

Jack moved in and kissed his wife affectionately before giving his daughters a shared hug. Tommy had never seen such a spontaneous show of affection before; this freedom of expression towards loved ones. He had certainly never seen it in his own house, that was for sure. He couldn't remember the last time he saw his dad kiss his mum when returning from work. The only time he saw them kiss was when they came back from the pub late at night and they were a bit drunk. But then it wasn't nice kissing, it was desperate kissing, and his mum would always say 'you dirty little devil', then whisper in his ear before running up the stairs, pulling her skirt down as she went. He much preferred the Ravenscroft home. He wished he lived there with them.

When the girls went to bed that night Stella dreamed that she and Tommy were walking down the aisle in church. Tommy looked just the same in her dreams as he did in real life, except he was wearing a top hat and tails. She was dressed in a beautiful gown of white, and the vicar, who was Valentino, waltzed her slowly up to her new husband. The organist played 'Roses Are Blooming in Picardy.'

Dancing-class started at ten-thirty every Saturday morning and Stella and Sadie had been the first there since joining at the beginning of the month. Most of their friends spent Saturday mornings huddled up in a seat at the Odeon cinema, watching Flash Gordon trying to outwit Emperor Ming, and failing to do so until about chapter thirteen or fourteen. But they weren't envious, they loved their dancing: they loved the whole idea of being in showbusiness.

Mrs Bunting, and her seventeen-year-old daughter, Donna, ran the Gaynor School of Dancing for tap, modern and American, ballet, and classical movement. They charged one and six an hour, two and six for private tuition. Understandably, not many of the parents wanted their children to have private tuition.

The dance-hall was large and cold and had a very noticeable echo. The floor they were taught on was hard and lumpy, and left many splinters in as equally many bottoms.

The girls fought their way up the spiral staircase with twenty-eight other anxious legs. On arriving in the dance-hall itself the correct procedure was to go up to Mrs Bunting, curtsey, and say, 'Good morning, Mrs Bunting'.

Mrs Bunting was a long, thin woman who looked capable of bending into a hundred and one surprising positions, and most probably did. Outside of her work she wore all the same clothes as her idol, Miss Janet Gaynor – hence the name of the dance school – and the woman who made up these clothes for her was allowed to send her son along for lessons free of charge. The boy was destined to grow up to be either a delicate man or a sex maniac.

Also, her hair was dyed to resemble, as closely as possible, that of Janet Gaynor's. It was some years before Mrs Bunting found a colour photo of Janet Gaynor and discovered to her horror that she didn't have bright red hair after all. She also discovered at the same time that Miss Gaynor was sixteen years her junior.

With one sharp clap of her large swollen hands she caught the attention of her wild young class. 'Now, children,' she whispered, so as to avoid the repetitive pounding of echo, 'this week we're going to learn a new variation of the time step.'

She gave her prodigies a hopeful smile, which was duly returned by a sea of blank expressions. She tapped carefully at her crisp red hair as she examined her mothers of tomorrow. They were such a mixed bunch of girls. Some fat, some thin, some short, some tall – and just the one boy.

Their ages ranged from six to fourteen. Some had no idea of dancing and never would, while others showed minor talent but lacked the necessary enthusiasm to make anything of it.

She marched slowly behind the second row, from where she could see all thirty-four stationary legs. Mildred's caught her eye in particular. She had short, stubby legs that had to support a solid mound of body. Only twelve, she already weighed nearly eight stone. For a moment she thought 'poor girl', then consoled herself by thinking 'money in the bank'.

She clapped her hands twice, the echo making it sound like fading applause. 'All the girls in the front row go into the far corner of the room with Donna.' Dutifully, they accompanied her to the selected area. As they moved eagerlessly across the room she knew that there was little hope of the variation on the time step being learnt this week. 'Now the rest of you stay with me.' The little boy looked confused as to which group he should be with. He was an enigma, and Sadie always pitied him.

For the Ravenscroft girls the lessons went quickly. They were quite competent and, more importantly, they enjoyed their dancing and the challenge of a new step. For Mrs Bunting and daughter it dragged miserably slowly. The challenge wasn't there any more; just the money.

Sadie and Stella were always last out of the school, both wanting the thrill of being in showbusiness to last as long as possible, and until they turned professional one day, Mrs Bunting's dance-school was the sole representative of showbusiness. 'Thank you, Mrs Bunting. See you next week.'

'Okay, girls,' she replied, with a tired weak smile, the kind she used on her husband when serving up his dinner in the evenings.

Tommy hid under the cover of a shop doorway near the dance-school, waiting for his loved one to come out. The two sisters were now once more traipsing wearily down the crisp, white street, their shoes crunching and imprinting themselves on the ground in a snaking trail. They huddled close together as they went through the city centre, looking like one body with four legs. 'Hey, bugger off,' said the shopkeeper as he waved a firm fist at Tommy.

'It's all right, mister. I'm just waiting for my friends.'

'Sod you and your friends. You're putting customers off, so bugger off.'

'Misery-guts,' mumbled Tommy with a grimace.

He dug his hands deep into his pockets and stepped forward into the weather. When the shopkeeper had strutted back inside he scraped up a handful of snow in his gloved hands and tossed it violently at the shop window. 'Yer little bastard,' screamed the man, and Tommy ran for all his worth, not stopping until he'd caught up with the girls.

They deliberately ignored him, as it wasn't the done thing to be seen talking to the male species outside of the school grounds. They increased their pace, but Tommy matched them step for step. They swung left into the arcade, quite often using this route as a short-cut. Tommy gallantly skipped ahead of them to open the large swing-doors, but, although he was strong for his age, the doors were a lot stronger for theirs.

The springs on the doors started, very early on, to establish their superiority and the girls only just managed to squeeze through before they closed.

A little embarrassed, Tommy forced it open to let himself through, the girls now waiting for him on the other side, having decided that, although they wouldn't talk to him, they would let him accompany them.

Just as Tommy had managed to re-open it a stream of people filed through the arcade, oblivious to the fact that he was holding the door open for his own benefit and not for theirs. Many thank yous were uttered as they barged by him.

Eventually he escaped from his 'door duty' and trotted back up to the girls. They stopped outside the Palladium cinema to look at the photographs of the stars. A Janet Gaynor film was now showing. 'Well, we can guess where Mrs Bunting will be spending her evenings this week,' said Stella with a chuckle, and her younger sister laughed – as did Tommy, which immediately made the girls go quiet.

'Oh, come on, give us a break,' he pleaded as the three of them walked on. 'I'm only trying to be friendly, like.'

'So Molly Chadwick tells me,' said Stella in a most sarcastic tone.

'I DON'T LIKE MOLLY CHADWICK,' he declared in a very loud voice, which convinced Stella he was telling the truth. She was a little surprised to have brought out such a reaction in him and it gave her an inexplicable thrill. However, once she had achieved her confession she wasn't the sort to continue torturing her victim.

10

'Are you bothered about seeing the Janet Gaynor film?' she asked him.

'No,' he droned. 'It'll be a right mushy one that. I'd rather go to the Kingsway and see *The White Hell of Pitz Palu*. Aye, that'll be a grand film.'

'Who's in it?' asked Sadie with genuine interest.

'Eh?' Young Tommy had never been asked such a technical question before. As far as he and his mates were concerned a film was a film was a film. Who starred in it was of little consequence, so long as someone did. The important thing was how the villain died. Did he die slowly and in great pain or quickly with just a little pain because he had a likeable mum who'd contracted an incurable disease?

'I said, who's in it?' repeated Sadie softly.

'I . . . I've forgotten.'

'Forgotten,' sighed Stella, picking up on his slip.

'That's right,' he said defensively.

'Well, what's it about then?' she persisted.

Tommy looked blankly at Sadie. He needed her support. She was gentle and kind. She gave him some support. 'Is it a love story, perhaps?' she assisted.

'Bloomin' 'eck no.' He felt himself blush bright red. He crossed his left eye to see if his nose had gone red. It had.

'Then it's probably an adventure story.'

'Aye, that's right. They're always adventure stories with swear-words like "hell" in it. It'll probably be about caves and savages and furnaces . . .' He petered out of description.

'Yes, I'm sure you're right,' said Stella condescendingly. Tommy wished he hadn't mentioned anything about the Kingsway.

They drifted by the market and stopped at the fish stall to say hello to 'Pop'. Everyone knew Joe Billings as Pop. He was a youthful seventy; that is, he was young at heart.

Pop had a round, wizened face and kindly attitude like everyone's grandfather should have, and this was how he came to be called Pop. He helped out Saturdays on the stall since retiring as a trawlerman a couple of years back. Sitting on an upturned crate, he was shelling a bucket full of shrimps.

Stella thought he looked like a big shrimp himself: all pink and puffy and a curved back. 'Ello, kids. What do you know, then?'

'Hello, Pop. Nothing,' said Stella. They always started conversations in this way.

They gazed hungrily at the piles of shelled shrimps in a large carton. The dancing had made Stella hungry. Tommy just loved shrimps more than anything else, and Sadie could eat anything, anytime, any place.

Pop smiled and his face wrinkled all the more. 'Go on. 'Ave a few. I've plenty there.' They didn't need any further encouragement and dived in with eager hands. 'Steady on, now. Don't go spillin' 'em.'

Pop stood up to serve a customer. 'What'll it be for Bob's supper t'night then, Mrs Robertson?'

Stella nudged Sadie. 'You've got more than me,' she complained.

'No I 'aven't.'

'Y'ave. Don't argue 'bout it.'

'Here yer are, Stella,' said Tommy, coming between them. 'Have some of mine.'

Stella blushed. 'I don't want yours, thank you, Tommy Moran.' She gave her sister a fiery glare. 'I want hers.'

'Now, now,' calmed Pop, as he returned to his position on his crate. 'You've all done well enough.'

He began rummaging in his pockets and at once the children's eyes lit up. This was the moment they liked best. Pop was famous throughout Lancaster for his giant pockets on his black great-coat. They'd been a source of much mystery to children for many years. They were always filled with 'goodies', and the girls had been told by their mother that they were the deepest pockets in the world – probably bottomless. They didn't believe her, though. Maybe six or seven feet deep, but surely not bottomless? 'Here y'are. A coupla green arras each. Suck 'em slow.'

Green arrows. Red hot peppermints. Maybe they should be called red arrows, thought Stella.

They thanked him, popped them into their mouths and with fleeting cries of goodbye, they trotted away. Pop shook his head as he put a green arrow into his own mouth.

'You should come and watch Sadie and me dancing some time, Tommy,' said Stella, suddenly.

'Oh, no. I couldn't do that,' replied Tommy.

'I'm not asking you to join in, you know. Just watch us. We're ever so good, aren't we, Sadie?'

'I suppose so,' she said doubtfully.

''Course we are. We're going to be dancers when we leave school: rotten, smelly, pooey school. Aren't we, Sadie?'

'I suppose so.'

'Stop saying that,' Stella snapped. Sadie stopped saying it. 'Come along next Saturday, Tommy.'

He pondered for a moment. It would be worth his while going, just to be near Stella, his sweetheart. But at what price? What would his mates say if they caught him coming out of the dancing school?

Stone the crows I'd never live it down, he thought. 'I can't make it Saturday. I said I'd go with me dad to see Morecambe play.'

Stella scowled at him. It was a poor excuse. Kick off wasn't until three; even *she* knew that.

'As you like, but don't expect to see us any other times if you can't accept our kind invitations.' She held her nose up to add more aloofness as Sadie wished she wouldn't include her in every decision she made.

He had only himself to blame that they didn't talk to him for the following three weeks. Well, Sadie did once or twice, but she made sure her sister didn't find out.

Chapter 2

'Stella!' beckoned a voice as she made to leave the Gaynor School of Dancing. She turned to see Mrs Bunting advance. 'Just wanted to thank you for filling in for me this week, dear.'

'That's okay. I hope the cold's much better now.'

Stella studied her wiry body, which had lost much of its vitality and flexibility during the last six years. She was as thin and as active as ever she was before, but her body had taken on a certain stiffness, as though she was gradually solidifying.

Stella, at sixteen, was now virtually running her dancing classes, whether Mrs Bunting was away ill with a cold or even in attendance at the school. She'd taken on the role of a supervisor, allowing Stella to carry out the more physical exercises.

She had never been that immersed in the workings of the school, and, now her twenty-three-year-old daughter, Donna, was married and settled in a small village in the Pennines, what little enthusiasm she had ever had had now finally ebbed away altogether. If it wasn't for her fondness of Stella, and the girl's desire to succeed in showbusiness, she would have seriously considered closing down the establishment some years ago.

Stella and Sadie had grown closer to each other through maturity. In fact, Stella found that she was sometimes too protective towards her 'little sister'.

Sadie had what she termed a 'real job'. She was an assistant

14

at the cake shop in Corn Street. And Tommy was still a fundamental part of their lives. The three of them would meet up most evenings at the girls' home, and, whilst Stella would prattle on about her dreams of stardom, Tommy would be half listening and half wondering if Blackpool would reach the Cup Final.

He had little ambition, and always did as he was told, especially by Stella, although his boyish feelings of love for her had long since dissipated. It was Sadie to whom he had diverted his affections.

She'd developed into a beautiful young teenager who seemed to have been spared the puppy fat and acne that most young people endure. She was gentle, full of charm and personality, and happy with her life. Sadie could also laugh at herself, which he had noticed Stella was unable to do. If Stella said or did anything that wasn't quite accurate she would argue with you until you finally weakened and gave her the benefit of the doubt. It was always the other person who would inevitably end up apologising.

Although Sadie didn't possess a wealth of topics she enjoyed discussing, she wasn't as limited as Stella, who could only think 'showbusiness' to the point of obsession. Not only had Stella decided where her own career was going to take her, she also knew where Sadie's was going to go. She was going to give up her regular job in the cake shop and be her partner in a dancing act. Already they had been rehearsing a few things together; the only problem now was to find somewhere to play.

It was their father who fixed them their first showbiz date. He worked at Heysham Harbour, and, while waiting for the bus to Lancaster one day, he stood in a queue next to a man he had been at school with. It was Frank Bland, and at school poor Frank was considered to have been not all there. He'd never played games or participated in any rough or mischievous activities.

The growl of the red bus could be heard as it assaulted the steep incline up to the bus stop. 'So what are you doing in Heysham?' asked Jack. 'I've never seen you out this way before.'

'I work at Mission,' came the reply.

15

'Mission? What Mission?'

'*The* Mission. You must know the Church Mission?'

'Bloody hellfire,' swore Jack through a short, sharp laugh, before adding, 'Sorry, Frank, it just came as a surprise.'

'It's for old folks really. I don't work for the Mission proper, like. I just try and help 'em out with the old folk.'

'I see.'

They both glimpsed the front grill of the bus as it levelled on the crest of the hill. 'I try and keep them occupied and so on,' continued Frank. 'I've just been down there now.'

'Oh, I see.'

'We try and arrange for them some entertainment and so on. Do a few songs on the piano and have a singer. That sort of thing.'

The bus jerked and squeaked as it pulled up in front of them. 'It must be difficult to get entertainers, regular like' said Jack. The thought of his talented daughter looking for work was making his interest in Frank grow with each passing second.

'Good 'uns, it is, yes.'

'I see.'

'It's a bit difficult 'cos we can't pay them owt, so we end up with the same old faces who don't mind doing it for nowt.'

'It must get boring for them,' said Jack with feeling.

Jack put a penny in the conductor's outstretched hand. 'I know some youngsters who would be interested.'

'Oh aye,' said Frank. He was always looking for new talent.

The bus lurched forward, seemingly propelling him into conversation. 'Well, if they'd like to come down to the Mission next Saturday I'll give 'em a try-out.'

The bus swung off the main route and pulled up a few minutes later. Jack peered through the dirty windows where some kids had drawn their own version of the female anatomy. It was Jack's stop, and as he climbed down from the bus he smiled to himself in the knowledge that he had secured his daughters their first date.

Still smiling from the good news, Stella trotted to Gaynor's and informed the caretaker that they had a special booking come in and so would require the rooms for a while longer that evening. He smiled and nodded, though she doubted that he had understood fully as he was hard of hearing.

16

As the girls lay in bed that night, exhausted from their work-out at Gaynor's, Stella began to consider the finer details of their act. 'What do you think we should close the act with?' Sadie fought to keep her eyes open, knowing how much her sister wanted her to share in the excitement.

'You'll think of something,' came her bland reply. 'You always do.'

'Maybe the military routine is a good one to close with,' she mused. 'It's a bit too serious, though. No, maybe the selection from the Broadway musical.'

She gave Sadie a firm shake to make sure she hadn't fallen off to sleep. 'Now, there's one important thing I want you to listen to, Sadie. When we introduce . . . Sadie, wake up and listen.'

'I am, I am,' said Sadie feebly.

Stella watched her for a short while, making sure she didn't shut her eyes. When satisfied she had her full attention, she continued. 'When we introduce the songs and dances I want no Lancashire accents. We mustn't sound common; we must sound posh. Understand?'

'I can only talk the way I talk,' said Sadie, almost apologetically.

'Look, I'm Lancashire, Sadie, but I don't have to talk it,' said Stella in a forced southern accent.

She sighed, and then smiled down at her sister. Sadie's head was rolling loosely round her neck. 'Now, just before you leave the land of the living we must decide on what we're going to call ourselves. We can't use Ravenscroft, it's too long. People'll forget it.'

'Let's call ourselves the "Goodnight Sisters",' suggested Sadie, as she let herself slip further under the warm covers.

'You're a fine help, you are. I suppose I'll have to think of everything from now on.'

Stella curled up but continued to think. There was no point talking aloud any more. Sadie was beyond her reaching.

The Champagne Sisters, p'rhaps? No. Too fancy. The Ravenscroft Sisters . . . Yuk! The Raven Sisters? Hmmm.

Stella blew out the candle. Had Sadie stayed awake she would have heard what her stage name was to be from that night onwards.

The concert at the Mission wasn't quite up to Stella's expectations. They had arrived at precisely six o'clock, with Sadie having spent the day secretly hoping the building had been burnt down, flooded, or undergone any other equally dramatic disaster.

Stella had insisted that they enter by the stage door, which proved exceedingly difficult to do as it turned out that the Mission didn't have one. They settled on filing in with the audience, with Stella carrying the music and Sadie carrying all their props. One of the younger men in the audience volunteered to assist Sadie with the props, but he was at least seventy years old – albeit a young seventy years old – and Sadie ended up assisting him to his seat.

Stella took an audience's view of the stage, which looked more like a coffee table with a piano perched on it. As they made their way to it Sadie kept her head hung low so she wouldn't be seen, while Stella lifted hers defiantly at them, so as to show she had no fear. As it happened, it wasn't possible to see their faces because the Mission was full of pipe smoke.

She whispered to Sadie, 'They're too old to inhale.'

'Is it a full house?' asked her sister nervously.

'From what I can see through the smog, it is.' She paused to count the audience. 'Yes,' she said at length. 'All seventeen seats are taken.'

They stepped behind the curtain and, to Sadie's relief, out of sight. The Reverend John Wright was awaiting them there, calmly pacing the floor with his hands behind his back. 'Hello,' he beamed encouragingly.

'Hello,' replied the girls suspiciously.

'You must be the new talent we've heard so much about.'

Stella and Sadie exchanged furtive glances. 'Yes, that's right,' said Stella confidently.

'Oh, good. Mr Bland said you'd come highly recommended.'

Sadie put the suitcases down. She felt as though her arms had been elongated. 'Please step this way,' requested the Reverend with a gentle swaying motion of the hand. 'Mr Barnes is at the rear.'

Wondering who Mr Barnes was, the girls headed for the rear of the building.

18

'Hello, kids. I'm Joey Barnes. I do compering. I've done plenty afore, so don't go fretting that I'll make right fool of myself . . . or yourselves.'

'Your names?' enquired the Reverend. Stella spoke at Joey Barnes.

'Just say, "Ladies and Gentlemen, you're about to be entertained by the fabulous Raven Sisters, with their own brand of song and dance and high-class comedy."'

'The Raving Sisters?' laughed Joey Barnes.

'No. Raven. R.A.V.E.N. That's Raven.'

The Reverend started to blush and moved awkwardly from one foot to the other. 'Er, like the bird, perhaps?' he offered, hoping he was right. Stella nodded. Sadie remained silent, with head hung even lower than before. Joey Barnes couldn't help but notice it.

'Is there owt wrong with her neck?' he whispered to Stella. 'It isn't broken or anything, is it?'

'It's called fear,' she explained, at which Sadie dropped it even lower which would have seemed impossible until she actually did it. Then Sadie asked, 'Could someone show me to the dressing-room, please?'

The Reverend looked to the compere for advice, and he in turn looked at Stella and said, 'I'm afraid you're standing in it.'

'Don't worry, my child,' said the Reverend, putting a reassuring hand on her shoulder. 'Once we get started, no-one will disturb you here.'

The curtain burst open and a middle-aged man bounded in with the sort of expression that said this wasn't the first time he had worked at the Mission. 'Evening, Vicar. Watcha, Joey. Sorry I'm late, the bus was running late.' He glanced at the girls. 'Hello, 'ello. Who picked these dainty little flowers from the Garden of Eden, then?' The Reverend blushed again, as he so often would.

'These young ladies are on our show tonight, Mr Rodgers.'

He offered his right hand. 'I'm Rodgers, alias Magico the Master Magician.' Stella told him who they were, emphasising the word Raven.

Magico took Barnes to one side to discuss his act and a fragile old man wavered up to them from behind the curtain.

19

The girls both jumped with fright. It was like watching the walking dead. 'This is our pianist, Mr Baxter,' said the Reverend, feeling that there needed to be an explanation.

Without saying anything the old man reached forward and gently pulled the music sheets from Stella's grasp. Having studied them from behind half-moon glasses for a while, he said, 'Sorry, girls, I don't do any of these.'

'But it's all there for you,' said Stella. 'All you have got to do is read it.'

'I only play by ear,' he said, indignantly.

'Only by ear?' she repeated, dumbfoundedly.

'Let's go home to Mam and Dad,' suggested Sadie, who must have got to know every inch of the stage floor by now.

'So what you're saying is that you can't play any of our music?' said Stella.

The old man didn't like this forthright young woman's attitude at all. 'Don't you shout at me, Miss Wonderful,' he croaked. 'I once played with G. H. Elliot.' And with that, and a body that tremored so much it seemed on the brink of falling apart, he shimmied over to join Barnes and Magico.

Eventually, in the old showbiz tradition, the show went on. Magico succeeded in making the audience disappear – most of them to the toilet. Joey Barnes, because the pipe smoke had blanketed the stage, walked straight over the edge, struggled back on, and then introduced the girls as the Crow Sisters.

Mr Baxter played all the songs he knew and none of the ones the girls had rehearsed to. Of all the free concerts put on at the Mission, it was the first where booing had been heard.

Stella stormed out at the end in a raging temper, stating that she would never work there again – not even if they paid her. And Sadie, who did manage to finally lift her head for the briefest of moments, left in floods of tears.

Reflecting on the affair and the injustice of it all in the comfort of their home, Sadie categorically stated that her brief flirtation with showbusiness was at an end. The same humiliation had had the reverse effect on Stella. It made her more keen to succeed, and more motivated about improving the act and finding the right places to play. The Mission was merely a hiccup on her way to becoming a great performer, one day to be idolised by the public. At least, that was how she intended looking at it.

There were two important things she'd learnt from this unfortunate experience: always make sure that the piano-player was capable of playing their music and that the compere said their names right.

It took nearly two weeks of kindness mixed with animal cunning for her to persuade Sadie to make a return to the dancing classes. By making Sadie understand her own importance to their act, and the fruitlessness of embarrassment, outrage, and humiliation, by the third week she had her making suggestions for an act of her own.

When they came to the time when they felt the act was as polished and presentable as it could ever be, Stella made it her job to find them a public gathering to perform it to.

She kept alert to any opportunities, and, at the very low fee of nothing, she managed to fix them a job in the very high-class venue of the County Hotel, Lancaster.

It was for a firm of brewers, and drink was top of the bill. She got them the job because the previously booked double-act had had a major bust-up and was consequently cancelled.

They did very well that night. They were bright and young, and the audience were drunk enough to enjoy two young teenagers cavorting about in costumes they couldn't envisage their wives in. They did well enough to be given a pound to split by a very drunk landlord, whose wife never forgave him.

Over the next twelve months their act blossomed like summer flowers, as did their figures. They were tall, easy movers, with natural blonde hair. Unsurprisingly, the only thing of importance to Stella was the act, and Sadie was willing to go along with this, for, as yet, she had no other interests or distractions.

Chapter 3

At weekends Tommy joined the girls at their various venues. He enjoyed helping out wherever he could. He was a strong boy, and his prominent muscles kept over-enthusiastic male admirers under control.

He was employed at the Lancil factory, making – or rather assisting in the making of – oilcloth.

He had become Sadie's all-time favourite hero, and secretly they had shared kisses, as long as he promised to do it romantically, like in the films she had seen. Tommy went along with this. He went along with anything that kept her happy.

Towards the latter part of 1932 they were working the cream of anything that was going, even as far afield as Preston, and had twice worked Manchester.

Their post-office savings books had never looked healthier. Sadie had managed to save nearly every penny she had earned – after giving her mother an allowance. Stella had spent most of her earnings on clothing and on the act, realising that they wouldn't progress without spending on themselves. Fashion was an important part of their song and dance act, and Stella didn't want anyone thinking they were cheap and scruffy. Anyway, it was far easier for Sadie to save as she had kept her job going at the cake shop.

Tommy received a flat salary of five shillings every time he worked with them. It didn't matter how large or small the date was; five shillings he received. Half of this went into his own post-office savings account, the rest he spent on treating himself.

Unlike the girls, he didn't have to pay anything to his parents towards his keep: it had always been that way. Now and again he'd go to the market and buy in a load of vegetables as a gesture of his gratitude, and by doing it this way he guaranteed that his dad wouldn't blow it all at the pub.

Sadie was quite content to drift through life without any changes. After all, she had never had so much money, so why should she want to change things? She thought they had become legendary figures when she saw a piece about them in the local press: 'Stella and Sadie Raven are now household names throughout the whole of Lancaster.' It also went on to say that Stella was renowned for her fashion sense and Sadie for her gentle personality.

One morning, during this busy period, Stella declared that she had discovered the opportunity for them to make sensational progress. She'd seen in a theatrical paper, *The Stage*, that there was to be a talent contest held in the north, called 'The North–West, Go as You Please Show'.

The first prize wasn't money – it was far better than that. If you won you were given a full week's work at your nearest main theatre. For the girls that would mean the Winter Gardens, Morecambe.

The first instalment of the competition took place at the Alhambra Theatre, Morecambe, where they had to win the local heat. If successful, they would then go to the Hippodrome, at Ardwick Green, Manchester, for the second heat. This was followed by the semi-finals in Liverpool (no theatre confirmed as yet, due to dispute betweeen various managements) and would conclude back in Manchester at the Palace Theatre. Stella entered them for it at once. 'It won't be easy for the others with us performing,' she said confidently – maybe too confidently.

'It's a bit scary, though,' said Sadie. 'They'll be some awful good uns' having a go, Stella.'

She ignored Sadie's reservations. If she took any notice of her sister they'd be permanently out of work.

On the day of the first local heat Sadie just managed to overcome a severe bout of nerves and Stella gave one of her most perfunctory performances. She'd made the classic mistake of having her mind already on the stage at the Palace, Manchester. They came second. An Irish pub tenor won the first heat, singing, 'Mother Macrea', followed by 'I'll take you home again, Kathleen'. He was awful but – and this is the part Stella couldn't comprehend – the public liked him. He was a short, fat man, well into his forties, who didn't touch upon many right notes. *But the public liked him.* 'Better luck to us next time,' was Sadie's only remark as the theatre emptied.

'How on earth could they have liked him?' cried Stella, gazing up at the heavens in stunned disbelief. 'How could a garden gnome come in first? Did you see that orange doormat he wore on his head?'

'I think that was a wig,' said Tommy, keeping his distance as Stella was looking positively volatile.

'Course it was a ruddy wig, which makes it all the more stupid that he won.'

'Well, *I* thought he was quite good,' said Sadie, very generously.

'But Sadie, dear,' she said with frustration in her emotion-filled voice: 'if he was only "quite good", as you say, *and* he went and won the thing, and we came in second, does that make us not quite as good as quite good?' Sadie was confused. She never had understood Stella's logic.

Tommy stood several feet away with his hands dug deep into his pockets and a look of bemusement on his pallid face. 'I'll bet you he won't get past the next round,' said Stella. 'In Manchester they've seen real pros, real talent. They have four or five number-one theatres in Manchester and so they know real talent, I'll stake my life on it.'

'I wouldn't want you to go as far as that,' said Sadie, seriously.

Stella studied her sister despairingly before saying, 'And neither one of you is to go backstage and wish that big idiot luck for the next round.' She turned on Tommy, who had moved even further away. 'You hear that, Tommy Moran?'

He swung round with an angelic expression upon his face. 'What was that?'

'You heard me.' She sighed heavily. 'Come on, there's nothing here for us any more. Let's go home and tell our folks the worst.'

Once on the tram Stella managed to calm herself considerably. 'I'll give him this,' she said, preparing to offer her first piece of praise for the tenor singer: 'He knew exactly what the audience wanted. He sang the right numbers for the occasion.'

There was a glimmer in her eyes as if she was registering on her own words as she spoke them. 'Yes, that's the secret, isn't it? You give them what they want; not what *you* want.'

'I think that's quite so,' said Tommy, bravely. '"Live and learn" is what my old man taught me.'

'What's *he* got to do with the business?' she said, hurtfully. Tommy cowered and stared out of the window.

'Don't be mean on him,' defended Sadie. 'It's not Tommy's fault.'

'I know, I am sorry. I just can't believe we're out of the stupid competition.'

Within two days Stella had a plan. They would go to Preston, put their names down at the theatre there and re-enter the competition. They could use their Aunt Alice's name and address to avoid recognition. She lived in Garston, which was nearer to Preston than Lancaster. 'But only by about two yards,' Tommy pointed out. She was very pleased with herself, and even more pleased when Tommy revealed that he had a relation in Preston itself, and that they could use *her* address.

After an awkward journey they reached Preston, did their performance using Tommy's relation's name and address – and came in third. They were beaten out of second place by a young man who did the worst impression of Charlie Chaplin Stella had ever seen. 'I didn't even realise he was supposed to be Charlie Chaplin,' declared Sadie. He, in turn, was beaten out of first place by a crippled accordionist and his dog that howled to all his tunes, hitting the right notes more often than his owner.

Stella asked Tommy if he had any relatives in Blackburn, but both he and Sadie were quite adamant that, as far as this particular competition was concerned, they were finished.

Stella was almost frantic from the lack of worthwhile work

there was about during the ensuing period. The one thing that gnawed away at her mind more consistently than anything else was the question, would they ever really make it big? Both of them were now members of the VAF union, and they read the papers and periodicals appertaining to any form of entertainment. All Stella wanted was for them to have just one good job in the business so they could prove their worth.

Sadie had lost much of her enthusiasm since the big competition. She didn't in any way blame her sister for their failure, but felt that, having put all her faith and trust in her for so long with such poor results, she'd be better off spending more of her time at the cake shop, doing an honest day's work. She was also falling more and more in love with Tommy Moran by the second, and in recent years he hadn't stopped being in love with her for a moment. In fact, if the truth had been known, his main reason for continuing to participate in their work as travelling chaperone was to now gradually save towards buying an engagement ring. He knew they were both too young for marriage as yet, 'but there's no harm in saving,' he would keep telling himself.

What neither of them realised was that Stella was so blinded by her ambition to succeed that she hadn't noticed their blossoming love. They'd wrongly assumed that she simply wasn't interested.

The next two years were traumatic ones for Stella but not too unpleasant for Sadie. Work had come in fits and starts, and when they did work it was received with little remark or enthusiasm. One night, when her sister was already asleep, Stella lay wide-awake in bed, her eyes filled with bitter tears. The next morning she intended dissolving the partnership and going in search of a real job, as she'd heard Sadie call her own work at the cake shop.

When morning came, she descended into the kitchen to break the news to Sadie, knowing that it would probably come as a relief to her younger sister. But an historic occurrence took place that was to change the whole pattern of their lives. For the first time since they had lived in Corkell's Yard, a postman delivered a letter. It was addressed to Miss Stella Raven, c/o the Raven Sisters.

26

Mrs Ravenscroft gingerly accepted it from him when he knocked at the door – there being no letterbox, indeed, until then there had been no need for one. She gave a brief curtsey and carried it indoors, delicately held between thumb and forefinger as though she was going to take it away to have it tested for fingerprints. She placed it by the oil lamp for a while, then decided it should be on the mantle-shelf, where it would be more prominent. Then she sat down and watched it do nothing.

Glumly, Stella reached for the first mug of tea she saw poured out and drifted into the best room. Her mother had got the open fire alight, but it was still cold as yet. 'You all right, Mam?' she asked, when seeing how immobile she was in her seat. She nodded at the mantle-shelf as if it was holding her at gun point, and Stella gave a curious frown before picking up the letter that rested on it. 'Stone the flamin' crows,' she gasped.

'Don't open it,' begged her mother, and with unexpected animation she leapt forward, snatched it, and returned it back to what she felt was its correct position – on the mantle-shelf.

'It's got to be opened, Mam. It's a letter – and it's addressed to me. It could be urgent.'

'I suppose you're right,' she agreed. Then she said, rather smugly, 'Mrs Milligan saw him deliver it, you know.' Her face began to beam. 'We'll be the talk of the neighbourhood.'

Stella opened it and read in silence for a moment or two.

'Who sent it, then?' asked her mother.

'It's from a theatrical agent I wrote to in London some weeks back.'

'London?' she gasped, as if her daughter had just said Hades.

'Yes, Mam, London. You know it; it's that place down south with big buildings.'

'Watch your tongue, young madam,' she warned. 'You're not so big that I can't put you across my knee if needs be.'

'Do you want to hear it, then?'

'I'm not moving till I do.'

'It says, "Dear Miss Raven, Thank you for your letter of the twenty-first inst. To confirm the advert in *The Stage*; yes, we are seeking new young talent to represent. We are a young agency with as much ambition as the artistes we have on our lists. Please call in to see us, accompanied by this letter. Yours sincerely, Brooksie (Ronnie Brookfield).'"

Stella put the letter back in its envelope and replaced it on the mantle-shelf. 'What happens now?' her mother asked.

'How do you mean?' Stella fenced with her.

'You know. What happens now? Do you write to him again or what?'

'Yes. I'll write to him telling him I got his letter. Then I'll go to London and visit him – probably fix up an audition with him and get any other work that's about. There's more prospects down there. Sadie and me may get good theatre work.'

'And what do you think your dad's going to say when you ask him if you can go to London?'

As far as Stella was concerned, her father had nothing to do with her decisions, and so she answered her mother with as much nonchalance as she could muster. 'Well, Mam, for one thing I won't be asking Dad, I'll be telling him I'm going, and if Sadie and Tommy can't come with me I'll just have to go alone.'

Then her nonchalant air began to fade as she saw her mother's eyebrows raise in shock. Stella raised a hand as she said, 'I'll have no rows about it. I'm not wanting to lose my temper, but I've made up my mind, no matter what. I have my own money and Sadie has more than enough to pay her own half.'

'Sadie'll pay half, will she? And where did you get that idea from? It was you that wrote to the agency, not our Sadie.'

'Mam, I'll be going down to try and find work for the both of us. It's always been me that's taken care of fixing everything up. I even do all the music, the dance arrangements and everything else to do with the act.' She paused for a second, conscious that she may have been playing for too much sympathy. 'Look, she has a nice little nest-egg in the Post Office, and I doubt she'd even have to give up her job at the shop to come with me, but she will have to pay her own fare.'

'She won't be allowed to leave work just to take fancy trips down to London,' said her mother firmly, as if she, herself, employed her at the shop.

Inwardly Stella sensed that her mother's concern was over

the loss of keep-money rather than the temporary loss of two daughters. 'You know, Mam, when you talk like this it's easy to see why you and Dad never got anywhere.'

Was she really speaking to her own mother like this? she quickly thought. 'You have no spirit of adventure, which is why one day you'll die in this horrible little prison and nothing of interest will have ever happened to you. There's a land of opportunity out there; not here in Lancaster, Morecambe, or Preston, Mam. It's down there, in London.'

Stella had once seen Miriam Hopkins do a similar speech in one of her films substituting Lancaster, Morecambe, and Preston for Palm Beach, Long Island, and Pasadena.

Her mother stood up, walked over to a taper, and lit the fire. She was having difficulty in quelling her anger. 'If your father could hear you talk like that he'd tan your arse, Stella Ravenscroft. And I'd help him. Now set the table, Miss Upitty.' With a touch of resignation Stella opened the knife-drawer, making as much noise as she could. Her mother left the room and quickly Stella reached for the letter on the mantle-shelf. 'And you can leave that where it is,' said her mother's distant voice. 'Your dad's to read it before it goes walking.'

Jack and Lilly Ravenscroft were still thumping the kitchen table and laying down the law while Sadie and Tommy were at the station waving Stella off on the London-bound train for her first-ever trip 'down there'.

Within a few days Jack and Lilly received a postcard from their wayward daughter, as they began to refer to her. It just said that she had arrived safe and soundly, and that the weather was no different to that in Lancaster. She sent her love to them all and put a PS, 'saying that Mr and Mrs Gosling, the people she was staying with, send their very best, and a PPS, saying that 'Streatham is really quite lovely'.

The postcard became another ornament for the Ravenscroft mantle-shelf.

Ronnie Brookfield's tiny office at the back of Charing Cross Road was as drab and dirty as he was. The only promise of work came through such expressions as 'As soon as I can fix anything for you, I will' and 'Believe me, you will be the first to know', and 'Is your sister as pretty as you?'

To her surprise, he also asked her if she minded doing stag parties. He produced a pen from his cheap-looking, badly stained blazer. 'What, no phone number? Er – Oh well, no matter. I'll be in touch by post. Goodbye, Miss Ravel, er, Miss Raymond, er, Miss Raven.'

She went round at least another half a dozen more agents, some quite prominent, others as dubious as Mr Brookfield's outfit. More promises were made and more time seemingly wasted. Her money was running short. It was time to vacate the 'Big City' and return to the smaller one of Lancaster, hoping that the fare and various other expenses hadn't proved to be money down the drain.

She'd been home six weeks. Her letter was still on the mantle-shelf and just beside it was the postcard. Both were memories of London, but what worried her more was that both were rapidly becoming memories of a career that seemed destined not to happen.

At about this time Corkell's Yard received another rare visit from the postman. This time he delivered a larger envelope than before. 'Telegram for Miss Raven,' he announced, pushing it into Mrs Ravenscroft's hand. Her head was swimming with excitement as she signed her name in full: Lilly Elizabeth Ravenscroft.

She could sense the neighbours peering at her from behind closed curtains. Stella hurriedly made some tea, allowed it to brew for only a moment, and then poured it out for both of them. As she finally reached for the telegram her mother said, 'Let's have a biscuit.'

Stella went to the tiny pantry and returned with a tin with Peak Frean stamped on it. The Peak Frean biscuits had long since been eaten and the tin had been purchased some years ago. It now contained a lower vintage of biscuit but good enough for them to dunk in their tea. 'Read it out,' said her mother, with crumbs all over her lips.

She opened it and read: 'Miss Stella Raven, Corkell's Yard, Penny Street, Lancaster, Lancs.' Her mother nodded a few times, as if giving her approval. 'Can fix you Babes rehearsals Dec Five Six weeks Ten joint own fares Theatre Royal Portsmouth Phone Affirmative Brooksie.'

Her mother waited some moments before asking, 'Is that

showbusiness talk?' Stella shakily reached for her tea and sat down. 'Well, come on. Explain it all to me. Remember, we're just plain simple folk up this way.' That was a gentle dig – a small attempt at revenge – for the comments she'd made about them some weeks ago.

'What it means is, *Babes in the Wood* pantomine rehearsals, starting December fifth with a six-week run for ten pounds a week each between Sadie and me. We have to settle our own fares and I must phone them right away if the answer's yes.'

'Where's it say all that?' asked her bewildered mother, turning the telegram over and over in her hands as if the missing words would magically fall out onto her lap.

'A telegram's like code, Mam. They do it that way 'cos it's cheaper.' As she spoke her mind was already way ahead of her, carefully planning what sort of digs she would be looking for and how much she would be able to spend whilst in Portsmouth.

'I see,' said her mother. 'Well, be a good girl and put telegram on mantle-shelf for your dad to see when he's back from work.'

She sat back, looking at the three pieces of correspondence and sighed. 'My, we'll soon be needing a longer mantle.'

'Ten pound a week's not a bad starter in the big time, is it, Mam?' She felt she mustn't let her change the subject until she had been given a definite go-ahead. She couldn't keep Brooksie waiting. She had to phone him before her dad was back from work or it might be too late.

'Hmmm. But you've got to split it with Sadie. That makes a big difference doesn't it?'

'Yes, Mam, but five pounds a week is twice as much as Dad gets.'

Before she'd finished the sentence she knew that she had made a grave mistake.

'Two pounds five your dad gets, and he has to work hard for it, not singing and dancing about the place, but solid hard work. Your dad's got a good name. Everybody says what a good worker he is, everybody says that.' Her cheeks were crimson with anger, though Stella wasn't sure whether it was because she had insulted his name or because her mother wished he could earn as much as five pounds a week. Either

31

way, she appeared to calm as easily as she had flared. 'How much will the railway be?'

'About twenty-five bob return, third class. Then Sadie will be able to earn more than she can in the cake shop.'

'A guinea a week she earns,' established her mother with a pointing, almost threatening, finger. 'Our Sadie's like Dad. She's a good worker. Why, only just the other day I went into the cake shop for a pennith of broken biscuits and Mrs Coverdale, she's manageress there, said "Hello Mrs Ravenscroft. What a good worker your Sadie is . . ."'

Stella wondered if it would be best to hunt out good digs that cost more or bad digs and so save more. '". . . I've never known any girl work as hard as your Sadie."' Her mother nodded at least five times as if to say, there now, so no more argument. Stella wasn't arguing.

Stella's mind returned from Portsmouth. 'Yes, okay, Mam.' She had stopped listening after 'a guinea a week she earns . . .'

'I'm off to see Sadie to tell her to give up her job at the cake shop, come home and get packing, ready for our long journey down to the wicked South.'

'You'll have your dad to see about all this, and don't think I'm going to stick up for you either.'

'Going to Portsmouth is no worse than going to London, Mam. And going to London isn't like going to Hell. You can always come back from London.'

'Watch that language. You've been there once and look at the swear-words you've picked up.'

'Goodbye, Mam. see yer . . .'

She was out of the house before her mother could say 'Jack Ravenscroft'. She fell into the cake shop and saw Sadie serving Mrs Pritchard three coconut macaroons. 'That'll be fourpence, Mrs P.'

'How much?' challenged her customer.

'Ooh, sorry, Mrs P. Er, threepence please.' Out the corner of her eye she could see Stella doing an uncanny mime of Mrs Pritchard quibbling over the price. She had to stop looking at Stella to prevent herself from breaking up into laughter, which she was prone to do at the least amusing comment or action her sister made.

Mrs Pritchard checked her change and, with a groan and a

frown, turned and stomped out of the shop, not even acknowledging Stella's presence. The bell above the door rang and she slammed the door shut. 'What are you doing, visiting me here during hours?' whispered Sadie with a mixture of concern and excitement. Stella related the story about the telegram and her subsequent discussion with her mother. 'Portsmouth!' gasped Sadie. 'That's further than London, that is.'

'You're sounding like Mam did.'

'But it's a long way.'

She spied Mrs Coverdale coming out the back office. 'Quickly, order something or I'll be for it.'

'Yer what?'

'Order something, quickly,' urged Sadie. She smiled sweetly at Mrs Coverdale, who eyed her with an amount of suspicion.

When Stella saw Mrs Coverdale she said to her, 'One of your cakes just spoke to me.' Sadie felt herself age by a hundred years.

'What you on about?' growled the manageress.

'It's one of your delicious cakes. It spoke to me. It said, "Please eat me, I'm so delicious." I'll just have to buy it.'

She looked from one sister to the other. 'I hope you're not as daft as yer sister?' she said to Sadie, at length. Sadie shoved the cake forcefully into Stella's hands.

'There's your cake.'

'And how much is that?' she asked sweetly, producing a purse and pretending to hunt through it for change.

'Sixpence,' was Sadie's reply.

'How much?' asked Stella, reverting back to her impression of Mrs Pritchard. Sadie just managed to contain herself.

'Sixpence, please.'

She held out her hand and Stella pretended to put money in it. It was something they had done before. She rang up sixpence and rattled the change about in the wooden till for effect.

Mrs Coverdale, ever-suspicious of youth in her shop, marched over to see what was going on. Stella quickly warned her sister. 'Ooh, and Mam says you're to bring home twelve black puddings for Dad's tea.' Sadie closed her eyes and opened them again, hoping she would be many miles away.

'Twelve?' said a disbelieving Mrs Coverdale as she stopped in her tracks – much to Stella's relief.

'No. I said two, Mrs Coverdale,' she corrected, innocently. Mrs Coverdale squeezed a finger into her ear and shook it about.

'I must be going deaf. Could have sworn you said twelve.'

The shop door opened and another customer stepped inside. She moved to serve her and both Sadie and Stella dropped their shoulders with relief.

Stella found a public phone and rang up Ronnie Brookfield, 'confirming that they would be in attendance of the first rehearsal on the fifth of December. She had found it easy to convince her sister that eight weeks away from Tommy was not the end of the world. 'Think of all that money you will be able to save towards a wedding dress,' she'd remarked glibly, not expecting a 'that's true' reply.

Jack Ravenscroft had also been easy to convince. He'd considered the extra few bob that they would pull in for them during their absence. With a big, hearty smile, he'd then given his decision. 'Of course you can go, my darlings. Why, I couldn't think of anything better for you.'

Lily Ravenscroft had muttered under her breath about the dangers of ill-doings that went on in the south, but no-one was paying her much attention on the matter by now.

Stella and Sadie Raven – Sadie, in all honesty, a little reluctantly so – were now in showbusiness proper.

Chapter 4

It was last-night party time in Portsmouth and, as was the custom with end-of-run parties, it was held three nights in advance of the last show.

The 'binge' was set to start half an hour after final curtain. This would give the cast time for a quick breather and the caterers an opportunity for the auditorium to clear before setting up the tables and bar on the stage. It wasn't unusual to have the party on the stage: it gave the cast a chance to mix together and discard any 'us and them' attitudes that may have hitherto existed.

When the party was in full swing one of the stage-lads nodded at the empty auditorium and said to the lighting man, 'The theatre seems fuller than normal.' His comment reflected what kind of season it had been.

Stella and Sadie were sitting on two stools, the sort used by ventriloquists for their act, when Billy Clay and his side-kick assistant, Doug Lambourne, glided over. 'Here we go,' sighed Stella, and she took a firmer grasp on her bottle of ginger beer, holding it menacingly on her lap.

Sadie, being Sadie, gave him a courteous smile and took a large bite out of one of the four sausage rolls she had taken from the service table. Her appetite was as enormous as when she was small – and, much to Stella's envy, she had never put on so much as an extra pound in weight. 'Ouch, it's hot,' cried Sadie.

'So am I,' remarked Billy, 'and you don't need to pick me off the service table.'

Stella glowered at him but he wasn't looking at her. He had learnt she was the tough one of the two – of the whole show, most probably – and so kept clear of her. 'You'll need picking up off the floor if you carry on irritating my sister any more,' she warned, sternly.

Billy chuckled but he soon stopped. His wife appeared at the side of the stage. He hadn't been expecting her to show up. He hadn't *wanted* her to show up.

Stella noted his rapid change of expression and glanced across her shoulder to see what could have caused it. 'Oh, how romantic,' she gloated. 'You and the missus together for a fun-filled evening.' Billy sneered at her and, muttering one or two obscenities, he went to greet her. Lambourne dutifully – and silently – followed him.

'Thank God they've gone,' sighed Sadie as she planted a rock cake in her mouth, shortly followed by two hard-boiled eggs.

Stella was about to remark on Sadie's digestive system when she stood up and fetched herself two lamb chops. She bought her sister another ginger beer. 'Home on Sunday,' she mused as the last of the food went down.

'Yes. You'll probably be glad to get back to a good meal.'

'Yes, I will.' Sadie didn't catch on to the sarcasm. Then she said, 'You don't mind me not coming with you to London, like? That I will be going home and you'll be hunting for work?'

'Of course not, pet. But just be sure to tell our Mam and Dad that I am working for the two of us and not just for myself.' Then she added, 'There are times I believe she thinks I'm on the game, you know.' Sadie laughed at that.

'Oh dear,' she suddenly sighed.

'What's up?'

It's the Sheriff of Nottingham,' she explained. 'He's hogged the last custard pie.'

'Well, I'm sure you won't starve. Now tell me what the time is.'

Sadie checked her rolled gold Samuels watch that Tommy had given to her as a special going-away present. 'Half past six,' she said.

'Don't be daft.'

36

'That's what it says.'

Stella glanced at it. 'When you see Tommy again tell him from me to buy you a watch with the works in it next time.'

There was a sharp cough and an announcement was made: dancing beginning in ten minutes.

'Come on, Sade,' said her sister. 'Unless, that is, you want me as a dance-partner?' Sadie firmly shook her head, and they made their way to the dressing-room.

The doorman strutted across the stage with a gramophone and promptly tripped over as the lights were dimmed for atmosphere.

For two minutes it was chaos. A long, loud, girlish giggle was heard coming from somewhere in the stalls, followed by a long, loud girlish scream from the same place. 'Drinking is bad for you,' warned Stella with a smile. 'But what follows is worse.'

The pantomime finished with a dull thud. Portsmouth was left and forgotten by the artistes, and the artistes that left were forgotten by Portsmouth. It hadn't been a very happy show, and from the management's point of view it hadn't been a successful one either. Profits had been made but not fortunes. Managements were not content with just making profits, they wanted fortunes, each and every time. As for the artistes themselves, whenever asked where they played last Christmas, they would invariably reply, 'Somewhere on the south coast.' Portsmouth was not a name to mention.

On the Saturday, the actual last night of the pantomime, Stella was called to the phone. It was Ronnie Brookfield. Apparently, an act had dropped out at the Palace, Grimsby, and could they replace them? Money would be the same as they were getting for the pantomime and third-class fares would be paid for one way only. He needed an answer then and there, and, of course, Stella was quite incapable of turning down any work.

She dashed back to the dressing-room to tell her sister the good news, and perhaps, not surprisingly, it was met with much apathy. Sadie was more excited about meeting up with Tommy. 'Okay, then,' she said, finally surrendering to her insistent sister. And Stella made her the promise that all show business is run on.

'We're just filling in for the week.'

Mrs Fisher brought into the warm, compact front room of her home five desserts on a tray: four prunes and custards and one prunes without custard because Billy Manners didn't like custard.

Stella and Sadie cleared away the dinner plates and stacked them haphazardly on the sideboard for Mrs Fisher. It was eleven p.m. and these were the best digs in Grimsby; clean, warm, and the food was excellent if you were used to mediocre food.

The furniture was in a class of its own – instant depression. The sideboard looked like a coffin with drawers and could have been the one used to ship the body of Count Dracula into the country.

Sat around a highly polished wooden table, *circa* 1934, were Stella, Sadie, and Billy Manners – a new, young comedian with an American style to his act. He was full of one-liners, smart comments, and a smart suit to match. His idea was that you don't have to look funny to be funny. His jokes were sharp, much too sharp for Grimsby – that only served to dull his razor wit. The other couple at the table were Grace and Karl Kent, a husband-and-wife team. She sang and played the harp while he drank and played around. Their act was like their earnings – on the way down. What had once been a salary was now a wage.

Sadie looked at her prunes and said, 'Sailor!' The others looked up. 'According to my prunes I'm going to marry a sailor,' she explained to the questioning faces.

Billy said, 'According to mine there's going to be a queue for the bathroom tomorrow.' Grace Kent pulled a suitable face to show her disdain.

'I'm going to marry a rich man,' said Stella, 'because Mrs Fisher gave me five prunes to your four.'

'Looks like you'll be first in the bathroom, then Stella,' grinned Billy.

'Ah yes, but what about Grace and Karl?' remarked Sadie.

'A lot of people have been saying that just recently,' sniggered Billy, and the girls laughed at this.

'Grace doesn't enjoy her prunes,' announced Karl in an

aloof manner that made them laugh all the more, though they did have the decency to try to disguise their amusement.

'We should have got together, Grace,' said Billy. 'I don't like custard!'

Mrs Fisher tapped lightly and came into the room. She brought in a tray with a pot of tea, cups, sugar, and milk. Billy spoke. 'Mrs Fisher, I have some news for you. In the morning keep clear of the bathroom. There's going to be a long queue there, though it looks like Grace might be a late entry.'

'Oh, yes,' said Mrs Fisher in a kindly voice. She had had many young comedians lodge at her home in the past. She accepted that they were all as mad as each other.

Sadie took the tray off her and placed the teapot in the hearth by the glowing fire. 'Now, if you want any more hot water just give me a shout,' said Mrs Fisher. 'It'll be at least another hour and a half before I've to see to all the washing up. I don't like coming down to dirty pots and pans in the morning.' She turned for a final inspection of her boarders. 'Any special calls in the morning?' No-one replied. 'Good! I'll be saying goodnight then.' Five incoherent goodnights were voiced back as she shuffled through the doorway in her threadbare tartan slippers that clicked against the floor. Stella poured the tea out. Karl was immersed in the sporting page of the paper and writing down racing tips as he read. Grace had turned her narrow back on everyone to soak up the heat of the fire, not too concerned that soon everyone else was shivering. Billy silently, and mis-chievously, nodded at the table and both girls knew what he meant. 'When they've gone to bed,' mouthed Stella, then furtively checked over her shoulder to make sure she hadn't been seen.

Grace, a dignified, sexless, thirty-eight-year-old blonde, looked up, giving the impression she couldn't see more than a foot beyond the end of her husband. She rose in a serene manner that almost invited everyone else to stand and, with a forced, seemingly painful smile, she announced, 'I'm going to retire now. Karl – if you please.' Karl mumbled under his breath and folded up the newspaper. They made their grand exit from the room and immediately Billy rubbed his hands and pulled out a packet of lettered cards. Stella moved to a cabinet and returned with a stemmed glass while Sadie racked the fire with the poker.

'I hope you're both going to take it seriously and not lark about like you did last night,' said Sadie.

'She means it,' confirmed Stella.

'I know, and, yes, I'll try and take it seriously,' Billy smiled.

'You're smiling now before we've even started,' said Sadie.

'I'm just getting rid of them before we begin; that's all – promise.'

'Stop it, Billy,' said Stella, but with no real authority. Billy was too likeable, too effervescent to be firm with.

'Come on, then, let's get started before the vampire arrives and bites your necks,' teased Billy.

They each placed a finger lightly on the rim of the upturned glass. Sadie said, 'Concentrate everyone, and no pushing.' After a short pause she said in a solemn voice, 'Is there a spirit there?'

The glass screeched around the letters and spelt 'YEF'.

'It must mean YES,' was Sadie's explanation.

'But it spelt YEF', argued Billy.

'Maybe it's a child who can't spell.'

'Maybe it's all a load of . . .'

'That's enough, Billy,' ordered Stella.

'Let's stop jabbering and give it a full chance,' pleaded Sadie.

The next time it spelt YEP. 'I suppose it's an American child, this time,' teased Billy.

'Shut up, Billy,' said Stella.

'Americans do say YEP, that's all I was saying.'

'Have you a message for us?' asked Sadie, putting on her same mysterious tone again.

The glass spelt out SARAH DEF. 'Hard of hearing, are you?' enquired Billy.

'Stop it, Billy,' ordered Stella – yet again.

'Sarah is *my* name,' said Sadie, excitedly. That was very true, as Sadie was only a nickname derived from the name Sarah. 'Sarah Def,' she pondered. 'I've no idea what it means.'

'So far, both words spelt have sounded loosely like real words,' said Billy, remarkably seriously for him. 'By that method you could assume, then, that DEF means DEATH.'

'SARAH DEATH,' said Stella. 'Well, that's charming, that is, Billy Manners.'

'Only an idea,' he said, weakly.

'And he's right,' agreed Sadie. 'That's just what it could mean.'

'Come on,' said Stella. 'Let's give it a rest for one night.'
She pushed back a chair and collected up the pack of lettered
cards.

They huddled around the dying embers of the fire. 'Hey, I'll
tell you girls something,' whispered Billy.

'Tell us what?' said Stella, tiredly. She thought they must
be mad, staying up so late when they were working.

'I've never shared digs with two such smashers before as you
two – and that's truth.' He chuckled as he began reminiscing
over a past incident. 'Usually I end up with two Russian
acrobats, or four midgets who can't quite reach the table: I end
up having to feed them, and then my own dinner gets cold.'

He gave the girls a full smile that glimmered in the firelight.
'You've got lovely teeth, Billy,' remarked Sadie.

'Thanks. I've another nice set in a glass upstairs. I'll show
you those tomorrow night.'

'Billy,' Stella chided. Then she said, 'Where are you working next week?'

'Palace, Newcastle. Then I've got two Moss Empires;
Empire Swansea and . . .'

'God, that's a helluva journey. Swansea to Newcastle.'

'No. Newcastle to Swansea,' Billy checked.

'Does that make it shorter?'

'And then I'm at the Empire, Edinburgh.'

'Swansea to Edinburgh?'

'I'm trying not to think about it,' he winced.

'Who's your agent?'

'Michael White of Theo Connell Associates.'

'Doesn't he like you?'

'Well, they are the Moss circuit,' he defended.

Sadie said, a little too honestly for Stella's liking, 'We
haven't played a number-one yet.'

'We will do, though,' promised Stella, and Billy couldn't
imagine much stopping her. She glanced up at him. 'In fact,
we may have to fill in for an act at the Hippodrome, Bristol,
straight from here. *Then* we'll have done a number-one.'

'Which act is that?' he asked.

'Tip or Tap.'

'Oh, I know them,' chuckled Billy. 'I was working with
them only six weeks back. Do you know them?'

'Only *of* them. Never worked with them.'

'Two very nice girls there,' he said with a wink.

'I thought they were fellas?' said a naive Sadie.

'Almost. They walk with a limp, if you know what I mean.'

'Are they – you know what?' asked Sadie, delicately.

'Oh, yes. I know what. And they know what as well.'

'One of them got done by a sailor,' revealed Stella, recalling a story she'd heard about them from Ronnie Brookfield.

'Eh?'

'It's true. They were returning to their digs in Plymouth after a show one night when a sailor pounced on them.' Billy started laughing. 'This sailor ran off with the small one.'

'And what did the other one do?'

'He fainted.' Now Billy exploded with laughter. He thrived on these sort of stories. They gave him a basis for fresh material.

Sadie said, 'You shouldn't laugh at someone else's misery, Billy.'

'That's the best time to laugh. You don't want to laugh at your own.'

'Keep your voices down,' urged Stella in a hushed voice. 'You'll have Mrs Fisher down on us.

Billy rubbed his hands together excitedly. 'Tell me more about Tip or Tap,' he begged.

'Well, he finally went to the police station to report the abduction of his friend. The police officer thought he was describing a girl. You can imagine his face when Tip or Tap came out with lines like "going bald", "double-breasted suit", and "dance together". Of course, he turned up in the end, having left behind him a very satisfied sailor.'

Billy cried hysterically into his hankie for a minute. 'C'mon. Bedtime, you lot,' announced Stella as she collected their mugs.

'Is that an invitation, by chance?' asked Billy with bright eyes. She kicked his shin.

'You wouldn't be able to handle the two of us.'

'Maybe not, but think of the fun I'd have in trying.' He grinned as he stood up. 'That sailor-man managed on his own with old Tip and Tap.'

'SARAH DEATH' was all Sadie could think of as she

switched out the lights and snuggled up. Eventually she did fall asleep. Under her pillow was a letter from Tommy. She never slept without it. She thought it the most wonderful love-letter in the world, though she would have preferred it that he hadn't signed off 'yours sincerely'.

A little typical of Tommy, she'd thought.

Stella stayed awake a little longer than her sister. As usual, when she could enjoy a tranquil moment, she considered her work.

Can't always be song-and-dance performers. We must branch out a bit. Maybe break into the films.

It was thoughts like these that gave her her motivation. The way the future was going to go for her, she'd need all the motivation she possessed.

Chapter 5

After Grimsby, Sadie went straight home into the waiting arms of Tommy and Stella went to London in an effort to find them more work. Sadie had no problem in getting her old job back in the cake shop, though her mother made a point of telling everyone that it was because she was such a good worker – just like her dad.

Tommy took the rolled gold watch to Samuels, though instead of having it repaired he did a direct swop for a rolled gold neck chain, with a petite black ebony cross attached. The chain was a little too long for Sadie which consequently caused the cross to become lost in her cleavage. It wouldn't have been important, except that the cross was very slim with severe edges and sharp corners. She endured the pain so as not to disappoint Tommy, though she would have preferred to wear the watch that didn't work.

Stella thoroughly enjoyed every second of her latest stay in London. Just to walk up Shaftesbury Avenue was enough in itself to have made her stay there worthwhile. To see all those theatres showing hit, or at least, semi-hit shows, with billboards outside, boasting names of their famous artistes. They were names she had only read about, but she felt as though she knew each one personally – as if they were related to her.

I wish Sadie was with me, she said to herself as she bent down to study every front-of-house photo as she had done a hundred times.

'One day, Sadie and I will play here,' she announced, boldly. A bowler-hatted gent moved up to her and whispered in her ear, 'How much do you charge, then?'

After that incident she stopped loitering and began looking more purposeful.

Some of the agencies had heard of the Raven Sisters, from their part in *Babes* in Portsmouth. One agent told her that their playing of *Babes* was one of the funniest things he had ever seen. When she asked him why, he said, 'It's the first time I've ever seen Babes taller than the principal boy and older than the principal girl.' Stella smiled, but there was little humour in it. He did go on to say that he thought they had a good act but that it was wasted in pantomime. 'Always remember: in panto the kids want a lot of blood and gore and shouting, the grown-ups like a few naughty gags, and the old folk want to see knickers and have a good sing-song.' She could see some sense in that. 'The other bit of advice is never play Portsmouth, Plymouth, Catterick, or Aldershot. You're too sophisticated for them.'

After a couple of weeks of knocking on doors she had fixed them up the odd work here and there. Moneywise there was little being offered, but at least she had found them some work. She returned to Lancaster, exaggerating how good their prospects were. It cheered her up in pretending things were better than they were, and it also kept her parents off her back.

Talking of her parents, one thing that struck Stella more squarely than anything else was how much their little world was identical to when she left it. It was as though they were counting time between when they became married and the day they died.

Previously she had found inspiration from observing their empty lives but now it caught her so unawares that it depressed her. What increased this feeling was that Sadie had reverted back so easily to this way of life, and that wasn't a sign of someone who seriously wanted to strive forward in showbusiness.

When Stella prepared herself for yet another visit to London a few weeks later she insisted that this time Sadie accompanied her. She intended to enlighten her younger sister

45

to the harshness and difficulties of finding work in their profession. 'And I don't want to hear Tommy or the cake shop as an excuse,' she warned her. Sadie agreed to go.

Over the following two months it became rapidly apparent to them that they weren't bringing in enough money to keep them both down in the City. Sadie, rather quickly, volunteered to go back up north, stating that by working in the cake shop she could put some money by each week for them. Stella was in no position to argue. The act needed every penny they could lay their unemployed hands on.

It was a Sunday, and Sadie had been home one day. Early in the morning she and Tommy were stepping down off the Ribble bus at Morecambe's Euston Road Station. It was a bitterly cold morning, and as they walked along together they huddled up tight to keep each other warm.

The weather on the deserted promenade was even colder. Having crossed the road, they stood at the entrance of a closed Central Pier. For a while they just stared down on a scattering of fishing boats that bobbed and dipped on the angry, grey sea. The clock on the tower next to the pier struck nine, making a dozen seagulls spring three or four feet into the air before floating down again onto the shoreline.

They turned right, looked in the general direction of Scotland, and started to walk towards it. Both of them were suitably dressed to battle with the harsh conditions. Tommy wore his cap down over his ears, holding them close against his head and pulling up his eyebrows into an expression of permanent surprise. His scarf covered his mouth, and his overcoat was nearly as close to the ground as his feet. Sadie's beret had started out from Lancaster at a saucy but fashionable angle, and the cold, blended with common sense, had made her pull it so far down that the rim rested on the bridge of her nose. Tommy glimpsed her red-button nose. 'Do you want to sell that poppy?' he asked in a muffled voice. She gave him a friendly punch on his arm, which to Tommy – him being so big, her being so slight – was like being prodded by a feather.

They veered inland a bit, and headed for one of the coast road's bus shelters. Tommy pointed. 'You can see Grange,' he said in a loud voice, but struggled against the wind.

'And Barrow,' said Sadie, with equal difficulty. 'Sometimes you can even see the Cumbrian mountains. That's a sign of rain, or so experts say, whoever they may be.'

'Oh. I hadn't heard that.'

'Don't think it'll rain today, though.'

'More likely start snowing.'

He pulled her gently by the hand. 'Come on. Let's head back to Central Pier and nip down Queen Street to the bus station.'

Tommy had been trying hard all morning to find the suitable moment to tackle Sadie about when she would be going back down to London. As the Central Pier grew before them it seemed that the moment had arrived. 'I guess you'll be wanting to get back to the show stuff soon?'

Sadie had hoped that the subject wouldn't arise, but she knew it had been naive of her to think that it could have been avoided.

'Well, er, Stella reckons, er, Stella says I'm to be back up next Wednesday.' She paused for some reaction. None was forthcoming as yet. Tentatively she continued. 'We've to start rehearsals fairly soon, you see, on a new revue – a touring revue, it is.'

'What's revue?' he asked, darkly.

'It's like variety,' she explained, 'but has sketches and numbers, songs . . .'

'Okay, okay, I get the picture,' he snapped. 'I'm not as bloody daft as you all like to think, you know.'

'I know you're not. I mean . . . Oh, I don't know what I mean,' she said. 'I'm not the least bit eager to get going at the act with Stella again. But no doubt I'll still be saying that when I'm fifty.'

Tommy dug his hands deep into his coat pockets and hunched his back a little to show her how miserable he was feeling. 'Yer didn't mention about Wednesday. I thought we had ages left together.'

Sadie said, 'Sorry, I thought I had.' Both of them knew very well that she hadn't thought at all but it was her way of expressing to him how much she had been dreading having to break the bad news. 'Anyway, I've 'til Wednesday lunchtime and it's only Sunday, love.'

47

'I'll be working Wednesday,' he said, sourly.

'I know that, but you can see me off at Green Ayre Station at one o'clock. You can come straight from work during your lunch break. I'll bring some food and we can have a picnic on the platform. You'd like that, wouldn't you?'

Looking ahead, Tommy asked, 'How long is new revue lasting?'

'Only eight weeks,' she replied, knowing herself just how long eight weeks sounded.

'Two whole flamin' months,' he groaned. He nodded in the approximate direction of the pier. 'What's wrong with here?'

'Eh?'

'Here – Morecambe. They have shows here, don't they? You could work here.'

'It's not as easy as that Tommy. Neil and Claxton will be putting their own show on and they'll use their own dancers.'

'You could tell'em you'd work cheaper if you could appear at Central Pier.'

'Tommy, you know that's not possible. And, anyway, Stella and me are booked for Shanklin for the summer . . .' The sentence filtered out. She hadn't intended letting that piece of devastating information slip out.

He stopped half-way through a stride and pulled her to a halt. 'Shanklin?' he cried, as if someone had said he owed them a thousand pounds. Sadie glumly nodded her head, and wished she'd kept her big mouth closed. 'You mean, Shanklin in Isle of Wight?' To Tommy that could have been Australia. 'Bloody hellfire!'

They started walking again but much slower. 'I won't see you all summer, then?' He shook his head with despair. 'It'll be six months or more before I see you.'

'I'll be back first week in October,' she promised, hoping the freezing tide would sweep over her and take her away.

'Hellfire Sade!'

'Or maybe I'll even be able to get back in the last week of September. It depends how it's going. They've got an option on the last week.'

Tommy had stepped up his pace and she was struggling to keep up with him. 'It's a good date for us, Tommy,' she said. 'Stella's thrilled we're going there.'

'Sod Stella.'

'Oh, Tommy,' she cried, pulling up in her tracks. He walked on a few more paces before turning round to look at her.

'Well, she'll be seeing you and I won't, will I?'

'I know, but we have to look on the bright side. October isn't too far away now,' she lied.

'Sadie, it's seven months.'

'Yes, but it's only a short season from the first week in June when we open, and we only rehearse one week before and not the usual two.'

'It doesn't matter how you juggle it,' he said wearily. 'Seven months is seven months. I can't take time off to visit you, and even when I take my holidays I can't afford to go all the way to the Isle of flamin' Wight.'

They drifted down Queen Street. 'I'll have to go there, Tommy, it's a good run and other dates Stella's got in the book amount to seven months, like you said.' She was being firm with Tommy now. 'I can help you with the fare if you'll say you will come down.'

'No,' he snapped. 'No woman is going to keep Tommy Moran, and that's an end to it. You know my motto: "If you can't afford it, you don't have it." I've always lived by it and it's suited me just fine up 'til now.'

'Look, I'll ask Stella if she has any bright ideas.'

'Oh yes, you ask precious Stella. Stella rules your life, she does.' Now Sadie pulled Tommy to a stop.

'She does not.'

'She does.'

'She doesn't.'

'She bloody well does.'

'Don't swear.'

'I'll bloody swear if I bloody well want to.'

'No you won't.'

'How is it that every time I suggest or say something you always say, "I'll see what Stella says?"' Tommy was trying to imitate Sadie's voice as he said this, but it sounded more like a midget with a groin strain.

'I don't speak like that.'

'Yes you do.'

'No I don't.'

'Okay, you don't, but you can't go denying I'm right about you and Stella,' he said. 'Stella's got this and Stella's got that for us.'

Sadie stormed off for ten quick paces, stopped, turned round, and came briskly back. She looked up at him, staring straight into his eyes, her own having become taut slits of anger. 'I'm going to tell you something Tommy Moran. You say, "Stella's got this and Stella's got that."'

'She takes you over, that's all I'm saying,' he interjected.

'That's right, because if she didn't take over as you say who would do all those things? Me, that's who. I would be in London right now looking for work and walking round all the agencies. Now, you tell me, would you like that?' Before he could answer she continued. 'I'd have to be the one fixing the digs, the music, the costumes. It would have to be me traipsing round, getting everything ready, so I agree with you when you say Stella does this and Stella does that, and I'd like to tell her how grateful I am because if she didn't I wouldn't be able to be here now having a flamin' row with you.' She took a long deep breath. 'Now – I'm going home.'

She stomped away, leaving a stunned Tommy watching her diminish with every angry step. She knew that he would come round and see her later, all soft and meek, probably with a quarter pound of green arrows and a liquorice stick as a way of apologising. Maybe that was one of her frustrations with Tommy, she wondered as she jumped into the Lancaster bus: he was so predictable.

Tommy watched the gulls and the boats for a while longer, as if hypnotised by them. Suddenly he turned and sprinted for the bus station, his eyes swollen with tears.

Stella climbed into the underground train at Balham and headed for the West End. She had a couple of agents she wanted to call on: she had read about them in *The Stage*, and they'd sounded promising. She could hardly wait to see Sadie that night to tell her they had another two weeks' work in the book.

As Tommy waved Sadie off at Green Ayre Station Stella returned to her one and a half roomed flat she was renting, thinking bitterly about *The Stage* and promising agents. She busied herself going through music and costumes and writing off for digs in areas they'd be working in.

It was when the train was about ten miles north of Watford that Sadie began to feel really nervous about telling Stella she was going to leave the act. Stella met her at Euston Station, and Stella, being Stella, already had a porter poised to carry her sister's luggage. 'That's her,' Stella told the porter.

'Which one, miss?' he asked. 'There's a lotta people coming off the train.'

'The one with the beret; that one, there.' She pointed.

The porter nodded approvingly. 'Ah, you mean the pretty one?' He gave a genuine smile on what was inevitably a sad face.

'You look fantastic,' Stella told her sister after they had hugged each other for a few moments. The porter shuffled awkwardly on his feet. He hoped his mates weren't watching. 'There was no-one to touch you walking down the platform, and I love the beret.'

'Wanna taxi, ladies?' enquired the porter.

'No,' replied Stella very definitely. 'Just take the case down to the tube.'

The porter grimaced as he thought of the long walk to the tube, knowing that by the time he had returned there wouldn't be a traveller left for him to make on. The next train wasn't due in for another half an hour.

As they walked Stella rambled on about everything she had been up to in town. Sadie was unusually frugal with her words, and restricted herself to just 'fines' and nods of the head.

'Here we are,' gasped the porter, putting down the case and putting out his hands, all in one motion. 'Phew! a long walk that,' he hinted.

'Yes, it was. Thank you.' Stella pushed two pennies into his hand. He gazed briefly down upon the two copper coins, and then, without further word, ran back to the station in the hope that he would catch a late arrival.

Stella said to her sister with a canny glint in her eyes, 'I've had to learn to watch the pennies carefully.'

51

Forty minutes later they were mounting the single flight of stairs at the Balham flat. Stella instinctively moved to the kettle and filled it. Sadie unpacked a few things and freshened up. Stella couldn't understand why Sadie had brought so little luggage with her. But, stranger, she couldn't understand why she didn't dare ask her about it. 'How's the tea doing?' asked Sadie, now joining her in the kitchen.

'Just brewing.' Stella leant against the sink and looked closely at her sister. Sadie dropped heavily into a stool and began unwrapping a pork pie she'd bought at Kinloch's, the butcher's, just behind Corkell's Yard. She didn't have to look up to sense Stella's questioning stare. 'What's the pie like?'

'Fine,' she replied, curtly.

'Kinloch's pies usually are,' said Stella.

Stella began wondering if Sadie's odd behaviour had anything to do with her parents. 'How are Mam and Dad?'

'They're fine.' Again, she didn't seem to want to expand on her answer.

They sipped at their tea in an awkward silence; so unusual was it for two such close sisters. Sadie finished the pie and wiped her mouth on the back of her sleeve. She took a deep breath and asked, 'What would you say if I told you I was getting married?'

Stella took her time answering. So *this* is what you were building up to, she thought. When finally she did answer, she kept her stare downwards onto the dregs in her cup. 'I'd say, do you have to?' Sadie briefly glanced at her.

'I don't have to – no. I mean, I'm not pregnant or anything.'

Stella looked at her with an angry frown. 'Well, what on earth are you on about then?'

'Didn't you hear me right?' Sadie asked her. 'I'm talking about marriage. Marriage out of a natural love, not a convenience to avoid family shame.'

'You asked me what I'd say and I've told you. Don't even think about marriage.'

'But you don't understand, do you? You've never been in love. We're in love.'

'Of course I understand,' she said. 'What do you take me for, a monster without feelings? I understand exactly.'

She lifted the lid off the teapot and began stirring to occupy her hands. It was either that or put them round Sadie's neck and start squeezing. 'I understand very well that you love Tommy Moran. But marriage? There's plenty of time for all that domestic bit. What do you want to get married for, anyway?' She poured the remainder of the pot into her own cup. 'If you love him proper and he loves you proper then you'll both be able to wait a while. Go back home when you can and sleep with him if that's what you want . . .'

'It's not like that,' squealed Sadie. 'You're making it sound dirty and . . . and . . . well, just horrible.'

She moved up close to her sister and clasped her hands in her own. 'You're not Joan Crawford love, and he's certainly not Gary Cooper. In Lancaster, once you're married, you end up like Mam and Dad. Just waiting for the end of time, and filling it in by doing the pools and drinking beer at the weekends.'

'But we're in love,' she wailed, as if desperately trying to establish this fundamental point.

'Of course you are. If you weren't we wouldn't be sitting here now talking about it all. But do as I say. Get married, fine – but wait a while. Give yourself a chance to live. Give us a chance to launch our careers.'

'Our career is all you think about. You bully me around for your own ends. Well, I've had enough of it.'

Stella couldn't say anything. For the first time in her life she was stunned into silence. She felt a twisting hurt in the pit of her stomach. 'I see. I didn't know that you saw it as being like that,' she finally managed to say in a hoarse voice.

Sadie shook her head a few times, and freed her hand to rub her troubled brow. 'I'm sorry,' she said in a level voice. 'I really didn't mean that – really.'

'And what do Mam and Dad think of all this, then?'

'They're for it,' she replied quickly, sure she'd trumped Stella's trump card.

'I don't believe you,' said Stella, as if she was a bad loser. 'You're under twenty-one, which will worry Dad, and also Mam knows that if you get married then it's goodbye to that extra few bob a week in keep.'

'Write and ask them, then – then we'll see who's right.'

'What's the point of that? The letter will only end up on the mantle-shelf until the end of time.'

Stella picked up the pot and cups and began washing them in the sink. When she had turned the pot upside-down and left it on the draining board to dry, she said to Sadie, 'You know that if you leave me now I'm in big trouble? I've got us the next six months booked. It's the biggest break we've had. And they're good dates, Sadie. Number-ones, some of them.' She felt a bit strange talking to her own reflection in the kitchen window, but it was easier than turning to face her sister. 'I've got us this agent chap. His name's Johnny Burton, and what can I tell him? He'd most probably thump me – he's that type.'

Now Stella did turn round. There were tears streaming down Sadie's face yet she wasn't flexing a muscle. Stella went for a hankie and gave it to her. 'I read in the paper the other day,' she said, changing the subject with a shattering abruptness, 'that Hull fishermen had the biggest catch they've ever known.'

Sadie looked up with a tear-stained face, but her composure returned. 'Pardon?'

'I was talking about the trawlermen. They've caught the biggest catch ever. I suppose they were just lucky to get into such a big shoal.'

'I suppose they were.' She gave a solid blow on her nose which sounded like the signal to launch a lifeboat. Then she said, 'But I'm still going to marry him, Stella.'

Stella took a few deep breaths. She could feel the anger welling up in her. She hadn't anticipated Sadie's return to London bringing such upset and misery. 'Look, I know how you feel. Honest I do. But what about me? Let's face it, Sadie, I've signed a contract and I've signed it for both of us. Can't you, just for my sake even, wait until we've done these dates? That's all I'm asking. And think of the money you'll save – that'll be a great wedding present in itself. Dad won't be able to afford to give you much of a wedding, so we'll both put into it and make it special.'

Sadie kept quiet: she thought it best to. Stella was coming to the boil and she didn't want to accelerate the process. 'I don't want to have to give up the business, Sadie. I'm not like you; I don't want to go and spend the rest of my life in Lancaster raising kids.'

The negative response she was receiving made her change her pleas into offers of compromise. 'Look, just give me three months,' she said. 'I think I could manage to find a new partner by then. Even two months would be a help; but don't let me down now, Sadie.'

Sadie gave a single, firm shake of her head, which made her hair drift across her face. 'Jesus!' shouted Stella. 'Don't you realise what you're doing, you selfish bitch? You're cutting my lifeline; you're killing my future; you and that stupid git from next door.'

Stella had reached bursting-point. 'He put you up to this, didn't he, eh? It was him, wasn't it? And what can he promise you? I'll tell you what – sod-all, that's what. You stupid girl, you'll end up like our Mam – seventy years old at twenty-one.'

She would have continued overflowing with frustrated anger if they hadn't been interrupted by the dull ring of the hallway telephone. 'That'll be Tommy,' said Sadie, in a soft, unaffected voice, as though she'd been out of the room all during her sister's remonstrations.

'Give the bastard my love, won't you?'

Sadie trotted from the room and Stella heard her muffled voice. Ten minutes later, with Sadie still on the phone, Stella wrapped a coat across her shoulders and drifted past her and out through the front door. She wandered aimlessly down the street. She followed the pavement, staring in windows at shoes, handbags, and dresses, but she didn't really see them.

It's eight weeks to the show, was all she was thinking. If Sadie can be persuaded to stay on for that time I'm sure I'll be able to get myself another partner.

Her attention fell on a wedding dress displayed in one of the shop windows. She nearly spat at it. Making her way back to the flat she wondered how she was going to survive on fifty-six pounds, which was the sum total in her post-office savings book.

She opened the door and discovered that Sadie had finished on the phone. The bare bulb on its ragged cord, was still weakly illuminating the kitchen. Resting on the upturned teapot was a note. Stella read it.

55

'Dear Stella,

I'm sorry but I waited as long as I could for you to come back. Tommy wants me to come home and there's a late train tonight. I've given it much thought and have decided it best I go home. I want to be with Tommy more than I want to struggle along in showbusiness. I love you Stella, and always will, but Tommy needs me. Please don't think I've run out on you, as I was never much good in the act as it was. You're the talented one. It'll take a brave man to stop Stella Raven from making it.

I've left two pounds ten shillings under the plant pot for my share of the flat for this week. Don't think too badly of me. Tommy and I will be getting married soon. I'll let you know when the wedding is,

Your loving sister, Sadie.

PS: I've packed all my own stuff and left the stage costumes under the bed in the big case.'

Stella reread the letter a couple of times and certain parts of it several more times. She cried on and off for nearly an hour, then she washed her swollen face and looked at her dishevelled state in the mirror.

She went to her bed and, perched on one corner, munched at an apple and thought about her career. After that night it was a long time before she thought about Sadie again.

Chapter 6

'C'min,' said her agent, Johnny Burton, in answer to her knock. He didn't have a secretary. He couldn't afford one.

She entered his Charing Cross Road office, which was all of twelve feet by twelve feet, and walked up to a desk that would have been old when Charles Dickens was a boy. She sat down in the only seat that faced it.

Johnny Burton was in his late thirties, and had all the trappings of someone who had never quite made it but intended pretending that he had. His suit was obviously expensive – and obviously not his. His late thirties body was turning to late forties fat, and when he smiled, which wasn't very often, he revealed a lack of teeth.

His pasty face tilted up from the desk to frown upon Stella. She thought it resembled an unhappy pancake. 'Sit down,' he instructed, grumpily.

'I am sat down.'

'Oh yeah. So what was all that crap you were giving me on the phone about your kid sister?'

'Mr Burton, I'm very sorry about all this but, like I said, she's decided to give it all up. It was totally unexpected, I assure you.'

Burton gave her his most piercing stare and she shuffled uncomfortably in her seat, trying to attain a relaxed posture. She couldn't find one. 'You've really got me into a right bleedin' mess haven't you?' He massaged his forehead and cheeks firmly enough to momentarily alter the shape of his face.

'I'm very sorry,' she whispered, meekly.

'Sorry? *You're* bleedin' sorry,' he growled. 'That's a lotta bleedin' good that is, girlie.'

Stella glanced down, noticing how white her clenched hands had made her knuckles. 'All morning I've been sat on the bleedin' phone and some cow of a secretary at Cranbourn Mansions* kept me waiting fifteen minutes before I could speak with anyone in authority to do with Moss Empires' bookings.'

He jerked back his desk drawer and took out a single cigarette. As he lit it Stella noticed it wasn't for the first time. A puff of grey smoke swept across her face but she refused to flinch or cough. He released a couple of bronchial-sounding coughs, then pointed several times at the telephone with a loose finger. 'Twenty minutes I've been on that bleedin' phone to the producer of the Shanklin summer show.' He coughed, agonisingly. 'You'll never get the chance of Moss Empires again, I can promise you that, girlie. You've Friar Tucked your chances there, kid.'

Still coughing, he began to wipe away the tears that filled his beady eyes with a sheet of used blotting paper that he'd pulled out of the waste-paper basket. 'Have you brought your date book?'

'Er, yes.' She fumbled hurriedly through her bag.

He lunged forward, rudely swiped the diary from her hand, and began rifling through the pages with stubby, nicotine-stained fingers. 'You've had it with Moss Empires,' he repeated, thinking that maybe it hadn't registered the first time.

She tried to muster a weak smile but it came out as more of a grimace. 'I might, and I mean *might*, be able to save you the summer show,' he said. A slight ray of hope ran through her body. 'But I'll have to work bleedin' hard on that one for you. I mean, it isn't worth a bleedin' miserable ten per cent.' Stella kept quiet. He tossed the diary back at her and it landed on the floor near her feet. She reached down in a slow and dignified manner and retrieved it. 'Moss Empires don't want

* Cranbourn Mansions in London's West End was the head office for Moss Empires

to know. They've already got another act to take your place.'
She thought that was remarkably quick replacement work.

'I'll have an act ready for the summer show,' she said. 'You
see, I've got this idea for a solo act where I sing more than
dance, and joke a bit with the aud . . .'

'Solo?' He gasped. His eyes hardened. 'For Christ's sake
don't go and tell them it's solo. As far as they're concerned
they've booked a duo. They'll want to pay less money if they
know it's solo. Keep that bleedin' piece of news to yourself,
girlie.'

'Yes, yes, of course. And do you think that there's any
possibility of getting me anything in the next few weeks – to
tide me over, sort of?' Though her voice was steady, she
couldn't disguise the begging tone. He took a long time to
answer.

'I might.' He stood up and he was nearly taller sitting
down. He waddled over to the curtainless window and tried to
open it, but it was stuck, so he dropped his cigarette-end on a
stretch of bare floorboards where the carpet had worn out,
flattened it with a cruel foot, and returned to his chair. 'You're
lucky,' he finally said. 'The producer of the summer show likes
you. He saw you working with that bitch of a sister of yours
and he liked what he saw.' He gave Stella a slow, meaningful
wink. 'You know what I mean?'

Stella played the innocent and said, 'No, I don't.'

'Well, you should do, 'cos he wants you in the show and he
wants you to feed the comic, Allan Walker, as well. Ever
heard of him?' She didn't reply, and she wouldn't have had
time to anyway. 'Bleedin' awful. Twenty-five and thinks he
knows the game backwards.' He winked at her again. 'You
must have played it pretty smart with that producer then, eh?'

'I've never even met him,' she replied, honestly.

'I bet. He's the biggest crumpet king in the business. Had
'em all, he has. His name's Ken Hutton. Come off it, girlie,
you must have heard of "Huttons Mutton?"' Stella gave him a
long, cold look with a smile to match. 'Anyway, he says he
likes you – fancies you a bit maybe. Have to keep your hands
on your drawers with him about.'

'Do you think you can get me some work within the next
couple of weeks, so I can get my act together?' Her tone was

businesslike, and the frown on Burton's face showed how it aggravated him.

'I might,' he said with little optimism, and then started to leer across his desk at her. He rested his face in his hands as if to stop it running down his shirt. 'Depends on what you can do.'

'Anything; anything at all.'

'That's nice,' he groaned. 'Can you lock doors?'

'Lock doors?' she asked, her eyebrows raised in a questioning arch.

'You heard me,' he said firmly. 'Lock doors.'

His eyes looked over her shoulders, asking her to follow them. She turned round and saw the key in the lock. She turned back, giving him a seductive smile. 'I would say that was easy enough,' she said, tossing her head casually back at the door. 'What about being disturbed?'

'No chance,' he croaked as if he'd just eaten three slices of sandpaper.

She stood up slowly, and walked rhythmically to the door, her hips playing a rumba as he watched.

Burton could feel stirrings in his trousers and a trickle of sweat running down his chest. She pulled the key out of the lock, opened the door, walked out of the room, closed the door, locked it, put the key in her handbag, and, with all the time in the world, moved elegantly down the stairway and out into the bright, noisy street.

The winter sun felt good on her self-satisfied face. She glanced up to the second-floor window and saw the great Johnny Burton trying to open it. She waved to him and he mouthed something back, followed by violent gesticulations of his fist.

Taking the key out of her bag she held it high for him to see. He went very still, clasping his hands together as if in prayer. She laughed, then dropped it down the drain.

She knew Ken Hutton's address from *The Stage*, and if by chance he had really thought something of their act, and not just their figures, then it had to be worth a visit. She really had very little to lose at this present time. She'd already succeeded in losing her partner and agent within about twelve hours of each other.

60

She went directly to his office, hoping she would beat Johnny Burton's phone call informing him, and the rest of showbusiness, to avoid Stella Raven like the plague. Mind you, she was fairly sure that there weren't too many bookers and agents in the business who would take much notice of an oversexed shark like Johnny Burton.

Minutes later she was in Beak Street, just off Regent Street. She apprehensively entered through the glass door marked 'K. Hutton Productions'.

A smart young secretary smiled up from her typing. The front office was empty of people but there was still a sense of activity and success. 'Good morning. Can I help you?' enquired the smiling face.

'Yes. Is Mr Hutton in?'

'Who shall I say is calling?'

'Miss Stella Raven.'

'And what time was your appointment for?' She was looking down a long list of names on a large diary page.

'Actually, I'm here on the offchance of seeing him.'

'Oh, I'm so sorry,' she said. 'But Mr Hutton only sees people who have appointments.' The smile didn't once leave her face, which irritated Stella more than if the girl had been insulting to her.

'It *is* rather important,' said Stella, raising a serious expression.

'I am sorry, but he's very busy today. If you'd care to ring in some time, perhaps then we could fix you an appointment.'

She began to type, now oblivious to Stella's presence. Even her smile was waning. Stella didn't go away, though. She stood there for a moment in thought, wondering what her next move should be. 'I've *got* to see him,' she blurted.

'Then please ring for an appointment.' Her tone was much firmer now.

This secretary had obviously been instructed on how to deal with the desperate, off-the-street artiste. Stella knew that there must be a dozen a day like her who came wandering in hoping to have the chance of seeing Mr Hutton. To this secretary she was no doubt just another piece of animated flesh, young and ambitious, and who would never be heard of in a million years. 'Well, could I leave a message then?' The secretary stopped typing and looked at her cautiously.

'A message – what kind of message?'

'It's a personal message,' she explained. 'And I'll have to wait here while you deliver it, as it does need an urgent reply.'

'I understand,' said the secretary, not really understanding. She reached for a pad and pencil.

'Will you tell him that Stella is here, and that all our fears have been verified – I am pregnant, and I'll be phoning his wife this afternoon.' Stella inwardly smiled as the secretary went the colour of sunset and, with shaking fingers, tore the sheet away from her pad. 'And tell him that if he doesn't see me now, then I have a sneaking suspicion that both his wife and my husband will be round to see him this afternoon.'

'Er, yes. I . . . I'll be right back.'

'Remember, it's Stella. Stella Raven.'

With the message in her hand she hurried in to Ken Hutton's private office. 'Stella Raven to see you, sir.'

'Do I know her?'

'Miss Stella Raven, sir. Yes, I believe you know her very well,' she said bitterly.

'Oh, okay. Send her in.'

Stella marched boldly in and the secretary went back to her work but her hands were shaking too much for her to type properly.

Fifteen minutes later they emerged from Hutton's office, Stella adorned with a triumphant smile. During her quarter of an hour she'd told him the traumas of her sister leaving and of Johnny Burton's crude, unprofessional behaviour. Despite his reputation, she'd found Mr Hutton one of the better agents she had come across. 'Goodbye, Miss Raven. I shall do all I can to help you,' he promised.

He smiled at her departing back, and carried the smile across to his secretary, who returned it with a sharp, fiery glare.

He returned to his office wondering what he had said to upset her so much. She punched the typewriter, hurting her knuckles, and said aloud, but not loud enough to be heard by anyone but herself, 'That's the last time you come back to my place, you bastard.'

As she massaged her tender hand one of the phones rang. 'K. Hutton Productions,' she said angrily as if warning the caller they'd better have a damn good reason for calling.

'Put me through to Hutton, please,' demanded the caller.

'Who is calling, please?'

'Burton – Johnny Burton.'

She informed her boss of the call. 'Who?'

'A Johnny Burton. He's a theatrical agent, I believe.'

'Oh, yes. Tell him to get stuffed.' The briefest of pauses followed, then, 'And is it okay if I drop in tonight, say tenish?'

This was followed by a longer pause, then, 'Yes, fine,' she said casually, and reconnected herself to Johnny Burton.

Tommy Moran splashed ice-cold water across his freshly shaved face and gingerly tapped it dry with a cloth. A thin trickle of blood drew a route from his chin to his Adam's apple.

Quickly, he tore a corner off the newspaper, a piece without print on it, and held it against the cut until it had sealed itself in place.

His brother Colin, who was, much to Tommy's concern, his best man, was upstairs fighting with a very new, very stiff collar.

Their father was in the 'Red Lion', fighting with a very full pint of beer. Their mother was in the bride's house, next door, applying her special gift of getting in everyone's way.

Tommy was relieved to have the kitchen sink all to himself. He gazed thoughtfully through the rain-soaked window, hoping the disappointing weather wasn't a bad omen of some kind.

He thought of Stella, his first love – a childhood fantasy of woman. How sad he was she wouldn't be there to share in the joy of this special day. She hadn't even sent a letter or telegram wishing them well. Sadie still believed she would make a surprise appearance at the service but Tommy doubted it. He had a more realistic conception of how deep Stella's wounds were. Dissolving the partnership had dissolved a part of Stella's life.

Tommy sighed and went upstairs, saying, as he went, 'Hurry up, Colin. We don't want to be late.'

'I am hurrying,' grunted back Colin's voice.

Once upstairs, Tommy pulled out a long, slim box from beneath his bed. Opening it, he saw a thick dark suit that felt as though it had been made from sacking. It would be his best suit for the next few years and last him the rest of his life.

As he changed he pondered on how strange and unreal it all was. Tonight he would be in Blackpool with his new wife: tonight, Saturday and most of Sunday, and then back home for Sunday night – well, next door at the Ravenscrofts'. Then a couple of more weeks and they should have a home of their own.

Shirt and trousers in place, he struggled into the jacket, which was designed in the latest style – high-waisted, single-breasted, peaked rolled lapels, slanting pockets, double vents – and then skipped back downstairs, ready to make tracks.

Colin was hovering by the back door with a guilty expression on his face. Tommy said to him, 'What are you up to?'

'Er, I thought I'd just tell our Dad to drink up,' he replied, awkwardly.

'Like hell, you will,' frowned his brother. 'I'll go with you, otherwise we'll end up with both you and Dad missing, presumed drunk.' He pulled open the door and took a positive step in the direction of Saint Luke's Church – and the 'Red Lion' pub.

'He's not in there,' announced Colin, emerging out of the entrance to the 'Red Lion' and wiping a sleeve across his mouth. 'I wonder which one he's at.'

'Sod him,' said Tommy. 'C'mon. Let's get to the church.'

They sat next to each other on the edge of the front pew. 'I've a splinter in my bum,' moaned Colin, in a voice that echoed through the old stone building.

'Shush. You can pick it out later,' Tommy told him.

They lowered their heads in prayer. Tommy asked for a happy marriage, a nice house, a few kids, and enough money. Colin asked the same person to make sure Tommy and Sadie had a good time in Blackpool, that their mam found their dad, and Preston North End beat the living daylights out of Manchester City on Saturday – thanks a lot, Amen.

At the conclusion of Colin's prayer the arched door swung open with a bang, and Mrs Moran came bounding down the aisle in a more meaningful fashion than she had done thirty years ago.

She was short and dumpy, and resembled Colin more than Tommy. 'Where the flamin' hell's yer father?' she snapped.

'We don't know,' answered Tommy with open palms.

'He's not in the "Red Lion",' said Colin. 'I've checked.'

'I'm not fussed where he's *not*, I want to know where he *is*.'

'How about the "Dog and Partridge"?' suggested Colin.

'The taxi driver's been there and four other blood . . . flamin' places, and he's not in any of 'em.'

She nodded sharply towards the entrance where a poor excuse for daylight was seeping in. 'Poor Sadie's sitting on her arse in that taxi with no-one with her.'

'But it's Jack Ravenscroft's job to give Sadie away,' said Tommy; 'Not our Dad's.'

'Jack went looking for him and now he's gone missing,' she said.

'I think the vicar wants us to get a move on,' remarked Colin, as the agitated clergyman came slowly across to them. 'Are we Catholic, Mam?' asked Colin, seriously.

'Don't ask flamin' stupid questions at times like these,' she replied.

'I hope Dad gets here all right,' said Tommy.

'Bugger 'im,' swore Colin, and he promptly received a short, sharp clip around the ear from his mother.

The vicar 'ahemmed' to the congregation – which numbered, in total, eight – and then stepped forward, summoning the two brothers to do likewise. Mrs Moran slumped into her seat. The organ wheezed into Wagner's Bridal March, 'Lohengrin', and Tommy estimated that it would cost him another thirty bob on the day – and it did.

He whispered in Colin's ear, 'Have you got the ring?' His brother rummaged in his pocket and clinked about in his loose change until he found it. Tommy breathed a sigh of relief.

The vicar lifted his head as the bride appeared in the doorway in a light-blue two-piece outfit, with a pillbox hat glued firmly at an angle on her head.

She didn't look as incongruous as she could have done, walking up the aisle on the arm of an unshaven taxi driver who looked remarkably calm and experienced in this sort of fill-in role.

Jack arrived as they were all leaving the church and Mr

Moran didn't arrive at all. He was later discovered to have gone straight to the reception being held above the Palladium cinema.

It could have been a more enjoyable reception had Colin tried to avoid making a speech that consisted of jokes about sex-starved brides and a German doctor called Dr Kuttithoff.

Heads turned when Mr Moran collapsed in a drunken heap on the floor. To give him credit, he did manage, though it took him three and a half minutes, to climb back into his chair. Tommy was more irritated that, out of the forty guests, none of them had bothered to attend the service than the fact his father didn't even know why they were there and what was being celebrated.

Tommy's mother was upset that someone had invited 'Lancaster Lil' – the biggest scrubber north of the border. She was locally famous, or infamous, for being able to drink any man under the table, her chain-smoking, her free lessons in sex to beginners, and charging only two and six for professionals. She wasn't the wealthiest or prettiest of people. She cradled Tommy's dad in her arms, and began rocking him as if he was a baby she was trying to put to sleep.

There was a tense and embarrassed atmosphere by now mainly encouraged by Colin's speech but decided by Mr Moran's behaviour. Mrs Moran looked coldly at the spectacle of her husband swaying in the arms of Lancaster Lil, both singing 'You were meant for me', then quietly walked over to Colin and whispered in his ear. Her son dutifully followed her across the room as she made for his dad.

Sadie, who had been observing them, nudged Tommy nervously. Colin hoisted his dad out of Lil's arms, him still singing away, and his mother landed a firm punch on Lil's nose, sending her sprawling across the floor, dazed and blooded, and unable to move for several minutes.

Colin took his dad downstairs and out into the open where he sat him against a lamp post. He returned to help his mother lift up Lil and lay her across the food table, face-down in the sausage rolls. When they returned to their seats they were given a spontaneous round of applause, and the rest of the reception was fairly enjoyable.

Tommy and Sadie, contrary to tradition, were last to leave

their own reception. 'Tommy darling,' said Sadie as they finally made to go.

'Yes, love?'

'There was no telegram from Stella, was there?' It was a statement more than a question. Tommy thought for a second before replying.

'It might have been mislaid.'

Chapter 7

It took Stella just two days to find a new place to stay and a week to put her new act together. She'd had one or two ideas in her mind before Sadie had left but they were ideas created specifically for a partnership – not a solo performer. Therefore she'd had to make alterations and refinements to suit the new and unexpected position she found herself in.

She settled in a small place in Mornington Crescent. In the same block were a couple of other acts who hardly ever seemed to find work and several prostitutes who never seemed to stop work.

She booked a rehearsal room and a pianist, and really started to work on polishing her solo act, which had now developed from just singing and a little dancing to also telling a few light-hearted anecdotes and sharing one or two jokes with the audience. There was one phone on the same floor as her flat, when it rang, she would take the gamble of answering in case it was some work coming in, but invariably it was someone asking what she would do for fifteen bob. As far as she was concerned, this place was somewhere temporary and cheap.

She wrote occasionally to her parents, telling them of any progress she was making, always painting a better picture of how things were. She would never make reference to Sadie or Tommy, and, at this time, didn't know or care that they were married.

Everyone, no matter what line of business they are in, needs a little bit of luck. Stella was given some, and it brought about a major step forward in her career.

In a way it began with Johnny Burton; the cheap oversexed agent she'd locked in his own office. He'd had to phone his way out. The locksmith who released him listened astounded to his story and told someone else, who in turn told someone else, and so on. Through the various agents and bookers it became quite a famous story, and with each rendition it grew more exaggerated. This made it easier for her to find work, as she was quite well known by managements even before making an approach to them.

She picked up an important week's work before starting rehearsals for the summer show in Shanklin, and she took full advantage of it to test out her new-look act. Being a town date, most agents and bookers came to see her – having read her letter saying, 'Stella Raven, comedienne extraordinaire, not to be missed' – and, although a little nervous and new, she did impress them.

The summer show in Shanklin opened and it was a big success. The landladies told their boarders to go and see it, and soon they were playing to packed houses. Much to Stella's own personal pleasure she found she was often approached during the daytime to sign an autograph or two: a new experience for her.

After it had been running for five weeks Mr Henry Charles came to the island. Henry Charles was *the* big West End impresario of the era. The reason why he should have made a personal call to the island was that his wife was born there, and was at present visiting her mother, who still lived there. He'd come down to join her for the weekend.

The moment he arrived, his wife told him of the glowing reports on the show. He drew heavily on a fat Cuban cigar he was rarely to be seen without. Once, a close friend and colleague had arranged to meet him at seven o'clock one morning for a pre-working day meeting. One thing's for certain, he'd thought. I'll catch him without that damn cigar in his mouth. But he didn't.

'Who's in it, then?' he asked, letting the ash fall onto his mother-in-law's carpet, and he rubbed it in uncaringly. He'd

69

paid for the carpet, the car, and the house: he felt he had a right to do as he wanted.

'I'm not too sure,' replied Mrs Charles, scowling at the mirror for revealing too many wrinkles on her face. She reached across the dresser for her make-up bag and began working on them. 'We'll have to take a walk out that way later and have a look at the names outside the theatre.'

'Good idea,' he agreed. He didn't like weekends away from London. His London office was his life. Weekends merely upset the pattern of his work. Just walking by a theatre was at least some compensation.

They walked arm-in-arm and reached the theatre at exactly six o'clock. They were only out taking the fresh air, and hadn't planned on going inside. The show was due to raise its curtain at six ten. At six five, having seen few names of interest, the Charles' turned to go home. Then the heavens opened and, with an endless sky of grey hanging over them, it looked like they intended staying open.

Henry Charles pointed with his cigar at the main doors and said, with a touch of irony, 'Fancy taking in a show?'

As they went to leave at the end of the performance Mr Charles was recognised by the management. 'Indeed an honour sir', and 'Come this way', and 'A few drinks with the artistes', were the types of comments bestowed upon him. With a shrug they followed him into a spacious back room and were handed a glass of 'first-night' champagne – beer and spirits from then until the last-night party being the only alcoholic beverages supplied – and duly met the performers. 'And this is Stella Raven,' said the manager with a quick flourish of the wrist, eager to move on to one or two more well-known faces. Charles pulled up in front of her.

'Stella Raven, eh?'

'Yes, sir,' she replied weakly, as if she'd just been introduced to the King of England.

'That song "Stormy Weather" that you sang – bit inspirational playing it for laughs like you did.'

'I was told it was bucketing down outside, sir, so it seemed the natural thing to do. Sort of cheer people up.'

Henry Charles gently nodded and moved on down the line. Afterwards, he pulled out a pen and put a little tick next to the

70

name of Stella Raven where it appeared in his programme. That was the biggest piece of luck she would ever have, and she would say in better times that it was 'heaven-sent.'

At the end of the seaon Stella returned to London with little money left in her post-office savings account but a fair amount of cash in her pocket which she put into her account at the earliest possible moment.

One of her first priorities was to find a small flat as near to the West End as possible, for that was where it all happened. Whilst she hunted, she took digs in Brixton – where very little happened. At least, that was what she thought until she received a message from Henry Charles, via Ken Hutton.

Charles had been told that Hutton kept contact with her over possible work-availability, and so told Hutton to tell Stella to pay him a visit in his London office at eleven thirty on Wednesday morning. It was then Monday, and Tuesday afternoon by the time Hutton had managed to get hold of Stella with the encouraging message.

The reception to Henry Charles' office was larger than any flat or digs she'd stayed in. 'Mr Charles will see you now, Miss Raven,' an attractive secretary informed her; one who'd been as carefully chosen as the furnishings surrounding her.

Impulsively, Stella glanced at her watch. It was precisely eleven thirty, and she knew it was accurate because she had checked it first thing that morning. Mr Charles was clearly quite a time-keeper.

The secretary minced towards the panelled oak door and gently knocked. Stella heard nothing from within, but the secretary, with her ear to the door like a sink plunger, suddenly smiled and opened the door for her. Smiling a quiet thank-you, Stella edged past her and inside.

Charles languished in an upright leather chair that was big enough to be a throne and, in this particular building, it *was* a throne. 'Come in, Miss Raven, and please sit down,' instructed a talking cigar.

If she hadn't been so nervous she would have laughed at the sight of this large man seated in an even larger chair, with what appeared to be a tree trunk protruding between moistened, pouting lips. But she *was* nervous – very nervous.

He said, 'How do you feel the summer show went?'

'We were told that it broke all existing records there.'

'I think you were told the truth,' he purred, knowing it had been a huge success. 'Would you care for a drink?'

Probably to help me relax, she thought. 'I wouldn't mind a small sherry, if that's no trouble.'

'If it was to be a trouble I wouldn't have asked,' he told her, and she could tell that he wasn't being nasty – just truthful.

He pressed a button on his desk and a bell could be heard from within an adjoining room. Another panelled door opened and another attractive secretary came inside. 'Sherry for Miss Raven; usual for me.'

Stella couldn't stop herself from peering over her shoulder to see where the drinks cabinet was kept, but there was no obvious cabinet on show in the room.

The woman pushed firmly against a particular wooden panel on the rear wall and there followed a humming sound. Then the wall turned on casters and, lo and behold, Stella could see a bar counter with an array of glinting bottles. 'Good God!' she exclaimed, and instantly put a hand to her mouth. Henry Charles chuckled in a calm, unenthusiastic manner.

'I take it you haven't seen too many contraptions like this?' he said.

'No, sir, I haven't.'

The drinks were brought over, his usual being a large Scotch with two lumps of ice. 'Are you represented?' he asked, not wasting any more time on small talk. The woman left the room and Stella waited until she had gone before replying.

'Not exactly. I don't have a contract or anything, though Mr Hutton has been kind enough to help me find some work here and there.'

'No-one's "kind enough" to do anything in this business,' he said, honestly. 'Ken Hutton is a fairly good agent, who saw a prospect talent come into his office of whom he wanted ten per cent. Trouble is, you're not really Hutton material. He needs established talent – that's how he's always got by. I like to find possible talent and then make it great.'

He looked at her for a while as if trying to weigh her up. Then he asked her, 'How would you like this agency to

72

represent you? My junior partner is one of the best agents you'll ever come across in this business, so if you say no, then you're as good as putting an end to what *I* think could be a great career.'

His words were bouncing around her head, making her giddy with excitement. 'Y. . .yes, I would like to be with your agency.'

'Good.' He was still quite placid and unflinching. His attitude would have been the same even had she said, 'No thank you'. He was a professional. 'The office is called Charles and Farrow. It is Farrow, Mr Michael Farrow, who I'll be directing you to. At the moment we're working on a new idea for a West End revue for about November time, and I think I'd like you to have a small part in it. I want you to do that stormy weather number.' He chuckled as he reminisced. 'It was really very good indeed,' he mused. He was serious again. 'I want you to get the kind of laughs you got when I saw you do it in the Isle of Wight.' He paused. 'Can you get those kind of laughs again?' he asked.

Stella nodded with self-conviction. 'Oh yes.'

'Good. There's nothing better than belief in your own talent, and there's nothing better in a revue than a lovely girl doing a "point" number and having the audience laugh *with* her, not *at* her. I thought you showed a great potential for comedy, and in due course I'd like to help you all I can to develop it – with the assistance of Woody Woodville. Do you know him?'

'The American producer?' she asked, a little dumbstruck. She was feeling as though she had just arrived in fairyland. Surely none of this was true. When she returned to the stark reality of her bedsit in Brixton she would realise that it was all just a dream to torment her.

'That's the man. Well, he's coming over here in a few weeks' time and then we start rehearsals, and then open a tour in the provinces – maybe Bristol, Brighton, Manchester, and Birmingham. Then, we hope, into the West End itself.'

His phone rang and it allowed her time to quickly swallow her drink. She noticed it was a very monosyllabic phone conversation. Perhaps he didn't want to talk business in front of her, or perhaps he just always had that sort of phone manner. He soon finished and picked up just where he'd left off, which impressed her immensely. 'But to get into the West End the show has obviously got to prove its worth in those provinces. Now, you must meet Mr Farrow and discuss a few things: no less than a contract itself.'

He climbed out of his chair in a way that suggested he didn't do it very often during the course of his day and that it was quite an inconvenience that he should have to do it at all. Briefly, he left the room to return with a handsome grey-haired man who Stella judged was on the verge of entering his forties, but reluctantly so.

They were introduced, and Mr Farrow crinkled his face, making deep wrinkles form around his laughing eyes. His suit was noticeably baggy and seemed able to allow him to move around in it while the suit itself remained still. 'Miss Raven. Henry told me you were a picture of beauty. He's rarely wrong and on this occasion he's right again.' He reached forward and, in chivalrous manner, softly touched the back of her right hand with his lips and nose. With a continuous grin he released her hand then allowed his suit to take him across to the other side of the room.

She said, 'I must stress, Mr Farrow . . .'

'Call me Mike – only my wife calls me Mr Farrow. Ha ha ha!'

'Thank you, Mike. I must stress I haven't done too much solo work, and I've very little work in the book, except next week. I'm in a variety bill at the Empire, Oldham.'

'Oldham, you say? I come from near there – Accrington.' She looked to Mr Charles as if with a need for verification. He grinned and gave a single nod. 'And let me tell you one thing, Stella, you will soon have so much work you'll hardly have time to eat and drink. You'll be begging me to let you have a day off, because when you look at me you are looking at a genius. Is that not right, Henry?'

'So you keep telling everyone, Mike, so you keep telling everyone.'

'And that's because it's the truth, Stella.' She didn't doubt it for a second. 'Now step next door, Stella Raven, star of the near future, and we'll produce a contract for you to study.'

He turned to Henry Charles, but his suit remained facing

74

the door. 'See you later, Henry, and thank you for bringing this wonderful star to my notice.' He asked Stella, 'Where do you live?'

'Brixton at the moment, but . . .'

'Now isn't that a coincidence.'

'You mean you don't live in Brixton?' she asked, incredulously.

'Tomorrow I might,' he replied, with a mischievous twinkle in his eye.

Stella was sure that things were starting to look up. She now had an agent, and a particularly good one, although it was early days in her representation, and Mike Farrow would have to prove himself before she could be certain: and one of the cleverest men in the business, Henry Charles, had shown her respect and wanted to consider her for a West End revue. 'Oh God, please let me get the job in the revue,' she prayed aloud as she sipped her third cup of coffee of the morning. 'If you do, I'll go to church every Sunday that I'm not travelling.'

She was sitting in her small Brixton flat, wondering who she could break the good news to. She thought about writing to her parents, but they wouldn't really understand, and the letter would only end up as yet another souvenir on the mantle-shelf.

She rang Euston Station to find out the times of trains going to Oldham. Playing Oldham was now the last thing she felt like doing, but she knew it had to be done, and done well. There was an overnight train to Manchester on Sunday night, leaving midnight and arriving at five in the morning. She booked a sleeper, then found herself adding, to her own surprise, 'Make it first-class.' It would cost her a small fortune, but she felt in the mood for celebrating.

As Shipton Bellinger made his way with the rest of the theatrical company towards Oldham in the grimy third-class railway carriage he looked up from the borrowed *Sunday Dispatch* to peer through a rain-streaked window at the gateway to one week of oblivion. The unheated carriages rattled through a long tunnel to emerge some seconds later into shafts of sunlit soot. 'Jesus!' he exclaimed, and then, crossing his legs, pulled his hat over his face as if to cut out reality.

He had no digs arranged but he knew that the stage manager would be able to recommend somewhere to stay – they always did, because most of them took a small cut off the landlord or landlady.

Leaving behind him the 'root-toot' noises of the incoming and outgoing trains he weaved an unsure path down various unknown streets. Like most artistes of the show, he had been given directions, and like most directions that are given, they are easy to understand if you are the one giving them.

Then he came across a street sign – Tunstall Street. He glanced at his wrist-watch through its fractured glass casing. It was about quarter past very early morning. He studied the street that ran way down a steep hill. It must have been a mile long and perfectly straight. It was drizzling, just as it had been when he left the train, and probably just how it had been when he boarded the train. It was fine drizzle, the sort that seemed to fall without touching you. It was a miserable day in what Shipton Bellinger was beginning to think was a miserable career.

The running, shouting children, or the walking quiet grown-ups, didn't seem to care about the damp. They didn't even seem to wear any protective clothing for it.

Nearly two hours after leaving the train, he knocked on the door of 287 Tunstall Street, a brisk twenty-minute walk from the station if you were fit, and going in the right direction. If the landlords or landladies of this randomly chosen street were unable to oblige him, he would report to the theatre and seek the advice of the stage manager.

He rested his suitcase down and his arms felt as if they could touch his toes without his bending. He knocked lightly at the door, trying hard not to stand on the well-scrubbed yellow doorstep. An evil-faced boy of about five answered it. Shipton had to work hard to raise a smile. He didn't like kids. He had played too many matinees where sweets and other edibles had been tossed at him. 'Is your dear mother at home, little boy?'

'She's on't lav!'

'Oh!' He really didn't know what to say after that.

'Who is it?' asked a muffled female voice.

'A man with a big hat,' shouted back the boy.

'Is it the rent man?' Shipton pursed his lips and shook his head at the boy. 'Is it the rent man?' was asked again, only louder.

'No, it's not the rent man,' replied Shipton. There was a short silence, followed by a toilet being flushed.

A door cracked open and a woman stepped briskly down a corridor and appeared behind her son. He looked at the woman, who was probably about thirty-five. She drooped a protective arm around her son's neck. 'Yes?'

'Who is it, Mum?'

'Shut up.'

'Good evening. My name is Shipton Bellinger,' he announced, with an actor's accentuated bow that made the mother and child take a step back.

'What's he say, Mum?'

'Shut up. Er, can I help you?'

'I'm appearing at your local theatre in a play – a comedy. A Restoration comedy, in fact.' He gave her the same smile that Gary Cooper gave to Jean Arthur in *The Plainsman*. 'I'm an actor,' he said, in a way that told them they should be impressed.

'Why's he talking funny, Mum?'

'Shut up!'

'The, er, theatre recommended Tunstall Street when supplying us with directions for lodgings,' he lied.

He had never been greeted by two such deadpan faces before. He knew he would have to play another card. He grabbed the back of his left knee and winced with pain. 'I'm sorry,' he said. 'It's the damp, you know. Brings out the war wound. Took in some shrapnel on November the eleventh, 1918, while serving in France. Just outside Bapaume, actually. His Majesty told me, while he was pinning the Victoria . . . the old gong on, that I was probably one of the last British officers to be wounded. All very well, but it doesn't stop the old pain.'

He leant forward to support himself against the front wall of the terraced house. The boy stared at his leg with curiosity, and the woman said, 'Well, you'd better come inside and rest it.'

He gave her the 'devil-may-care' look similar to the one

Clark Gable gave Jean Harlow in *Red Dust*, then allowed his chin to quiver as if bravely containing the pain.

"What's up with him, Mum?"

'Shut up!'

He followed them both inside, and had removed his hat and coat by the time they were in the sitting-room. 'You say Mr Jenkins said try a few houses in Tunstall Street?'

'Yes, Mr Jenkins – the stage manager. May I sit down for a moment? It's the leg.' He gave her the Robert Young tight-lipped smile of controlled agony. 'Always like this when it's damp,' he explained.

She pointed to an armchair, then gave its cushion a hefty thump, hard enough to make it gasp. 'Is he going to stay here, Mum?' Shipton glared at the boy and thought, Don't spoil my chances by rushing her, you little brat.

'Shut up!'

The little boy was fascinated by the man's pain, and Shipton was trying every trick in the book to make them welcome him. He placed the boy on his right – 'good' – leg and held him there firmly, with a loving smile on his face. He gave the woman his Robert Taylor look and she unconsciously returned it with a Joan Crawford look. 'Well,' she said, at length. 'I did ask Mr Jenkins to send anyone down he felt was suitable.'

That's a bit of luck. I stopped at the right place here.

'I just didn't think it would be so soon.' She giggled, showing her nerves. 'See, I've never been a landlady before. You'll be my first one.'

'There's a first time for everything,' said Shipton, blandly.

She pushed her hand out at him. 'I'm Mrs Jane Butterworth.' She didn't know what to say about rates – who should mention money; him or her?

'How much will you be charging?' he asked, sensing her awkwardness.

'For the, er, week, from this morning 'til next Satur . . . Sunday morning, all meals provided, of course, and tea when ever you're wanting it, umm.' She thought for a second. 'Thirty shillings?' she asked, rather than stated. He smiled.

'Thirty shillings sounds most reasonable, Mrs Butterworth.'

'Oh, does it?' she said, disappointedly. Perhaps she had undercharged him.

'Would you object to me calling you Joan?' asked Errol Flynn.

'Not really, though my name's Jane,' replied Myrna Loy.

'Ah. You Jane, me Shipton.' Spencer Tracy laughed, almost throwing the boy off his knee.

'Shipton,' said his new landlady, as if trying to get accustomed to the name.

'That's right – Jane.'

The boy was now standing next to his mother and lifting her dress to try and hide under it. She moved quickly away from the threatening danger, and clipped his head with the palm of her open hand without even looking to take aim.

'Shipton's a place near Leeds, isn't it?'

'You're probably thinking of Skipton.' He rose from the chair. 'Would it be possible to have a cup of tea and take a look at my bedroom? Then I'll go and take a look at the theatre.'

'Yes, certainly. Come on, Adolf.'

'Adolf?' queried Shipton, and looked with some bewilderment at the boy.

'Yes. My husband thought Adolf was doing a good job in putting Germany to rights. He decided to name our boy after him. His mother was German, you see.'

'Hitler's?'

'No, silly. My husband's.'

'Ah, I see.'

Adolf had gone very quiet once he knew he'd become the centre of attention. Shipton smiled down at him, but it was a sad smile.

You poor little sod, he thought. At least mine's a stage name.

She picked the boy up in her arms. 'How's your leg?'

'Leg? What le. . .?' He recovered in time. 'Oh, the leg,' he said as he massaged it. 'Much better, thank you.'

She drifted into the kitchen, still carrying one of Hitler's half-dozen English friends. Shipton watched her legs as she went. She was an attractive woman, and he was sure he'd have bedded her by Thursday. So long as her husband was at work all day, every day. He had a vision of himself and Jane entwined in a passionate embrace, their legs thrashing, their bodies heaving and convulsing, and their . . .

'How much sugar?'

He blinked himself back into reality. 'Just one, please. I'm sweet enough as it is.'

Of course, there was the child to consider. Perhaps he attended a nursery school. Mind you, he could always make a play for her late at night, after the show. He smiled at the thought of two performances in one night. 'What are you smiling about?' she asked, as she brought two mugs of tea into the room.

'Oh, I'm just happy,' he said, quickly dropping the smile. 'Happy to be staying here with such a lovely family, though I've yet to meet your husband, of course.'

A shadow passed over her face. 'I'm a widow,' she whispered.

'Oh, I'm sorry, I didn't realise. Please forgive me.' Bedded by Tuesday he thought, then reproached himself for being so callous.

'It's nearly two years since Kurt was killed.'

'Killed?'

'Killed coming back from a football match. He always followed Oldham. His ambition was to see the boy have trials for them.' She smiled softly, before explaining what had happened. 'He and three other mates went to see the team play North End in Preston. They went in one of his mate's works' vans, and coming back, having probably had too much to drink, they hit a bus head-on. Kurt was killed outright, and one of his mates, Arnold, died later in hospital. The other two came out without a scratch.' She gave an ironic smile. 'That's the luck of the draw, isn't it?' Shipton nodded. He felt awkward and guilty.

'I'm sorry,' he said, for the second time.

'You weren't to know.'

The boy was now playing a mountaineering game across the settee. Hearing his late father talked about wasn't upsetting for him, as he was so young. He had an image of his father, just like he had an image of the man called Jesus whom they talked about at Sunday school. 'It's not been easy

80

bringing the boy up on my own,' she said. 'I've had a couple of jobs but nothing permanent. That's why I asked Mr Jenkins to send me lodgers.'

'Seems sensible.'

'I also asked the manager at the music hall to do the same thing. I gave him half a crown – that was three weeks ago.' She sighed and nodded at the staircase, probably thinking it was money down the drain. 'Now would you like to see your bedroom?'

It was late that evening when Shipton returned from checking out the theatre. To his relief, the boy was in bed, so he had Jane to himself and he hoped a little bit of peace and quiet. They had had quite a major talk-through at the theatre, and he was thoroughly exhausted when he flopped into the settee and Jane had brought him in some supper. 'Show all ready for opening tomorrow night, then?' she enquired, interestedly.

'Think so. A few hitches here and there that need ironing out, but we'll make it in time.' He swelled his chest and grinned. 'Of course, *my* performance is all that really matters.'

'Of course,' she said, and then hoped she hadn't sounded too sarcastic.

Not for a moment did he believe that on his first night there his hopes for 'making it' with Jane Butterworth would come true. Tuesday, possibly, Thursday, definitely. But Sunday? Surely not.

'That was a delightful meal, Jane, and I shall now retire for the evening. Tomorrow promises to be as equally strenuous as today.'

'Very well. Shall I show you to your room?' It crossed his mind as being a slightly strange thing to say, as she had already shown him his room earlier on that day.

'As you wish.'

There was a hungry, sex-starved glint in her eye as she pointed to the bed and said, 'Well, here we are.' He was sure he hadn't misread it. But what if he made a lunge and discovered he *had* misread it? It would be exceedingly difficult, if not impossible, to find other lodgings at this time of night. She made the decision for him. 'I'll just switch out the lights and then tuck you up.' For a moment he thought she had been

81

living alone with the child for too long, but when he stretched himself tiredly out on the bed and she returned a minute or so later wearing nothing but a dressing gown he could see she intended to more than just 'tuck him up'.

She was clearly not used to this kind of situation. Momentarily she leaned against the doorway in a Bette Davis pose, then, switching off the light, moved towards him only to trip up over one of his discarded shoes. There was a loud thud as her head struck against the floor. 'Are you all right?' he asked worriedly, as he leapt off the bed and beside her on the floor.

'Yes, I think so,' she replied, dazedly, as he gently massaged her head.

He was close enough to inhale the scent of her flesh and he began to feel very hungry. He had another vision of thrashing legs and entwined bodies, and then she was slowly pulling his mouth onto her own and a minute later his vision had become a reality.

Chapter 8

On arriving in Oldham, Stella – mainly to kill a little time before band call – went in search of the stage manager to see if he knew the availability of digs in town. She found him in a corner of the stage, checking through the show's running-order. 'Digs. Let me think.' John Blocker was very busy, but he always had time for the shows' artistes. 'Mrs Winthrop's full up. Got a house-load of midgets from the travelling circus. They lost a caravan en route so they've had to find some digs – but I'm sure you don't need to hear all about that.' She didn't. 'There's our favourite bachelor friend, Thomas Davison, but I really wouldn't recommend an attractive young woman like you staying with a somewhat dubious character like him.' He gave his chin a slow scratch. 'Mrs er, what's her name. She lives in Tunstall Street. Yes, that's right. She said she was after lodgers. She's a widow, and appears to be pleasant enough. Why not try her?'

'I will. Can you give me her name and number later on?'

'Certainly. I think her name's Butterscotch or something. Anyway, I'll check up and let you know.'

After Chief Long Knife, 'The Best In The West', had done his band call Stella was called up. To her horror, she noticed a small pool of blood on stage, where the Chief had been practising his knife-throwing with his young female assistant. She grimaced, then got on with the job in hand, wondering how many pints of blood his assistant got through during the course of the season.

It was nearly one thirty when she pulled up on the yellow

doorstep of 287 Tunstall Street. Jane Butterworth opened the door and Stella made an instant appraisal of her. Lonely, bored, tired out by child or children, and widowed – which she already knew. 'Good afternoon. I'm from the Empire. Mr Blocker suggested I tried you for digs.'

'Oh, right, yes,' stammered a worn-out Jane Butterworth, not knowing how from having an empty house she could have gone to having a full one. Stella followed her inside. 'I charge thirty shillings a week,' she said confidently, 'all meals included and tea on permanent supply.'

'Fine. I've left my bags at the theatre, but I'll bring them back tonight, after the show.'

They entered the sitting room. 'This is my other lodger, Mr . . .'

'Good-day to you madam; *je suis enchanté*. My name is Shipton Bellinger – actor. If Jane can't fix you up with a bed I'm sure I can.'

Stella's eyes flashed with surprise as Jane Butterworth intervened. 'Well, if you two don't mind sharing,' she said a little naively.

'Ho ho ho!' said Shipton, his red eyes lighting up like ships in the night.

'You mean share with George Arliss over here?'

'The name is Bellinger – Shipton Bellinger,' he corrected.

'Well, change it. It sounds like the name of a pub.'

'I only meant share the room,' explained Jane, weakly. 'Anyway, no trouble. I can sleep with Adolf and Ship . . . Mr Bellinger can have *his* room.'

'Who's Adolf?' asked Stella, beginning to think that Mr Blocker had set her up for some sort of joke.

'He's my little boy. He's five.'

'Named after Hitler, isn't that right, Mrs Butterworth?' said Shipton, hardly able to disguise a smile and chuckle. He looked at Stella. 'You have heard of Hitler, I imagine? He's a German chap. Lives in Berlin much of the time these days.'

'I know who he is,' she snapped.

'I'll make up your bed,' said Jane, and immediately trotted up the stairs.

'Where's Adolf now?' asked Stella in dulcet tones after she had gone.

'At nursery school,' Shipton whispered back.

'And when did *you* arrive?'

'Just last night,' he sighed, and rolled his eyes at the memory. It was becoming very plain as to what the set-up was in this house, except for one thing.

'So where's the old man, then?' Shipton waved her down and whispered in her ear.

'He's dead. Killed coming back from a football match.'

'No need to speak so quietly, then,' she said. 'He can't hear you.'

'Madam, really. Respect for the bereaved.'

'Suppose you're right. All this travelling about tends to make me rather ruthless.' He nodded with sympathy. He knew what being on the road was all about. 'Mind you, he would have been better off staying at home and watching the reserve game.'

Shipton shook his head disapprovingly. He'd never met a girl with such a direct manner. 'And how did you get a name like Shipton Bellinger?'

'I thought it sounded dignified – a true actor's name.'

'Oh, it's not your real name, then?' she teased.

Jane returned. 'There's tea in the pot,' she said. 'I'll bring it through.'

'Thank you,' they said in unison.

'Actually, I'm looking for a new name; something really good,' confessed Shipton.

'Can't say I blame you. Shipton Bellinger may as well be . . . I don't know. Swan Vestas, or something.'

'Charming. And what is your delightful name that gives you the authority to criticise others?'

She told him.

'Hardly as formidable as Katharine Hepburn or Marlene Dietrich.'

'And what's your real name?' asked Stella.

'Paul Newman.'

'I can see why you changed it,' she said, sympathetically. 'Have you had any other names?'

'I was once Newport Pagnell,' he reflected. 'Oh, and Leon Solent.' He waited for a moment for it to sink in. 'Don't you see?' he said excitedly. 'I take my names from an AA book.'

'Yes, I see. Why not call yourself Milton Keynes, but spelt Keens, K.E.E.N.S?'

'Hey, I rather like that.' He lifted his head in an aloof manner. 'Arise, Sir Milton Keens. Rather dignified.'

'Tea, everyone,' announced Jane.

The weeks passed by like all weeks in variety – quickly if you were doing well, slowly if you weren't. For Stella, it was passing reasonably quickly. It was also passing quickly for Shipton, but not because he was finding much success with his play – he wasn't – but because he had something to look forward to each night after work, and it wasn't just dinner.

Stella tried to remain well out of the situation, knowing that men like him were not too serious when it came to love affairs whilst touring. The final night would be the actor's farewell, which is the same as a soldier's farewell, only quicker.

Poor Jane. She believed in love at first sight and Shipton believed in love at first opportunity.

Within a few weeks of appearing at Oldham things really began to move for Stella. She was with London's top theatrical agency, and Henry Charles rang her every three days to see she was well and to arrange various bits and pieces, such as a photo session and an advert in *The Stage*, announcing her representation.

She made a point of dropping in to see Ken Hutton – who, incidentally, had found himself a new secretary, much to Stella's relief – and thanking him for all his help and advice. He was very happy for her, and said, 'One day I'll be able to boast that I was the one who started you.'

What made life that much easier for Stella was that Mike Farrow was as good as his word – he really was a genius at his job. He put her on a short tour of 'one-nighters' with an improved comedy act he had helped her work on for a couple of weeks. She was thrilled with his assistance and advice, and felt he had added a new dimension to her performance – given her a sophistication that she had before been lacking.

It was the West End that mattered the most. As Mike told her, 'No-one to my knowledge has gone to New York or Paris direct from Watford or Grimsby.'

Looking up to him admiringly she had said, 'You're a genius, Mike.' He had just smiled back at her.

'Maybe so,' he had said. 'But the important thing now is that I have to make *you* into one.'

Henry Charles would turn up in rehearsal rooms once in a while, just to see how she was progressing, but most of his advice came with his regular phone calls, as he didn't want to tread on the toes of his younger partner.

She felt it slightly significant that an important occasion like her twenty-first birthday should have been celebrated in London with her new-found friends and colleagues and not with her own family. But that was how it was in the late summer of 1935, with a rosy career ahead of her, and nothing, seemingly, to upset it.

Chapter 9

Beneath her tough surface Stella was an innocent young woman. She had never had a boyfriend, let alone slept with a man. Sexual activity, even the awareness of it, had not been permitted time and space on the Stella Raven agenda of important things in life.

There had been admirers that she was aware of – including her own agent, Mike Farrow. But Mike was married, and because he had too much at stake to risk philandering with his artistes, she didn't feel threatened by his abundant innuendoes.

As she moved positively along Shaftesbury Avenue on January the third, 1936, she began to wonder if she would ever become involved with someone of the opposite gender. She doubted it.

Shaftesbury Avenue was bustling with people: people with either sickly expressions brought on from over-indulging on Christmas Day or frustrated expressions – of which Stella had one – brought on because they couldn't understand why the festive season had to drag on for so long.

She glanced up to the heavy sky and, as if this had been a signal, the black uneasy clouds decided to open. Biting rain swept down in torrents. As she approached the Cambridge Circus end of the Avenue she felt a bump and heard an angry sigh. Looking up, and ready to make an apology, she was startled to find her friend from Oldham standing before her. 'Well, stone the crows. If it isn't Mr Shipton Bellinger.'

He gave her one of his exaggerated bows. 'And the one and only Miss Stella Raven, of whom the world seems to hear a little more of each day, may I add with a large amount of envy?'

'A long way to go yet,' she said, discarding his flattery. 'So tell me how life is treating you, Shipton?' He delayed before answering.

'Actually, the name's Milton Keens. I took your advice and changed it.'

He was quite sure Stella would give an almighty belly-laugh on hearing this, but she surprised him by appearing to be genuinely pleased. 'It has to be better than Shipton Bellinger.'

People were nearly queuing behind them as they stood in the rain for some minutes, reminiscing over Oldham and Jane Butterworth with her son, Adolf. Eventually, he pulled her arm and they sheltered in the foyer of a theatre. 'Where were you going to in such a hurry?' he asked.

'Rehearsal rooms.'

'A new show?'

'Maybe soon, but just rehearsals at the present. I rehearse almost every day,' she said.

'Practice makes perfect,' he said, and she wasn't sure if he was teasing or not. 'I've been following your career with great interest. Even caught you on the radio last week. You must slow down a bit – you may become famous.'

'And how's it working out with the new name?' He shrugged despondently.

'A new name unfortunately doesn't create a new actor; but I get by. I've just finished touring in a musical. I didn't think I could sing, but you live and learn. Next week I audition for a new revue for *the* Henry Charles, called *Bits and Pieces*, so wish me luck.'

'*Bits and Pieces*? Well, now, there's fate in action for you. I start rehearsals for it in a couple of weeks' time.'

Milton lit up. 'How wonderful, to work together.'

'Let's hope you pass the audition all right.' There was a short pause. 'Look, I must dash now. They're funny about times at the rehearsal rooms. Where are you living?'

'In a flat at the back of the Windmill,' he replied. 'Let's say that even if I don't make the show, we'll go out together one evening.'

89

'Lovely. When?'

'I have a diary that's virtually empty, so you name the time. Better still, catch up with me after I've auditioned.' He smiled nervously. 'I could do with a bit of moral support.'

'Fine. See you on your big day, then.'

They went off in separate directions. Stella had found that meeting up with Milton had been oddly distracting, and she never did manage to get her routine together at rehearsals all that morning.

A week later she found herself sitting at the back of the circle at the Savoy Theatre, all on her own, watching the auditions. When she heard Milton's name announced, currents of nerves electrified her body. He emerged from the side of the stage, shielding his eyes against the intensity of the footlights as he tried to focus on the jury, who were slumped phlegmatically across the first row of seats in the stalls.

Henry Charles was propped on the edge of the stage with secretary and house manager in close attendance. He murmured something to them and then asked loudly, 'Are you Keens?'

'That I am, sir,' he replied, with his old-fashioned Englishness.

'*Milton* Keens?'

'Yes, sir, that's right,' his voice quavered.

The jury began to mumble amongst themselves as Henry Charles considered his long list of names. Milton stood there, waiting like a pupil brought before the headmaster for an imminent thrashing. 'Sorry to keep you waiting, Mr Keens,' he said. 'We thought you were someone else.'

'My name's Milton Keens,' he declared.

'Yes, we've gathered that. We had you down as a Shipton Bellinger, but I'm informed' – here he glanced at the house manager – 'that you are in the habit of changing your name?'

'Yes, sir. That is, I used to be.'

'I see,' drawled Charles, chewing on his extinguished cigar. 'Okay, let's get on with it,' he instructed.

'Er, Mr Charles, I thought I'd give you a small reading from *Pickwick Papers*, at the point where Sam Weller is taken into the employ of Mr Pickwick.'

'Mr Keens, I appreciate that your love and living has been

acting, but on this particular occasion I just want you to sing. Is that possible?'

'Yes, sir,' whispered back Milton. He nodded to the pianist, who at once began to play the out-of-tune baby grand.

Stella was positive her pounding heart could be heard down in the stalls. She looked at her hands, balled like fighter's fists in her lap, the whites of her knuckles so prominent they almost shone in the dark auditorium.

Milton sang quite well and did a passable impression of Jack Buchanan. He followed that with a not-so-memorable impression of Maurice Chevalier, which went into a very funny idea of a mix-up between both impressions – a sort of Jack Chevalier and Maurice Buchanan routine.

Stella laughed quietly in the circle and Henry Charles laughed loudly in the stalls. 'Thank you, Mr Keens,' he said, with a shade of optimism when Milton had concluded his act. 'Very good indeed. Leave your phone number and the name of your agent with the stage manager, please . . . NEXT. Ah, Miss Davenport – when you're ready, please.'

Stella slipped into the dressing-rooms to see Milton, who was so sure he had won himself a part in the new revue that he forgot to ask her to come out for dinner with him, as he had originally intended to do. She didn't really mind too much. She was as equally thrilled for him, also being as certain as he was that he had got the part. No doubt they would be seeing much more of each other from now on. There would be plenty of time for dinners together.

That evening she contacted Mike Farrow, who verified that Milton *had* got himself the part and that Mr Charles thought a routine with Milton and herself would prove highly successful – perhaps a spoof on Sonnie Hale and Jesse Matthews, two of the West End's bigger stars.

Rehearsals for the new revue began in a church hall on the Kilburn/Hampstead border, north London. It was cold, it was draughty, it was typical of all rehearsal rooms.

All the principals of the show were leaning against or hanging around the upright piano, while the chorus were shuffling, tapping, and talking. Stella recognised one of the chorus girls as being a dancer in the Shanklin show. She recalled that she had been the one living with the manager there, until his wife and kids came down during the school holidays. The dancer had quickly vacated his home until term recommenced, and then she was back as his free lodger. Her name was Nola, and it was her attractiveness that had caught Stella's attention in Shanklin. She had a superb figure and natural blonde hair; not the type you pour from a bottle.

For a moment their eyes met and they both half-waved, half-smiled in recognition of each other. Stella was thinking, I wonder if she thinks I'm good enough to be in the show? and Nola was thinking, I wonder if she knew about me and the manager in Shanklin?

It was now ten twenty-five a.m., and everyone had been told to be there on time in practice costume for a ten-thirty start. They had all been doing their warm-up exercises. All they were waiting for now was the arrival of the famous Mr Woody Woodville. He had briefly met up with the stars, but he hadn't met any of the chorus before, having had them chosen for him. Stella hadn't realised he was black, and when she'd met him for a few seconds in the theatre office she had been so fascinated by his colour that she failed to take in anything that he had told her.

Nola made the first tentative moves. 'Hello, Miss Raven. I thought it was you.'

Very formal, thought Stella, and then remembered that she had done a fair amount of radio work just recently, and to a chorus girl like Nola who was only really working so she could travel and find romance for free, Stella Raven was probably quite a well-known name.

'Call me Stella,' she said with a smile. 'It's nice to see a face that I know.'

'Have you met Woody yet?' asked the chorus girl.

'Just briefly. What about you?'

'The same.' She shielded her mouth with a hand. 'He's black,' she whispered. They both giggled at this. 'I've been told he's a terrific dancer,' said Nola.

'With a reputation like his, I can well believe it.' One of the chorus called out to Nola.

'Let's catch up later for coffee or something,' Stella suggested.

'Okay. See you later.'

Nola skipped off, hoping that she wouldn't mention the manager from Shanklin should she know about them. The last thing Nola wanted was a bad reputation, though unfortunately she rarely behaved in a manner that would prevent her having one.

Before Stella had reached the piano the door at the far end of the hall flew open, and a hundred feet above them, the church clock struck half past. Musical director Ron Berry entered alone, and everyone seemed to relax again.

Ron strolled over to the piano, not looking up, down or around. Anton, the rehearsal pianist, rose from his stool to let him sit down, but Ron shook his head and beckoned with his hands for him to remain seated.

Now he considered the cast, as they hugged against the piano. He was a great musician, director, and arranger, and usually received the respect of his players as the show progressed and they began to understand his genius.

His complexion was as pale as aspirin, and there were black circles around his eyes like rippling pools of water. His thin, wispy, golden hair seemed to float above his head as if waiting for permission to land. His skin had a creamy pallor to it, and looked as if it hadn't seen sunlight since he had had his school photo taken some thirty years ago. 'I hate first day of rehearsals,' he remarked, through a haze of bluish-grey cigarette smoke. Before he could go on to explain why he hated them the door banged open again and in strode Woody Woodville.

The black American paused after two paces, as if waiting for a spotlight to hit him. Then he continued forward, and for most of them in the show it was their first sight of Hollywood.

He looked slowly from the chorus to the principals, and smiled a smile so white anyone standing within two feet would have had to blink. He was under six foot by about a sixteenth of an inch, fantastically good-looking in a film-star way, and dressed in a suit that could only be Savile Row. His white silk shirt was French and from it hung a pearl-grey tie. He had a soft American accent, and his head would gently wobble at the end of sentences to help accentuate his meaning. 'Good morning, ladies and gentlemen,' he began, in a precise voice. 'I'm sorry I'm a little late – I offer no excuse, but please forgive me. Also, don't think any of you here can get away with it. Only the boss can do that.'

93

As if on cue, the door burst open once again, and in stepped another black man – one much older than Woody Woodville and completely bald. All eyes turned to this new figure. 'Ladies and gentlemen,' said Woody, again. 'I'd like you all to meet Lester. Lester is the poor unfortunate man who looks after all my needs.'

Lester had been through many such introductions and merely offered a weak smile as he stumbled up to the piano. 'Lester has been with me many years,' continued Woody. 'Now there are two reasons for this: number one being that I love him.' Stella wasn't the only one to blush. 'The other reason is, that I like to prove to people that not all blacks are full of rhythm. Lester couldn't dance barefoot on a tray of coals.' He laughed at this, though it was a line he had used many times before. The company laughed dutifully with him.

Woody clapped his hands for attention before the laughter had had a chance to subside. 'Okay, now,' he said. 'Let's get this show rolling.' He delicately removed his jacket and hung it up on a collapsible hanger he kept inside one of his pockets. 'I want everyone close up to the piano as they can get without falling in it, and we're going to go through all the music in the show.' An attack of nerves made Ron Berry go whiter than normal. Everyone squeezed up close, and when Woody clipped his fingers, Lester trotted obediently up to his side.

They were all hanging on to the piano as if it was a raft at sea. Ron Berry was conducting the rehearsal pianist for the tempos with an unlit cigarette, the company laughed where they were supposed to laugh, and maintained silence at similarly appropriate moments.

Woody whispered something in Lester's ear half-way through a number and he shuffled away up to Nola, taking her to one side. Lester asked her something and she shrugged as if to say 'Why not?' and then returned to the others without giving anything away, though she was thinking to herself, this could be better than the manager at Shanklin.

At eleven thirty Woody shouted, 'Coffee – or maybe I should say tea?' Everyone smiled, mainly from the relief of having a break. Woody snapped his fingers and from a distance of over forty feet Lester heard the sound and came sauntering over to his boss. With a satisfied grin and a mug of coffee, Woody wandered over to Milton and Stella, who were discussing a routine they now did together in the show. 'Hi, Milt, Stella.' He patted both their backs as though they were fellow gospel-singers. 'I thought this afternoon we could go over the maternity ward skit and the dance routine at the end of it. I'm going to call the skit 'Tea for Three', Okay?' He looked pleased by his own inventiveness. Milton looked worried.

'Er, could I talk to you about the dance routines, Mr Woodville?'

'Woody. Everybody calls me Woody,' said Woody. 'Only my dear Mama call me by my real name, and that name I tell to no-one – not even Lester.' He flashed his teeth.

'I understand,' said Milton.

'Okay then, Milt – shoot.'

'Thank you, Woody. Well, the thing is I'm really an actor more than anything else, and although I can put a nice little point number over all right and do a little bit of comedy, I'm afraid I just can't dance. Really – I can't.'

Stella felt she was intruding on the situation and subtly extricated herself by feigning a need for more coffee. 'Stella's a wonderful dancer,' said Milton. 'I wouldn't want to let either of you down just because of my own incompetence.'

Woody gave him a steady look. 'Milt, I'm going to ask you something, and I don't want to hurt your feelings. Do you mind?'

'Please.' Milton half-bowed.

'How old are you?' Milton glanced across to Stella to make sure she was out of earshot.

'Thirty-seven,' he whispered.

'How old were you when you had your first woman?'

'Well, Mr Woody, I really don't quite see how that piece of information benefits my problem over the dance routines, and . . .'

'I'm waiting, Milt.' Milton shrugged resignedly.

'Eighteen or nineteen, I suppose. Yes, about eighteen.'

'So until you were eighteen you had all the equipment but no knowledge?'

'I suppose it could be looked at in that way,' he admitted.

'And that's the way it is with dancing,' said Woody. 'You're thirty-seven?'

'Thirty-eight, actually,' confessed Milton.

'You're thirty-eight, and all this time you've had feet but no knowledge. Well, that first lady gave you the knowledge of what to do with your equipment and I'll be doing the same with your feet. You've heard of Fred Astaire? Well, not only will I have you dancin' like him but singin' like him.'

He dismissed Milton and clipped his fingers. Lester, who until that moment had looked hard and fast asleep in a corner of the room, jumped up as if he'd heard a fire bell. Then he slouched over to Woody as fast as his ancient body would permit. 'Stella?' Woody commanded, and she joined him at the same time as Lester, despite the servant having a considerable lead. 'I've got big hopes on you, kid. From what I hear, you're very good. I guess this is a big break for you, huh?'

'I'm hoping so. It's the sort I've always wanted – always dreamed of. I'm just a little surprised it seems to have come so soon.'

'Just make the most of it, kid. You're never too young to be famous.'

'I'll try,' she promised.

'You must do more than try,' he said, with a touch of annoyance. 'From tomorrow on you'll be workin' your butt off, I promise. And if you fail, kid, it won't be through any fault of mine.'

He softened again. 'You'll make out okay. It might cost our friendship though. No-one likes a slave-driver.' Did she see Lester give a nod of agreement? 'The good Lord provided you with looks and talent. It's not often someone gets such a good deal, so don't screw up on it. Anyway, I want you to know that all the help you need, I'll give you, kid. That's what ol' Woody's here for.' Brief pause and fade out on smile, and, 'EVERYONE BACK TO PIANO.'

They were allowed an hour off for lunch, and Woody let them leave at four, it being their first day. 'Principals here at ten tomorrow morning, dancers – nine thirty.' The room was cleared in ten minutes. The only people left were Woody, and Nola. 'Coat,' ordered Woody. Lester disappeared into the hall to fetch it. As soon as his back was turned he waved a hand at Nola to come towards him. 'I've been watchin' you close all

96

day, Nola, and I like what I've been seein'. I think you could make a good first girl – you know what a first girl is? It's the girl who has to learn all the routines from me, and when I have to do rehearsals for the skits and stuff she takes charge of the other dancers and makes sure they keep rehearsing in my absence. What do you say?' He showed her his teeth without having to take them out.

'I think I could do that all right, Woody.'

'Sure you can, but you know it could mean a few late nights back at my place, talking over routines and learnin' thin's?'

'Back at your place?' she gasped, with a pout you could lean on.

'Of course. I'm a busy man. I'm doing the whole show, I'm going to need help along the way and someone to talk with, relax with, maybe.'

Lester returned with the overcoat. Woody snapped his fingers twice and Lester abruptly halted. 'Surely Lester is someone to talk to and relax with?' she teased.

'Maybe you hadn't noticed, kid, but Lester and I do a finger routine. I could hold a conversation with Lester and break three fingers. Now come on. What do you say? I'll give you a raise. What are you currently on?'

'Three pounds fifteen shillings a week,' she lied. It was only three pounds ten shillings.

'Okay, let's make it er' – he knew very little about the English currency – 'three pounds twenty shillings.'

Nola laughed. 'Over here we call that four pounds.'

'Well, I'll give you five pound a week. Does that sound okay?' He knew he was in when he saw the surprised delight on her face.

'What do I have to do for that?' she asked, pointedly.

'Only what you want, when you want. I can't be fairer than that. Now, where do you live in town?'

'I share a flat with two other girls . . .'

'These girls aren't in the show, are they?'

'No. They work at the Windmill Theatre.'

'Okay, fine. Now tell me where you live.'

'Primrose Street, just at the back of Liverpool Street Station.'

'How far is it from here?'

'Ooh, I'm not sure. Ten minutes by cab.'

'Okay, I'll give you a lift. What are you doing tonight?'

'How do you mean?'

'Tonight. You know, when it gets dark.'

'Nothing.'

'Okay, so I'll give you my address.'

He wrote a street and number on the back of a card and passed it to her with a pound note. 'Come round tonight and we'll have dinner,' he said. 'The money's for the cab. Be there at seven – no – make that eight. Don't dress up – come casual.'

Nola collected her belongings and they stepped outside to Woody's car – a beige 1920 Silver Ghost – preceded by Lester, who opened the door for them. 'You've got me for three months,' said Woody. 'That's three wonderful months for you, kid.'

He squeezed her hand, and being a professional, she squeezed back. In her mind she had it all worked out. If the show ran for six months she would have one hundred and twenty five pounds – apart from the meals and the odd presents he would bestow on her. She hoped Stella Raven would keep quiet about the manager in Shanklin.

They were well into rehearsals and the show was looking quite polished. Nola was also looking quite polished. She would turn up each morning with eyes bright as diamonds and a cheerful, confident little skip in her walk.

Milton was feeling just as confident but for a different reason. He had to admit that Woody had been right; at least, he now gave the appearance that he knew how to dance. After each successive rehearsal he would stagger home to a hot bath and soak away the aches and pains of a ten-hour day, nine of which would have been spent dancing.

As for Stella, well, she was word-perfect: she was dance-perfect, sketch-perfect, and her comedy timing surprised even herself.

As the show progressed towards its opening, Woody attended rehearsals, looking more like Cricklewood than Hollywood. He was so tired that when he snapped his fingers Lester had difficulty in hearing him. And it wasn't the schedule that was killing him – it was Nola.

The thought of opening in Manchester in ten days' time made Stella buzz. She sensed that something special was going to emerge from it, as if all her life, and the hard work she'd put into it, had all been for this moment in time. She decided she should send her parents a couple of tickets: they'd enjoy seeing the show and telling all the neighbours about it. Woody had allocated each performer a reasonable amount of complimentary tickets – or at least, he arranged through the Manchester management that these 'comps' were to be put by.

Nola, like Stella, couldn't suppress her excitement at shortly opening at the Opera House, Manchester. She had never had it so good, and, looking at the drained Woody, never so often. She was looking forward to staying at the Midland Hotel in a single room very close to, and being paid for by, Woody.

Milton felt he was at the stage where he wanted to perform all they'd rehearsed in front of an audience. If he rehearsed any more he was sure he'd overpeak, and the show was too important for him to risk that happening.

They all travelled up to Manchester in a reserved compartment, their moods being one of excitement and anticipation. Milton made himself comfortable, waiting for the train to ease out of the station, and reflected on the journey he'd made to Oldham where he'd first met Stella. It was as though that episode in his life had been enacted by a different person; certainly not the dancing, singing Milton Keens.

They arrived slightly ahead of time on the Saturday night, which was a good thing, because it was a show with lots of scenery and costume changes, and so there was much ironing, hanging, and unpacking to do.

Sunday afternoon was to be dress rehearsal with the band. No doubt it was going to be a chaotic affair, but somehow it always works out by the opening night. Adrenalin keeps the stage workers going and money keeps the management going. All Nola concerned herself with was keeping Woody going. Woody summoned Lester with a feeble snap of the fingers. 'Is there any way you can keep her away from me; just 'til the show opens?' Lester smiled.

'But I thought you were the King?'

'Maybe so, but I'd like to abdicate for a couple of days.'

He'd reached the stage where he was hiding from her and telling her lies about why he couldn't come back to the flat, and now the hotel, with her. 'She's the best ever, but, wow, an insatiable appetite.'

'You's always been the lucky one, Massa,' said Lester, shuffling his feet like a comedy black manservant character from a film. Then he hung his head to give a round-shouldered appearance and, letting everything 'hang loose', he flayed his arms and drifted away.

Stella went into her dressing-room, which was a largish-sized box with a cracked mirror and uneven table. There was also a chair that, she'd discovered, left splinters in her behind and a tatty sofa so badly shredded she'd have been embarrassed to give it to her worst enemy. What was even more frightening was she knew it to be one of the better dressing-rooms.

She found a small pile of mail strewn across the table. One or two were from well-wishers, and there was one from her mother. She felt encouraged that her mother had ventured into the world of letter-writing: it had taken her some while to accustom herself to just receiving them. The note inside thanked her for sending the two comps and some money for the fare – both were accepted, gratefully. They would arrive in time to see the Thursday-night performance.

Stella twisted her mouth to form a bitter smile. She knew it wouldn't have taken her dad long to decide. Anything that was free he was interested in.

The last letter she had left to open had an Oldham post-mark on it, and if she hadn't been so weary she'd have noticed it was addressed to Milton and not her. In fact it was addressed to Shipton Bellinger, but then Jane Butterworth wasn't to know he'd changed his name again.

She hurriedly read through the letter, as if the faster she read it the less guilt she would feel about it being someone else's mail. Despite it only stating that she would be attending the Wednesday matinee performance – was that all right? – she couldn't help but feel a pang of jealousy. It went through her body like an electric shock, jolting her upright. In a wicked way she was glad that Milton wouldn't be able to reply in time. However, she wasn't wicked enough to destroy the letter and pretend not to know anything about it. In fact, with an air of reluctance she took it straight into his dressing-room.

The dress rehearsal – put on for a selected audience that included local hospital staff and three bus-loads of old-age pensioners – was chaotic and consequently a minor disaster. Fortunately, and not completely unintentionally, the press were not invited to pass comment on this, the first proper performance.

It was the following night, the Monday night, that they had that privilege. And on that night the ghosts and gods of the theatre were in sympathetic mood, for the show went through an overnight transformation. As far as the paying public were concerned, it went without a hitch, and what little did go wrong was forgiven because of the quality of one particular artiste who that night became a star. The audience hunted through their programmes. What was her name? Ah, yes: Stella Raven.

The show ran half an hour over time, but the management could see that as being easily rectified; for a start, some of the routines could be severely cut back without damaging their overall effect.

The National Anthem played as all the artistes involved stood in two regimented lines behind the curtains, whispering excitedly to each other that they were sure the show was a sensation. As the lines broke up, 'Stella, you were wonderful' could be heard twenty times, and 'Girls, you were great' almost as many times. 'Well done, Milton, you surpassed yourself' was heard half a dozen times.

The chorus girls hugged anything that breathed, unable to contain the emotion on completing a successful first night after such hard work and so many inevitable traumas. Henry Charles was the first of the management to come back-stage, where everyone was milling about with large grins on their faces. He gently pushed aside staff and artistes alike, as if they were obstacles deliberately put there to irritate him, and made his way up to Stella as she made for her dressing-room. Mike Farrow was only inches behind him. Henry hugged her until she started gasping. He would have been willing to kiss her but the cigar in his mouth prevented him, and there had to be a better reason than kissing to make that cigar come out. And anyway, he'd never really been into kissing his own artistes; it wasn't dignified.

He pulled back to allow Mike a look-in. 'I wouldn't go as far as saying you were perfection,' said the junior partner with a grin that told her she was, without doubt, perfection, 'but you came remarkably close to it.'

She said, 'You always did know how to keep an entertainer's feet on the ground, didn't you Mike?' Mike didn't object to stretching forth and kissing her. In fact, he couldn't wait. Why didn't his wife taste so nice?

Henry said, 'I've heard him use words like "not too bad" when he's meant "brilliant", so I think you can take it he's fairly knocked out with you.'

'You're giving away my trade secrets,' laughed Mike, and laughter was the theme for most of that night.

Because Stella had the biggest dressing-room, by about nought point eight of an inch, it was decided she should house the spontaneous party that Henry insisted on having: and when he also insisted on paying, there wasn't one complaint or refusal.

Everyone appeared to be in sparkling form, except for Woody, who didn't join the merry gathering until quite a while on into the evening. He'd been spending most of his time avoiding the ever-angering Nola. 'Stella, Stella, Stella, Stella,' he repeated several times as he approached her with arms out and head wobbling. 'Magnifico! That's all I can say, honey. Simply magnifico!' Then he added, feeling he needed a bit of self-appraisal as no-one had yet thanked him, 'Of course, I knew you would be; I trained you myself.' Like Henry, he didn't try to kiss her as he was trying to give up kissing women for the time being. But he did snap his fingers and the dressing-room door immediately creaked open and in creaked Lester – or was it someone closing the door again? Lester had with him a silver bucket crammed full of ice that supported two very green and refreshing-looking bottles of Dom Perignon champagne. Lester passed the bucket to Woody before retreating from the room.

Woody said, 'Stella, kid, drink a whole one of these yourself and get pie-eyed, 'cos there ain't no other way, honey, you'll be able to sleep tonight.'

Looking back at him with deep gratitude and immense respect

she whispered a 'Thank you, Woody. Thank you for everything,' and then she kissed him on both cheeks. 'There's just one thing,' she said, pulling back as she remembered there had long been something she'd been meaning to find out.

'What's that?' he said, a little confused. She clenched her lips and with a serious expression of full concentration she snapped her fingers. No Lester appeared. They all laughed at her unsuccessful attempt to copy Woody's technique.

'Has he gone away?' she asked, thinking she'd snapped her fingers perfectly adequately. Woody just smiled as he snapped his own. In walked Lester and everyone laughed even more.

Woody whispered into Lester's ear and he stepped back to open the champagne. The laughter didn't upset him; he'd long grown accustomed to being used as a focal point of a joke. If he made people laugh by being a fairly old, black manservant, then what should he care? His boss paid him well. And he also just happened to love his boss.

As the gathering raised glasses in unison to toast Stella and the show, the door was flung open and in stormed Nola. Her legs quavered and she seemed to be having difficulty in focusing on anything. In her hand hung a half empty bottle of Scotch. 'Hello, Nola,' welcomed Stella, hoping to defuse what looked to be a highly volatile young chorus girl. 'Join the party. By the way, I thought you did the Brazilian routine with Milton and me just great . . .'

'So you're here?' she snapped, finally tracking down Woody, most probably by his shade rather than his features. The others in the room started up small talk, anticipating a major Anglo-American confrontation. 'So where've you been, you big black bastard?' After this comment, even the small talk petered out.

'Why, looking for you, honey,' lied Woody, in a remarkably level tone. He was as anxious to avoid a scene as the others were. He didn't want to turn the sweetness of the night sour; not after the hard work his performers had put in.

He deftly poured her a beaker of the champagne and passed it to her saying, 'Welcome to the party, baby.'

'Fuck the party and fuck you.' Woody was glad that the latter sentiment wasn't a request. Stella was quick to jump in with, 'Why don't you get changed, Nola, and we can all go back to the Midland and have a bit of a party there?'

103

'Listen, you cow, I know all about you.' There was a stunned silence. 'You told him about the manager at Shanklin, didn't you? You're just a stupid, bleeding cow, that's all. Just a stupid, bleeding . . .' Woody slapped her hard enough for her to fall resoundingly against the nearest wall and slip down on her backside to the floor. It was a most effective way to curtail her accusations, as it left her unconscious. For some reason, no-one had given the expected gasps of horror that normally accompany such scenes. In the circumstances everyone felt that Woody had taken the most sensible line of action.

He snapped his fingers and in came Lester again. Nonchalantly, the old servant hoisted up the fallen female as if it was a regular part of his work – and it probably was. 'Let's hope she sobers up in time for tomorrow night's show,' joked Woody, and soon everyone had managed to overlook the tiny blemish to their special evening.

There was an unspoken understanding that Nola wasn't worth spoiling their celebrations for, and it was Woody's own attitude towards her that had seemed to cement this understanding.

Minutes later the door opened again, and there was a sudden hush as, just for the briefest of seconds, they thought Nola had come round and returned to throw out some more drunken abuse. But it was Milton who filled the doorway. He was naturally surprised that everyone had gone quiet on his entrance. 'Hi, folks,' he said weakly. Conversations welled up again as Milton moved sheepishly over to Stella. 'I'm not intruding, am I?' he said through an awkward smile.

'Of course you're not,' said Stella. 'It's "open house" here tonight. Everyone's welcome; especially you.'

He surveyed the smoky, busy room. 'I guessed it would be a little hectic here. That's why I changed and had a bite to eat before coming along.'

'MILTON!' cried Woody, with unnecessary fervour. He gave him the same open-arm treatment he'd given Stella. 'Just magnifico, Milt, that's all I can say.' Stella found herself clinging to Milton's hand. Was she afraid she might lose him. Should she let go? 'Jesus, Milt, didn't I tell ya, didn't I tell ya?' Woody was now clutching poor Milton's cheeks as he

104

spoke. It was the nearest Milton had ever been to a complete face-lift. 'Why, baby, you looked more like Fred Astaire out there than Fred Astaire would have done. You were so hot that when I was at the back of the stalls I heard some guy say to his friend . . .'

'Well done, Milton,' congratulated Henry Charles. He didn't realise he was interrupting Woody in full flow: and if he had known, he wouldn't have cared less. 'Mike and I thought you did a splendid job.' It was best he mentioned Mike. Mike was renowned for his acute appreciation of strong talent: if Mike said something or someone was good, then Henry invariably went along with it. He never told Mike this, of course. That would be like a milkman telling his workhorse he couldn't survive without him.

'Er, thank you, Mr Charles,' said Milton. Quickly he turned back to Woody. He was eager to hear what Woody had overheard in the back of the stalls. 'Excuse me, Woody.' Woody was involved in another conversation – another moment in time.

'Yeah?' he said, irritably.

'You didn't quite finish. What was it you heard someone say – about me being as hot as Fred Astaire?' Woody furrowed his brow in thought.

'Oh, right,' he said remembering. 'I heard him say, "Do you know that all those male dancers are fags"?' Woody moved away, leaving Milton motionless – quite stunned. As he resumed his other conversation he would have had no idea that he could have hurt Milton's feelings.

Stella gave the back of Woody's dinner jacket a severe frown, and she squeezed Milton's hand to comfort him. 'He's not always too subtle with his words,' she told him, but she knew she couldn't cover up for him: Milton knew Woody as well as she did.

Milton said, 'But if that's what he did hear, then how many times between now and last night am I going to be called "one of those fag dancers"?'

She shrugged in an easy way that said, who really gives a damn about the odd unpleasant remark? It served to catch Milton's notice better than if she'd dished out the usual selection of sympathetic sentiments. He said, with a respectful

105

glint in his eye, 'That's the remarkable thing about you, Stella Raven.'

'How do you mean?' she asked, suspiciously.

'Well, you push and push with grim determination, and eventually you overcome.'

'Maybe people give in just to shut me up.'

'I don't think so.' Now he found that *he* was squeezing *her* hand. 'You're a wonderful girl as well as being a wonderful performer, and what makes you all the more wonderful is that you don't even realise it.'

Stella had never been the bashful type, and normally she could reply to these sorts of compliments with a 'don't be so daft'. But this time the words struck right through her core, making her cheeks burn. What frightened her was that she couldn't understand why she was so defenceless. But then, she hadn't understood why she'd felt so nervous for Milton when he'd been auditioning.

Her embarrassment, if that's the right word to describe what had caused her hot flush, was all the more amplified when Woody approached, saying, 'Cut that out, you kids. Stop the loving looks. I've enough problems without having to arrange a wedding.'

Woody snapped for Lester. 'See you guys later,' he announced, as Lester handed him a walking-cane with a carved swan's head that he'd taken a fancy to being seen with.

When all had drifted their various ways Stella made Milton turn around whilst she changed into something more suitable for the Midland Hotel. 'It's too late for food,' said Milton, 'but I've got some brandy back at my digs just round the corner.'

'Is that an invitation?' she asked and at the same time told herself to refuse it if it was. Think positive, Stella. Think career, Stella. But I can't seem able to.

'There's certainly no reason why you shouldn't come back for a nightcap.'

'Tomorrow night's show is a good reason for not going back for a nightcap,' she pointed out.

A few more appealing smiles by the ever-appealing Milton soon dented her willpower; enough anyway, for her to go back to his place for a nightcap.

The digs he was in – Milton didn't like the 'togetherness' of hotel life on the road – was closer to the Opera House than she'd realised. In daylight it stood in its shadow.

The tramps and alcoholics that dotted the early-morning street did little to encourage her to give up hotel life for digs. She thought Milton quite mad to not only put up with digs but to take them out of preference. 'It's what I might have expected,' she said, as she fumbled with a switch before a bare bulb, hanging shamefully from the centre of the ceiling, threw a meagre amount of light onto the bleak furnishings.

He moved to a box, explaining as he went that he'd not had time to unpack properly. 'It's only cooking brandy,' he apologised, holding out the dark bottle as though it were contaminated, 'but it's brandy.'

'I think you'd better taste it first before confirming that.'

She pointed at a two-seated sofa that had a spiral spring climbing out from it. 'Mind if I sit down?'

'Sorry, how rude of me,' he replied, all a fluster. 'Well, cheers,' he said, with some apprehension as he raised his grimy glass and passed the other one to her.

She said, 'Cheers, and down the hatch as they say, whoever "they" are, and most probably back up again if it meets with the other stuff I've drunk tonight.' Milton winced. She couldn't tell if it was the brandy or her remark that had caused him to.

In an ensuing short silence she briefly reflected on the glass of Benedictine she used to share with Sadie at Christmas time. The house would be nearly as bare as Milton's digs, but much much cleaner. Their dad would be busy sharpening the carving knife ready for the capon or, if finances permitted, the turkey. It didn't matter how tight things were – how hard up they were, they'd always laugh, tell jokes, sing carols. Other folk thought they were strange, but then other folk wallowed in self-pity. Not the Ravenscroft family. 'How do you see me?' asked Milton, breaking in on her thoughts.

'With my eyes,' she replied, dryly.

'No, really. It's important to me.' She saw his seriousness.

How was she to see a man who had been knocking off the landlady where they'd been staying and who had cropped up in the same revue as her, and was now seemingly turning his

107

affections onto her? 'I suppose I see you as a kind, generous man, but who's prone to shyness and who'd rather see himself as being another Douglas Fairbanks than an original Milton Keens.' She was pleased with the way she summarised him.

But Milton twitched. She'd unwittingly touched the right nerve. 'You certainly answered my question with direct honesty,' he responded, and a little sourly too, she noted.

'Would you have wanted it any other way?' Then, before he could reply, 'I didn't say I objected to how you are.'

He shrugged off his hurt with a heavy chuckle and, with a large swig, finished off his brandy. Stella had taken just one sip. She didn't intend drinking any more. She'd tasted better cough-mixture.

Milton sensed there was something forming between the two of them: something that would go beyond a platonic friendship. What he couldn't understand was why he failed to visualise thrashing legs and heaving bodies, and hear the cries of ecstasy, as he normally did when lustful for a particular female. He could only assume he was either very tired, or that – which was rapidly becoming the more likely – he'd fallen in love with a young woman called Stella Raven. 'It's very late,' he suddenly said, leaning forward as if about to make her a proposition. She felt her defence barriers going up. 'Why don't you consider camping down here the night?'

'Because you've only one bedroom.' Now what can you say? she thought.

'I could take the sofa,' he offered, but not very convincingly.

'And I could take a taxi back to the hotel.' There was a pregnant pause before Stella gently said, 'Look, I'm not like Jane Butterworth.'

'I realise that,' he said. 'It's precisely that point that makes all I'm saying and doing seem so right – so clean and aboveboard.'

There was a tension within her, yet she didn't feel trapped. She made a conscious effort to relax, but her tired body wouldn't respond.

Maybe it's because I want him, she thought. But it seems wrong. I'm scared. No I'm not: nothing scares Stella Raven.

'It's hard for me to express how I feel in mere words,' he continued. She wondered if this was the actor speaking. But he seemed genuine enough. 'To say all the things I want to say; that I need to say.'

Did he use these lines on Jane Butterworth?

'And when I bumped into you in Shaftesbury Avenue, I could tell in moments that there had to be more to life than the Jane Butterworths of this world.'

'It's taken you a long time and many warm beds to discover that,' she said, a fraction more scathingly than intended.

'I know, I know. But if the field is there to be played in, then why not play in it?'

That sounded fair enough.

'All I'm saying is, I've finished with all that. I need to settle with one person, and well, personally . . . well, I want that person to be you.' He studied her hopefully. It's amazing the confidence a few too many stiff drinks could give a man.

She said, 'I know, too, that I'm very fond of you, but we can't go talking of love at the beginning of what looks to be an endless revue. We've all the provinces to do and then the West End itself.' She gave a tired smile. 'And then there's Woody: the shock would turn him white.'

'Yes, there are problems,' he agreed. 'But life is full of them, and very few turn out to be insurmountable. You must know that, or you wouldn't have tried to make it in showbusiness.' He sighed, dramatically. 'All I'm saying is, don't make too many excuses for not doing things, Stella, or life will pass you by and you won't have lived.'

She thought of her parents and could see the truth in what he said.

Almost sensing she'd conceded, he stretched forward and planted a long, hard kiss on her mouth. She made no effort to retreat; on the contrary, if anything she returned it with more vigour, more passion, more meaning. Without further word he lifted her up and carried her to the bedroom – the only bedroom. 'What are you doing?' she demanded, but very weakly.

'I'm going to show you what you've been missing out on all these years,' he replied, the familiar stirrings swelling in his body.

It hadn't been the magical experience she'd anticipated. Bells hadn't rung, tears hadn't fallen. All in all, as she lay

109

head resting on his chest, she thought it only unforgettable because of the pain.

'How was it?' he asked, his male chauvinistic ego needing filling.

She wasn't one to toss out the first answer that came into her head. For a second she pictured the way he'd torn desperately at her clothing, forcing her back onto the bed, spreading her legs open, tearing off his own clothes, forcing his way into her with such urgency – such need; his quickening movements, his gasping breath, his body-weight crushing her, nearly suffocating her as he pumped relentlessly away, striving desperately to achieve that one moment of personal satisfaction, totally oblivious to how she may have felt: then the lying there in the aftermath, listening to him wheezing, uncomfortably short of breath. And then the tranquillity, only to be interrupted by spasmodic remonstrations from the plumbing. No. It had been an awful experience. 'It was just perfect, Milton,' she whispered.

As she walked mechanically to the theatre Stella tried to recall the impassive way in which Henry Charles had broken the tragic news to her at the hotel earlier that morning – how he'd probably broken the tragic news to all the artistes. He could have been referring to the demise of his favourite cat when he said, quite simply, 'Nola is dead.'

Her own personal reaction had been to release a short laugh, as if expecting a punchline to follow, or for Henry to say he was only kidding. But no. It was a fact. Nola, the show's leading chorus girl, the 'good-fun-kid' from Shanklin, was dead. What was worse – could it be worse? – was that the police were convinced it was not suicide.

And now she, like the others in the show, had to be at the theatre to face interviews by the police and presumably make a statement. Only Woody Woodville wouldn't be there. He was supposedly 'helping police with their enquiries', as they worded it. She wasn't born yesterday. She knew that, in the circumstances, he had to be a major suspect.

The Chief Superintendent held his interviews in a back office that, prior to this, she hadn't even known existed; but then why should she? She was just another artiste to appear at the Opera House – nothing more, nothing less.

The insipid policeman was tall, dark, but notably ugly, with long ungainly legs, the knees of which he insisted on tapping together in gentle, unsynchronised rhythm. This irritated Stella, but she said nothing.

He smiled at her through humourless lips as she came in. It was a professional, perfunctory smile that merely saved him from the effort of saying 'hello, please take a seat'.

His junior colleague took down frantic notes and occasionally threw in what sounded a fairly aimless question. When he wasn't making notes he shuffled uneasily in his upright position, as if unconfident with his superior's laborious methods of extracting basic data. He concluded by informing her that he might need to question her further, at a later date.

'How did Nola die?' she asked, as she stood to leave, her voice hoarse and tinged with emotion. Death was something that had always upset her for as long as she could remember. It was so final and so personal; the only thing that, without choice, you had to face alone.

'There was a knife, the six-inch blade of which was driven deeply into the young woman's back.'

'So suicide is out of the question, then?'

He gave her a little smirk. 'Only if she was a contortionist as well as a chorus girl.' He liked his own sense of humour. Other than his late mother, he was the only one who'd ever liked his sense of humour. Stella took his meaning and left the room.

Something troubled her for the rest of that morning. It wasn't just that Nola had apparently been murdered, or that she herself had slept with Milton that night, or that she had a head-splitting hangover, or that she had to try and shine on stage that night through all of this. It was something else.

It wasn't until Mike Farrow made an appearance at around one o'clock – he wanted to pull the team together in Woody's absence – that it struck her what was disturbing her. She'd seen Woody jokingly brandishing a long-bladed hunting knife at the dance-school some weeks ago. It was during a coffee-break. He was telling some of the girls how his father had presented it to him as a twenty-first birthday present. 'It's a precaution in case slave-trading becomes fashionable again,' he'd quipped.

111

Stella was confused. She was positive, more than positive, that Woody was no murderer, just as she was positive that she would be giving a below-par performance that night. But how could she, or anyone for that matter, prove him innocent? Innocent until proven guilty is the law of the land, but with all the evidence stacked against him it wouldn't take long to have Woody looking as guilty as Crippen. She hoped his nationality would make a difference. Maybe he would only be extradited.

But the manner in which poor Nola had died; the fact that they'd argued terribly the previous night; and now the possibility of the knife. It would all stick together to form conclusive evidence. Yet she knew Woody was innocent.

Then she thought selfishly, perhaps humanly, for one moment. What would become of the revue? Would it come to an abrupt end under a cloud of bad publicity engendered by the murder of Nola? She wasn't the only one in the show with that thought on her mind.

The bad publicity created a macabre interest in the show that night. Outside the theatre, long before it was due to commence, large crowds had gathered. They were ticketless but this didn't concern them. They weren't there to enjoy any show; they were there to soak up the atmosphere that they hoped would permeate through the solid brick of the Opera House and into the night air.

The show itself was well received. Stella managed an 'all-right' performance, and Nola's stand-in – or rather, her permanent replacement – did an admirable job at such short notice and in such circumstances. The standing ovation at the finale was for her, and no-one else, that night.

The press hounded all of them after the show, and Mike Farrow took it upon himself to face the barrage of predictable questions in an effort to protect his artistes, who had enough to cope with as it was. But even the experienced Mike Farrow floundered just a bit. He'd had to handle the press over one or two bizarre matters before but never over a murder within the company, and especially one that suggested that the producer was more than just involved.

'What a nightmare all this is,' said Milton, pulling up a seat next to Stella in the artistes' bar. She played with the single ice cube in her orange juice. The simple way it dipped and bobbed gave her some inexplicable childish pleasure. 'Any news for me?' She shook her head. She was tired, and still partially stunned. 'Well, I can't see them taking it off,' he continued, as he rationalised the situation. 'With the nationals picking up on it, it makes sense to go full steam ahead. It could turn into the biggest smash-hit of the year.'

'A bit like a freak might,' she remarked, bitterly.

Milton glanced at her and realised that now wasn't the time to be thinking about his career. 'I see what you mean,' he said, softly.

But Milton was to be quite right: the sensationalism of the press over the ensuing weeks was to turn the country's attention upon Henry Charles' revue. And that, in turn, was to do amazing things for the career of Stella Raven.

Chapter 10

'Mrs Bennet said she heard our Stella on the radio last Monday,' remarked Sadie.

'Did she, now?' responded Tommy, with a blatant lack of interest. His eyes and mind were focused on the pools sheets splayed out before him.

'You weren't even listening, were you?' she said.

'Can you remember if you put last night's paper in the bin or next to the door?'

'I knew you weren't listening,' she sighed.

'Eh?'

'Nothing,' she groaned, despairingly. 'It's by the back door.'

'Be a pet and fetch it for me, love.'

Sadie looked across at him incredulously. 'What d'yer last slave die of?'

'Answering back.' He quickly turned and gave her a sweet smile. For Tommy it was quite a risky remark: he had to be sure she could tell he was kidding.

'Lord save us,' she cried, and then went to fetch the paper.

They had been married for nearly a year. Tommy was still employed at the Lancil factory and Sadie still worked at the cake shop, though not quite so many hours every week. The most exciting moment of their marriage, indeed their lives to date, came when they moved out of Corkell's Yard and into their very own corporation house in Willow Lane – fourteen and six a week; three up and two down.

It had its own strip of garden where Tommy spent many hours checking on his own vegetables. Other than a touch of gardening, and the regularity of his work, Tommy liked to take a pint with his mates once in a while: and, of course, do the pools.

With each passing day it was harder to tell the difference between Sadie and Mrs Ravenscroft. When she stood in the kitchen wiping her flour-coated hands on her black, sack-like dress there was no difference at all. Her dress was so plain and hung so limply from her body it disguised whatever figure she may have had beneath it. Her stockings were thick and the colour of strong tea. The only way you could have told that they had legs inside them was by the holes and ladders that scarred them from top to bottom – not that anyone saw the top area (except Tommy, and then only on Saturday nights). But it was to be expected. The dress, and the stockings, were both seconds off her mother. It was a gesture to help them save some money.

Tommy had pulled free the sports page before Sadie had had the chance to say, 'Here you are, your lordship.' Instead she said, 'I don't see how the paper will help you any. If they're all so good at predicting scores then everybody would be rich.'

'That's daft,' he said, without looking up. 'They're only there to act as a guide – to inform you of what the experts reckon. It's still up to you to make the decisions.' A distant smile smothered his face as his mind drifted back to something he'd read. 'I remember that fella from Scotland winning ten thousand, not so long ago. First time and, blow me down, he scoops ten thousand.'

'And how long have you been trying to win?' she asked, accusingly.

'On and off,' thought Tommy, 'about two years.'

'And he collected ten grand?'

'Aye, and he didn't have a system.' As soon as he'd revealed this, he knew he shouldn't have done.

'So all this listening to the wireless and checking the sports page is a waste of time?' There was a triumphant ring in her voice.

'Well, everyone has their own methods . . .'

'Rubbish! Let me have a go for you this week. I've just as much chance as you of striking the fortune.'

'Ooh, Sade. Can't you just let me . . ?'

'List our families' birthdays,' she said, overriding him. 'That's my system.'

'Everybody does birthdays, and anyway, that's not a system; it's just chance. A silly one-off thing.'

Sadie was not having it, and took his pencil away and ushered him from his seat. 'Okay,' he conceded. 'But just one line of birthdays – seven; that's all I'm needing.'

Rapidly she ran through the birthdays of those closest to her. Tommy was impressed. He had enough trouble just remembering his own. She handed him the pencil back. 'Finished.'

'Right; now read them back to me so I can get them down on't form.'

'My birthday is on . . .'

'Just the dates, please Sadie. We'll be here all night, the way things are going.'

'Stop moaning.'

'I'm not moaning.'

'Yes you are; and don't argue with me.'

Tommy was growing tired. He'd spent over an hour on the coupons. Over an hour to put down no more than seven draws: and he still had the copy to make out afterwards.

It took a further ten minutes, but at long last he was considering the numbers before him. His face lengthened with each successive one. 'Good God. How the hell are Huddersfield going to draw away at Arsenal?' With a dejected sigh, he shoved them into the envelope and sealed it shut. 'I think I'll just nip in the "Woolpack" when I post these later on.'

'All right if I come along?' asked Sadie. He knew he couldn't say no – and so did she.

'Of course it is.' His feeble tone didn't sound too convincing.

He was standing by the back door when Sadie came down the stairs half an hour later. He studied her best coat and Sunday hat with gaping mouth.

'What are you all dressed up for?'

116

Sadie said, 'We're going out, aren't we?'

'Only to the "Woolpack". He could see his mates laughing at him if he walked in with Sadie dressed like this.

'So what?'

'We'll only be in the tap room; not the posh bit.'

'Fine; tap room it is, then. It doesn't hurt to look smart, you know.' He knew what was coming next. 'And I hope you don't think you're going out in your cap and overalls. You look a disgrace. Imagine my embarrassment if we bump into Mam and Dad.' He couldn't imagine her dad worrying too much – so long as Tommy bought his quota of pints.

He gave as disgruntled a look as he dared, then stomped upstairs to re-emerge minutes later, a new man. 'Satisfied?' he muttered.

She kissed him lightly on the cheek. 'And proud,' she said.

Having posted the coupon, they nipped into the best room at the 'Black Swan'. It was a much classier pub than the 'Woolpack' and it gave Sadie the chance to show off her smart coat. What she hadn't anticipated was that they'd be the only customers in there. Tommy smiled at his reflection on the shiny copper bar-top and his reflection smiled back.

When he went to pay he discovered he'd left his money in his overalls. Sadie watched him patting his empty pockets and, with a shake of the head, she slipped a ten-shilling note into his hand. 'And I want that back when we get home,' she whispered. 'I'm putting towards a new three-piece suite.'

'Of course you'll get it back,' promised Tommy, who was wishing she'd shut up because she was making him look mean. It was bad enough he'd come out without any money.

They took a corner seat and stared at their drinks – half of best bitter and a Benedictine. 'Those fancy drinks you have cost a fortune,' he moaned.

'I only have two a year, and who pays for it?'

'You'll get your money back,' he said touchily, 'and I've told you that already.'

Sadie tutted. 'And anyhow,' he carried on, 'I don't know what you see in that coloured muck.' He raised his own drink with pride. 'Not like beer. Beer is good for you, you know. It flushes you out.'

Sadie said, 'Tommy Moran, don't be so vulgar.'

They sat silently and motionlessly for nearly ten minutes. If they'd taken their clothes off they'd have resembled two newly sculpted statues. For the two of them, going out for a drink together was about as exciting as being in the dentist's waiting room.

Tommy was thinking about Huddersfield drawing with Arsenal, and a little ironic smile had grown on his face, and Sadie was thinking about Stella. 'What's the time?' she asked, suddenly, making Tommy miss Huddersfield's equaliser.

'Nine.'

She smiled. 'Same as your Colin's birthday, then.' He didn't react. The pools was not a joking matter. 'What time do they close?'

'About ten thirty, I think. Why?'

'Drink up,' she said.

'What for?'

'Drink up, then take me home. You can nip over to the "Pack" and have a quick 'un with your mates.'

He'd drained his glass before she'd reached the word 'mates'. They walked home, making monosyllabic conversation. The first thing Tommy did on reaching home was to change back into his overalls. 'Bye love – shan't be long.' He quietly closed the door behind him.

Sadie picked up the local and reread the piece about 'Lancaster girl – Stella Raven – making it big' for the umpteenth time. The part that most interested her was where it said she would be going to Manchester with a big revue. She ignored the remark she was supposedly quoted as saying to a reporter about not having time to see friends and family in not-too-distant Lancaster.

As she folded the paper she had already made up her mind. The three-piece suite would have to wait if they were going to see Stella's show. And she knew she'd have to work hard on Tommy to convince him it would be worth it.

Chapter 11

It was celebration time for Woody Woodville, and that meant throwing a big party in a private penthouse suite of the Midland Hotel. The drink flowed, the merrymaking flowed – and Woody's money flowed. Why? Because he was cleared of the murder charge: he was a free man.

Nola's true murderer – Richard Smith, an unemployed docker of no permanent address – had been apprehended on a petty theft charge and, under questioning on that and other minor offences, also confessed to carrying out her murder.

The Chief Superintendent was informed at once. The confession fitted perfectly, right down to the last detail of how he'd deliberately incriminated Woody Woodville. His motive? Apparently he'd been having an affair with the 'free and easy' chorus girl just before the Shanklin season had commenced. He had threatened her during the season for admitting to fancying the manager there. When she went on to repeat the same thing with producer Woody Woodville it was all too much for him to bear.

He was a man prone to violent behaviour, especially when under the influence of alcohol. On the night of Nola's murder he'd been evicted from three public houses for abusive behaviour.

Had he not been so calculating in his organisation of her murder his offence may have been seen as a crime of passion. Instead, it looked probable he would be going down for life. However, his confession would play in his favour.

If Woody hadn't been black he'd have looked paler for his

nerve-wracking ordeal. As it was, he just appeared a little thinner beneath his camel-skin drape.

Someone tapped a table and conversations petered out. By one of the doors, Milton finished a mouthful of nuts that sounded like a passing stampede. 'Friends,' began Woody. 'That's all I can say of all you beautiful people.'

And so began a long, well-rehearsed speech. Stella believed he'd put as much into it as the show itself. 'When the chips are down, friends are all a man in need has got. I went through a rough time, I don't deny it.' Lester winced. He knew how many fabricated stories were going to develop during this speech. 'The bread and the water, they made me lose a few pounds; but then so did this party.' Courteous laughter emanated from the guests. It had to. He was host and he was paying.

After rambling on for another fifteen minutes he wound up saying, 'Well, that's the end of my few short words.' An audible sigh of relief could be heard. 'I'd just like to conclude by saying, eat, drink, and be merry: you are all brothers of Woody Woodville.'

Enthusiastic clapping erupted, and why not? It was the best way to ensure he didn't say any more.

Milton, who had moved across to Stella, whispered to her, 'Another speech like that and *I'll* frame him for murder.'

Mike Farrow was engaged in conversation with Henry Charles. They were discussing the press and Henry looked very pleased. He realised that Woody, being proven innocent, had unwittingly created excellent publicity for the show. Previously, the publicity had centred around a murder, whereas now it centered around a producer – their producer – having been wrongly accused. Henry could see the headlines and almost taste the money of the punters. People loved a show that was entwined with mystery. He said to Mike, 'C'mon Mike. Let's go down to the lobby and assist the press boys in their task.'

'Visitor, Mr Keens,' announced the doorman through a gap in Milton's dressing-room door. Milton lowered his hair-brush and frowned at himself in his narrow mirror.

'Oh God, I'd forgotten all about her,' he groaned. 'Better send her down.'

'Okay.'

Like Milton, Stella was staring into a dressing-room mirror – her own one. She was trying to concentrate on her eye-shadow, but her mind kept forming a picture of the late Nola, and she knew she would be glad when they left Manchester because they could leave behind them the air of death that seemed to linger over the Opera House.

She decided to get a second opinion on her make-up and skipped down the corridor to Milton's room. A tilted corridor clock warned her she had only fifteen minutes left until she was due on-stage. She burst in on him saying, 'Hey, Milton, what do you think of my eye . . .'

She glimpsed his visitor sitting primly on a stool in one corner. 'Hello, Jane,' she said. 'I forgot you were coming to the show today.'

She thought, That sounds so stupid. I wish I hadn't said it.

'Hello, Miss Raven. It's nice to see you again.' Stella couldn't believe Jane found it nice at all. In fact, she hadn't seen two such long faces as those that confronted her now.

Stella looked questioningly at Milton, and then said, somewhat dryly, 'Has there been a death in the family?'

'Er, look; I'll catch up with you after the show, Jane,' he said, ushering her out into the corridor.'

'Okay, Shipton,' she smiled.

'It's Milton, actually.'

'Oh yes. Sorry. Forgot.' Jane disappeared to take her seat in the stalls.

'That didn't appear to be the happiest of reunions,' remarked Stella.

'It wasn't,' came the blunt response.

'So I can presume you told her.'

'Told her?'

'Told her about us.'

He gave an ironic smile. 'On the contrary,' he said. '*She* told *me* about herself.'

'Explain that,' said Stella, understandably a little confused. She hadn't the time for Milton's usual evasion of the point.

'All right, then,' he said. He could have added, 'if that's what you want,' but he didn't. 'Jane Butterworth is pregnant and it seems I'm the proud father-to-be.'

He slumped back into a chair, burying his head in his

121

hands. If he could have reproduced it on-stage he'd have had no problem in achieving a long and successful career in straight acting. 'The things you women put us poor men through,' he said, accusingly. If Stella hadn't been so stunned she'd have rebuked him for making such a glib and controversial remark.

'What will you do?' she asked, tonelessly.

'That, my dear, would seem to be the ultimate question.'

'And what does *she* have to say about it?'

Was there venom in the way she said 'she'? he wondered. He stretched slowly across his dressing-table and picked up one of his cigarettes. They weren't his in the strictest sense, as he hardly ever smoked. Someone had left them there – most likely it was Mike Farrow – so Milton had claimed them.

He lit up and sucked the soothing smoke deep down into his lungs before releasing it through flaring nostrils. 'She says I should do the gentlemanly thing and marry her.' He gave a short, derisive chuckle. 'Gentlemanly! I ask you. How pathetically old-fashioned.'

Stella said nothing for a moment or two. Her mouth hung limply open as if waiting for a thermometer to be put in it. She attempted to detach herself from the situation by considering the problem objectively.

'I was always told that if a fella got a girl in trouble, next mistake he could make would be to marry her. It would be for the wrong reason and only bring about further disaster.' Letting her objectives fade away, she said, 'And also, I don't want to lose you, Milton.' She gave a tiny shrug as she tried to explain. 'I may not be as deeply in love with you as you've been claiming to be with me, but I know it will come in time. I know I've never wanted someone near me as much as I've wanted you.'

He didn't dare glance up, knowing that just seeing her gentle face and wide blue eyes after such lovely words would only serve to destroy him all the more quickly and totally. 'Thank you,' was all he croaked.

'TWELVE MINUTES, STELLA!' bellowed an echoing voice. She didn't bat an eyelid.

'Funny, I only came in here to ask your opinion on my eyeshadow.'

122

'It looks great,' he said emptily and without even glancing up.

She bent down and kissed him on the forehead, wondering as she did so if their futures were destined not to be shared.

The curtains descended on average applause. The performers weren't discouraged. Most matinees were poorly attended whatever the theatre, whatever the show. At least, they could be thankful it was an audience mainly consisting of elderly people who'd come in from the rain to warm up and have a little snooze. During school holidays it was scruffy kids whose only interest was in the chorus girls' legs and how many performers they could pelt with half-chewed toffees.

Back in her dressing-room Stella checked her watch. Another couple of hours and she'd be making up for the evening performance. It was a treadmill but it was one she'd chosen to step onto. She thought of herself working in a cake shop in Lancaster and all at once that treadmill seemed paradise.

Allowing time for Jane Butterworth to leave, she knocked on Milton's door. He poured himself a large measure of whisky from a bottle Woody had given him when discovering they both shared a love for a 'drop of the malt'. 'Well, she's gone,' he said. 'Sadly, I think it's only for the time being, though.'

'It's to be expected,' she said, generously. 'If a fella got me up the spout and tried to do a runner, I'd have his guts for garters.' Despite his dire situation, Milton couldn't resist a short laugh.

He pushed a beaker of whisky into her hand. She held it at arm's length as if it was contaminated. 'You're not turning into an alcoholic, are you?' she asked. 'You won't solve any problems by drinking yourself stupid, you know.'

'Don't cast such a lurid light over me, Stella.' He raised his beaker in salutation. 'I'm merely relaxing my overworked, overstressed mind and body. Cheers!'

He threw back the drink and then tossed the empty beaker at a waste-paper basket, missing it by feet. 'Come on,' he said suddenly, and then made a positive step towards his jacket. 'No point in hanging round here feeling sorry for ourselves. Let's take some air.'

123

Mr Adams began pulling out a trumpet from a deep case he'd brought with him. 'It says on your form,' said Mike Farrow, 'that you're a vent act. I didn't know you could play trumpet.'

'There are many people who don't know I play trumpet. There are many people who don't know I play trumpet after they've *heard* me play trumpet.'

Mike linked his fingers behind his head and leant back. It was turning into a long and tiring day. Why had he been the one to get lumbered with auditioning new acts for the revue?

Henry had said, 'They'll be two acts dropping out after Manchester. I'll leave it with you and Woodville to organise replacements.' He said who but he didn't say why. And Woodville had said, 'Mike, baby, I'll leave it all in your hands. I'll just take care of their routines once you've got them signed up.'

And now here he was with this third talentless act of the day. 'Would you like to hear my rendition of "The Last Post"?' enquired Mr Adams.

'With the word "Last" in it, how could I refuse?' replied Mike, a shade sarcastically.

He thought despairingly of the next act due in. Mr G. H. Duffy, 'genius of the glockenspiel', as he billed himself. There was a firm knock at the door and for a second he thought Mr Duffy had arrived early. Instead, Stella poked her pretty face into the office – the same office where the Chief Superintendent had held his interviews – and to Mike, it was like someone had let summer into the room.

Simultaneously, Mr Adams played the opening notes of 'The Last Post'. Stella immediately burst out laughing, thinking it was a comedy routine. Once she had started laughing it was all Mike could do to prevent himself from joining in. The effort sent him puce.

Mr Adams, with a look of indignation, flung his trumpet into the case, slammed it shut, heaved it down from the table where it was resting, and stormed out of the room.

Stella felt terrible. 'Oh, Mike, I didn't realise . . . I mean, it was for real . . . I'm so sorry . . .' He waved her down.

'Not to worry,' he said. 'I think you saved me a job. But try not to make a habit of it. God knows, one day we may get someone talented come and see us for an audition.'

He stood up to stretch his aching back. 'Now, what can I do for you, Stella Raven?'

'It's my parents,' she explained. 'They're seeing the show tonight. Do you think you could see to them a bit, just 'til afterwards?'

'Be my pleasure to,' he lied – but he lied well. 'And now I've something for you.' She looked quizzical. She couldn't guess what it could be. 'There's a beauty contest on Saturday. We've been approached to see if we could volunteer a judge. I thought it would be a bit original to suggest a female. Would it interest you?'

She didn't really like that sort of thing, though she knew Mike was only trying to please her. 'The local press will be there,' he added, 'and maybe a couple of the nationals, even.' All at once she was more interested.

'I'll go,' she said.

'Good,' said Mike, and the knock at the door told him Mr G. H. Duffy had arrived.

The show came and went that night, and so did Stella's parents. It had been an odd reunion between the three of them. Sitting in Stella's dressing-room, she listened as they told her they'd 'quite liked' the show, especially Milton Keens – much to Stella's irritation. More amazingly, she found that they could only see her position in showbusiness as being temporary until something more secure came up.

This was mainly the attitude of her mother, for her father wasn't complaining about anyone or anything once Stella had stuck a bottle of light ale in his hand. And then her mother started going on about Sadie and Tommy and how she should make up with them.

The only light relief came when Woody burst into the room. 'Hi, honey,' he said to Stella, in his familiar forthright tone. 'Wonderful show – truly.' Then he focused in on her parents. 'These your grandparents?'

'No, Woody,' she said. 'These are my parents.'

'Hi, folks. You must be mighty proud of your offspring. Ain't she just the best?' Then with a smile he was gone.

'What's to do with him?' asked Jack, in a low and startled voice.

'Nothing, Dad. He choreographed the show.'

'Sounded bloody funny to me.'

'Language, Jack,' corrected his wife.

'And he's black,' he said, as if it was a sin.

'He's American, Dad. One of the finest producers in the business.'

She knew it was pointless trying to explain: she knew it was pointless trying to explain anything new in her life. She could almost touch the distance that had grown between them. Basically, they had nothing left in common any more, other than being directly related. She loved them as they loved her, but only as family should always love their own. They didn't understand the first thing about showbusiness and, perhaps more significantly, they didn't *want* to understand.

They said their goodbyes at the stage door – though in reality they'd been said when she first left for London. There was a room arranged for them at the Midland, courtesy of Henry Charles, but she knew she wouldn't be seeing them off in the morning.

Despite the unease of their reunion the tears still flowed between mother and daughter as they hugged each other goodbye, and Jack hovered in the background hoping they'd get back to the hotel in time for a pint.

Mike Farrow hadn't been entirely accurate in informing Stella she was to be a judge of a beauty contest. It was, in fact, a fashion show – and she was pleased by his mistake. She could guess how he had come to the wrong conclusion: judges, clothes, women, beauty – a beauty contest, he'd have thought.

There were five other judges, all of whom had arrived just before she had. She was a little disappointed that no-one seemed to recognise her, though she did find when she told them about the revue they knew exactly who she was. 'Did you know that murdered girl very well?' was the most repeated question of the day.

Champagne flowed as the judges acquainted themselves with each other, then silence was called for as the mayor – all four feet nine of him, accompanied by a rather bulbous wife – strode confidently into the meeting-room of the civic hall to greet them. 'Hello, Miss Raven,' he beamed, when finally reaching her. She noticed how his head had a natural tendency to tilt backwards – hardly surprising, as there must have been few people he met of his own height and even fewer who were smaller than him.

She shook his tough little hand and smiled. She felt good. Mike had arranged for her to borrow an imitation mink through the wardrobe girl at the theatre. Only an expert eye could have told it was a fake. Looking around the gathering there today she couldn't envisage she'd be threatened by too many expert eyes.

There was one man who shone out among the rest. He was tall and good-looking in a suave, sophisticated way. She didn't think these sort of people existed north of London, and when she spoke briefly to him she discovered she could still be right. He was American. His name was Bernard Goldman, and she wasn't to know then that this man was to play the singularly most important role in her whole life. What she *did* know then was that he could well have had expert eyes.

The fashion show began, and the girls – and the occasional man – paraded through in their various costumes that would suit the oncoming season. Stella was attracted to a very smart grey outfit that clung daringly tight to the hips, accentuating the young model's form. She saw Bernard Goldman eye her up and down as she walked past and decided that if it had that effect on good-looking men like him she was going to have to save up for one.

As judges, they had to give points between nought and ten for each outfit. The points were then collated at the end, and the outfit with the most points would obviously be the winner. But this aspect of the occasion wasn't taken very seriously. The main purpose of the exercise was to show off the new designs and give the guests a chance to meet the designers. The model who was in the winning outfit was, however, allowed to keep it. A splendid little perk, too.

The grey suit came out the winner, so Stella hadn't been alone in her choice. She wondered if she would be able to strike up a cash bargain with the model. 'I see you're admiring the winning outfit,' remarked Bernard Goldman to her.

'Oh, yes,' said Stella, surprised by the sudden voice at her side. 'She's a very lucky girl to be keeping it.'

Other than the initial hello and inevitable goodbye that was to be the only conversation between the two of them for the time being.

The mayor made his excuses and left, and after a cup of tea and a sandwich or two, the other guests did likewise.

Stella returned to the Midland, trying to decide which she liked the most – the grey suit or Mr Bernard Goldman. As it happened, she wasn't going to have to decide; she was going to get them both.

Woody's end-of-run party hadn't exactly gone off with the 'bang' they'd all expected. Perhaps it was because Nola's death still hung over them like a dark cloud, or that everyone's thoughts were on the forthcoming provinces before hitting London's West End – or both.

When the curtain fell on the last night they all heaved a sigh of relief and hugged each other lovingly. It wasn't so much because the show had been a great success that they showed such affection and delight – though the show had been a great success so far – it was more because they knew it was one down and two to go.

Henry Charles had mentioned to them at the party that he might consider – as the show was doing so well and receiving such wonderful notices – paying off Birmingham and Brighton and taking it straight into town to make the 'big killing', as he referred to it. But when Stella aproached him next day about this he sounded less certain, and she could only assume that he'd contacted the two remaining provincials and discovered that their contract was more binding than he could remember. Most likely they were in for a share of the gross, and, having seen the success in Manchester, were in no mood to be 'paid off'.

After the final show at the Opera House, Stella, as did all the artistes, went to change out of her working clothes for the last time there. 'Some guests to see you, Stella,' informed the doorman.

'Oh. Who is it?' she asked from within her dressing-room.

'It's us,' replied two excited voices. 'Sade and Tommy.'

Stella froze. She felt like a trapped animal with no possible way of escape. If she'd been holding a glass, now would have been the moment to drop it. 'Can we come in?' asked Sadie, not understanding what the delay was for. Stella dumbly nodded, then remembered they couldn't see her with the door closed.

'Yes, yes,' she said, blankly. 'Please come in.'

'Ello, 'ello, 'ello,' Sadie said, and threw her arms warmly around her elder sister – a warmth that wasn't returned.

'Hello, Sadie,' Stella greeted her coldly and, turning to Tommy, said in the same tone, 'Hello, Tommy.'

'Thought the show was knockout,' he congratulated.

'Thanks. I'm glad you enjoyed it. I didn't realise you were coming to see it.'

'Strange thing, that, about girl getting bumped off, eh?'

Tommy's just as blunt as ever, thought Stella.

'Very unfortunate incident,' she said.

'I told you you'd be better off on your own,' said Sadie, refusing to believe that her sister could possibly still hold a grudge against her for terminating their partnership.

'I didn't have a great deal of choice, the way I remember it,' she said.

Tommy shuffled uneasily and took a step back – just like he always used to whenever that familiar glint appeared in Stella's eyes. But Stella was more controlled these days and had no intention of causing a scene.

'Would you like a drink?'

'What have you got?' asked Tommy. 'Have you a beer or anything?'

'Only champagne.'

'Our Colin had a bottle of that last Christmas,' he said. 'It sends folk daft, but then he's always been daft, our Colin, hasn't he?'

'That would be lovely, Stella,' said Sadie, unconsciously clutching at her sister's sleeve. Stella had to yank quite hard to disconnect them.

'We've heard you on the wireless,' remarked Tommy. 'So has Mrs Bennet.'

'Mam and Dad mentioned you have a house of your own, now,' said Stella.

Tommy beamed with pride. 'Aye, we have. A corporation house in Willow Lane. Very nice it is, too. You'll have to visit us when you're not too busy.'

129

'Yes, you *must* visit us,' invited Sadie, far more insistently than Tommy.

'That depends on work,' she said, evasively. 'After the revue is over in London I don't intend being idle too long. I may take a short break – out to the country, or abroad, even. But then I'll be back hunting down another part in a big show.'

After a little more formal conversation Tommy and Sadie took the hint and made to leave. 'We're catching a late train back,' explained Tommy, 'so it's best we're on our way, now.'

'Do keep in contact, love,' said Sadie – pleaded Sadie.

'I'll try,' said Stella, and a tiny lump came to her throat. As her younger sister went to the door Stella said, 'Sadie?' Her sister paused and looked back inside.

'Yes, love?' she said, hopefully.

'You take care, too.'

Sadie's face broke into a smile. They were the best words she'd heard since Tommy said 'I will'. She didn't need to reply.

Stella listened as their footsteps faded down the corridor. After going into Milton's dressing-room for a large malt whisky or two, she erased Sadie and Tommy from her mind once again. It took Tommy two hours and two hankies to stop his wife from crying.

There was a package addressed to Stella at the Midland when she finally returned there that night. She took it upstairs to her room. She hadn't a clue what it could be, and wondered if it was a mistake. After all, she wasn't even staying in Manchester after tomorrow morning. She tossed it on the bed and roughly tore off the brown wrapping-paper. Inside was the grey suit she had so admired on the model. There was no message with it.

Chapter 12

It was the first week in November 1937. Stella was twenty-three, a star, indeed one of Britain's number-one box-office attractions. This meteoric rise to the giddy heights of fame and acclaim was solely attributable to the enormous success of the revue. Having done so well in the provinces, the show had come to the West End and had turned into a six-month sell-out blockbuster.

Everyone involved with it had done well from the good run – except for poor Nola – and was guaranteed regular work for the forthcoming year. But it was Stella who had emerged as its star, and she was guaranteed that if she did anything she wanted to do, an audience would pay to come and see her.

Understandably, she was quite thrilled at how her career had so unexpectedly soared. She'd seen the revue well received by press and public alike, but she hadn't anticipated that it would be individually picked out as 'the rose amongst the thorns of London theatre-land', as one poetic reporter had worded it.

She was attractive, she was boundlessly talented, and she was ideal to fill the gossip columns of the time as torch-bearer of the revue. In fact, the papers often made it sound as though she'd brought the revue to London single-handedly. Henry Charles didn't object. He merely rubbed his podgy hands together all the way to the bank.

She found being a star was not quite the joy she had once

dreamt it would be. Mike Farrow was quick to point out that achieving stardom is rarely better than the hunting for it.

She went through a transitory period as she fought to build new routines into her new life. She could no longer behave quite as unrestrictedly as before. She couldn't use public transport; tell the press where to shove their criticisms (not without it being used as a quote); walk down Shaftesbury Avenue looking at the billboards without wearing a hat and dark glasses; or accepting she'd be mobbed by irreverent autograph hunters if she didn't.

The pleasures were that she no longer had financial difficulties; she didn't have to rent flats in Brixton; and she could shout back at management if she disagreed with them.

In the early part of 1937 she'd taken some time off to rest and reflect on her position. It was on the advice of Henry Charles that she'd done so, and it was the best thing she could have done. When she returned some weeks later she was revitalised, and still capturing the imagination of a nation of theatregoers – and the inevitable gossip-columnists.

Journalists hounded her when and wherever: 'Stella Raven – the Lancashire Hot Pot – [that was what they had dubbed her] has been reputed to have bought a six-bedroomed mansion in Knightsbridge. She has a swimming pool, a butler and many lavish furnishings. Neighbours say she holds wild parties there most nights, but they never complain as she is willing to sing for them from her bedroom window.'

She would chuckle at such write-ups. The six-bedroomed mansion was a three-bedroomed flat; the swimming pool was more a communal bath with predominantly green, stagnant water, and the butler a porter employed to service the needs of the whole block. She'd had only one party in the six months she'd been in possession of the flat, and to her knowledge it hadn't been a particularly wild one. And she couldn't recall ever having sung for the neighbours, though she had once played a long-playing demonstration record of herself on the gramophone just to hear that it was all right before it went on release. Such was the press in her life at this time.

Henry had given her a substantial cash advance to enable her to purchase the flat. He'd also gone about arranging her private use of the company accountant – at her own expense, of course.

Her contact with Milton Keens had become non-existent. His

problems with Jane Butterworth, it seemed, had not yet resolved themselves. Stella had received one letter from him since the show's conclusion, to which she had replied. He mentioned Jane only once, and spent the rest of the two sheets talking about his new role in a play that 'makes a pleasant change from those blessed dance routines Woody put me through'. And that had been all.

That was back in June, and now she hardly thought about him, or anything else, for that matter. Her biggest concern was her forthcoming pantomime – *Dick Whittington* – in which she was to star at the Empire, Leeds, commencing December the twelfth, and hopefully not finishing until some time late in March of the following year.

When she did think of Milton she couldn't help picturing him sitting in the small terraced house in Oldham, with Jane hovering in the background holding a pot of tea and a bald, red-faced baby bouncing up and down on his lap, while Adolf fired ink-pellets from somewhere across the room. She found it silly she should think like that. She couldn't even be certain if he'd moved in with Jane.

A taxi delivered Stella to the front steps of Henry Charles' office. She paid the driver, giving him a sizeable tip, and hurried inside, shielding her face to avoid being recognised by passers-by. If people did recognise her and approach, she would always joke with them and sign her name – sometimes on various parts of the anatomy, if so desired, but normally on paper.

'You should advertise for an assistant,' said Henry, when Stella had told him how tiring it was trying to keep her flat in order; deal with the press; do her work; and so on.

'Maybe you're right,' she said, 'but if I advertised, I'd end up with about two thousand applicants, one thousand nine hundred and ninety-nine of which would not be getting the job.'

Henry chewed this over for a moment as he paced the room. He also chewed his fat green cigar over. It played like a pork sausage on his lips, asking to be devoured. 'If I could get a short-list drawn up,' he finally said, 'I could say something about one of our artistes – no specific names mentioned – requires a personal assistant; a domestic help. That sort of thing.'

'That'd be great, Henry, and it would save me another chore.'

'Well, I don't want you overdoing it, Stella,' he ordered, as if he was her doctor. 'You've got *Whittington* coming up. I don't want you tired out with nervous exhaustion.'

'I wouldn't do such a thing,' she said, with mock-indignation. 'I'm far too professional.' They shared a laugh and Mike Farrow bounded in as if it had been to summon him.

'This sounds a joyous place. Mind if I move in permanently?'

'We've got to find Stella a live-in help,' said Henry, deliberately curtailing Mike's usual preamble.

Mike gave an easy shrug. 'Shouldn't be difficult,' he said. 'People are always after those kind of jobs. Jean – my wife –' He always explained who she was whenever her name came up in conversation, just in case they might have forgotten. 'She's got this friend who's just taken on someone who's supposed to be brilliant.'

'Fine,' said Henry, 'but that doesn't really help Stella much, does it?'

'It could do,' argued Mike. 'The thing is,' he explained, 'that they are all a bit like us in showbusiness; they stick together.'

'Can you fix me an interview with one of them?' asked Stella. 'I mean, that's all I want to know.'

'Sure, I can.'

'So that's that taken care of,' said Henry with finality.

'Please sit down, Miss –' Stella checked the sheet of file paper in her hands '– Baxter.' The woman sat down and rested her hands together on her lap. Stella thought her to be anything between thirty-five and forty-five; the type who seemed to be born old and grow younger.

She was smartly dressed – about twenty years out of fashion, though – wore little make-up, and her skin was taut and very dry. She didn't wear a wedding ring. 'Well, Miss Baxter, as you know through Mr Farrow, I'm looking for a supportive hand.'

'Aye, that's right,' she responded, in her flat northern voice.

Stella briefly wondered if Mike had chosen her because of her northern background.

'May I ask your first name?'

'It's Annie, love.'

'Can I call you Annie?'

'Yes love – it's my name.' She smiled a warm and simple smile. Her naturalness rather touched Stella. Annie reminded her of one of her aunts.

Stella was probably more nervous than Annie. She'd never had to interview anyone before. 'It's been cooler just lately,' she remarked, as she tried to gain some time.

'Aye, it has,' replied Annie. 'It's probably the weather,' she said, seriously. 'They do say "it's an ill wind that blows nobody".' Stella hadn't heard that one before.

'Er, yes. Now, have you ever worked for anyone in showbusiness before?'

Annie placed an index finger over her lips as she tried to recall. 'Just the once,' she got round to saying. 'I was a daily for a woman whose husband was an announcer on the wireless. He had a smashing voice,' she reflected. 'A very proper man, indeed.'

'Really?'

'Yes, really. I'm not having you on.'

'No, I know you're not, Annie.' What an eccentric woman she had found herself.

She decided to direct the conversation back to the purpose of the interview. With Annie it was all too easy to diversify in several directions at once. 'You understand what I would be expecting of you,' she said, 'were I to accept your services?'

Annie smiled inanely back, and Stella couldn't see her as the sort who'd object to any work as long as she was treated well. 'It'll be no easy job; there'll be no fixed hours. Each week will take care of itself, and I won't be able to say what time you can have off until that week has started.' Still no response from Annie; just the smile. 'You'd get a good wage to compensate for the long hours.' Annie didn't flinch at the words 'good wage', which surprised her prospective employer.

Then Annie finally spoke. 'What about men?' Stella's eyes widened.

'Men?' she said. 'What about men, Annie?'

135

'That's what I just asked.'

'Oh, I see. You're married. Actually, I didn't realise you were ma . . .'

'I'm not married,' she said, firmly. 'And I never will be. I live by the old saying.' Stella awaited the 'old saying'. It didn't come.

She just said, 'Oh, right,' and let Annie continue.

'And drink,' she said. 'I don't drink. Nor smoke. I don't smoke.' She narrowed her eyes as she tried to remember anything else she didn't do.

'I'm glad to hear it,' said Stella. 'I wouldn't want to go employing someone who was either promiscuous or an alcoholic – or both.'

'Well, I always say,' said Annie, ready to deliver another of her misquotations, 'people who live in glass houses should keep their clothes on.' What made Stella smile was Annie's sincerity. She genuinely seemed to believe that the quotations, from her long and confused repertoire, were all as they should be.

'I agree with you,' said Stella, 'and I'd like you to have the job. When do you think you'd be available to start?'

'Now,' she shrugged, in a manner that suggested it was obvious.

Stella was astonished. 'You mean, now?' she said. 'Now, as in right now?'

'Yes please.'

'But wouldn't you like to go home and get your things together and let a few relations, or whoever, know?'

'My relatives are all dead – or at least, the ones I liked are – and my things *are* together: they're outside your flat door.'

Within a few weeks Stella was going to learn that nothing Annie could do would come as a surprise. And after that interview Annie rarely left her side: she wouldn't let her. Although she'd never have considered it, Annie made a good foil for her, just as Sadie had done in her own way. A young woman amidst the chaos of showbusiness can be a surprisingly lonely experience; even to call it a harrowing experience wouldn't be an exaggeration. To have someone to share thoughts and emotions with can be the best stabiliser an artiste could wish for.

Annie very quickly went on to become Stella's cook, and, when she required it, her confidante. Annie was never happier than when she was working for her 'Miss Stella'. She never wanted any extra money or time off. To please Stella Raven was payment enough.

At first, this embarrassed Stella, who thought Annie more resembled her slave than her help, but as time went by the embarrassment turned to gratitude, and she would often think how lucky she'd been to cross paths with this funny little lady from Blackpool.

At the beginning of December, when Stella and entourage rolled into Leeds for the pantomime season at the Empire Theatre, the latest figures showed that the show was likely to be running as late as April.

Everything had been geared towards Stella's comfort, from the never-ending teapot to the new beige pile carpet paid for by – indirectly, as it went through on expenses – Moss Empires, who were putting on the show.

Annie made a point of being friendly with everyone, from the callboy up to the stage manager. And it always seemed to work. There wasn't a person there who wouldn't do or get anything she wanted, whether for herself or Miss Raven.

The first run-through of the script was a casual affair held on-stage, mid-morning on the first full day. All the local press were there, taking their flash pictures and asking sometimes pertinent questions, other times impertinent ones. Their main purpose was to track down Stella.

She drifted across the stage in a grey outfit – *the* grey outfit. She did it even more justice than the model had done. Eyes turned on her as she said, 'Hello, everyone,' with a bright, cheery, be-ginning-of-season smile: the sort of smile that evaporates by the end of the first week; sometimes sooner – never later. She chatted with Syd, the stage manager, awhile, asking after his wife and his son's croup.

News reached the front of house that Stella had arrived and was meeting various people on-stage. This at once brought the front-of-house manager waddling over to her from out of the dark depths of one of the thousand and one recesses in the Empire. Syd saw him coming, quickly smiled a see-you-later to her, and returned to his prompt corner.

'Stella, Stella, Stella, darling,' groaned the manager, as if in eternal ecstasy. He grabbed her beautifully manicured hands with the delicacy of a half-starved orang-utan and held them between the two wet flannels at the end of his arms, which he called his hands.

The part she was dreading soon came upon her. The kiss. He pushed his lips forward, soon followed by the rest of his rotund head. She waited until the last possible second before diverting to the right. That way she was only brushed by his moist lips on the cheek. As they slid off her face, like a pair of snow skis off Mount Everest, she said, 'Bertie, how are you?'

'My darling,' he said, putting his hands firmly around her tiny waist. 'I am fine, but we must get you together in the circle bar with the press.' He grinned, showing her his teeth, which reminded her of a badly kept set of dominoes. 'Please follow me.' Bertie could find his way to the bar even in his sleep. He led her up the steps that bisected the stalls. 'Business is fantastic,' he said, unprompted. 'We're not at final rehearsals yet and already we've broken all existing box-office records. We're sold out for a definite ten weeks, and there's a fight to get to the box office for shows thereafter.'

Even in the dimmed light of the circle corridor she could see he was beaming. 'It's got to run until April, don't you think?' He turned his head quickly to see her reaction and sent a spray of perspiration from his forehead, face, and chins. She didn't respond. 'We're here,' he announced, and pushed open two swing-doors.

The reporters and camera-men were huddled in a large group in a corner by a dusty window, contentedly drinking the free booze. 'Ladies and gentlemen of the press,' began Bertie, very formally. 'May I present to you the star of our show, Miss Stella Raven.'

He applauded with unnecessary exaggeration, and the press made a token effort to put their hands together – but they made sure they didn't have to move too far from their free booze to do it.

One of them smiled; one lit up a cigarette; two finished their drinks; and one went to a door marked 'Gentlemen', perhaps to bring back his drink. The door was locked. He tried to use force on it but it wouldn't give.

Stella shouted to him with a smile, 'What paper are you with?' He turned, a little red in the face by now, and prodded his own chest with a finger. 'That's right; you.'

'*Telegraph and Argus*,' he replied, gruffly.

'Well, you'll find plenty of those inside, once you get in.'

All the other papers laughed at the *Telegraph and Argus* man's understandable embarrassment. It was a start towards breaking the ice. 'Well, gentlemen and lady' – there was just one – 'who's to be the bravest and ask me a question?'

Bertie, standing and dripping just behind her, echoed with, 'Yes, now. Who is going to ask Miss Raven the first question?' She turned and stared at him for a second and he was immediately withered in an eye-to-eye confrontation. He backed away, leaving the 'stage' to his star.

'You,' she said, pointing to a man with a half-smoked cigar in his mouth. 'What paper are you with?' He was so taken aback by her picking on him that he inhaled midway through an exhale and consequently had a coughing fit, sending tears of discomfort running down his cheeks.

Another man said, 'I'm with the *Yorkshire Post*. What do you think of Leeds?'

'Oh, wonderful,' she replied, nodding to the window where the rain was teaming down onto the main thoroughfare of Briggate. 'It was a hard decision, choosing either Leeds or the south of France; but Leeds won.'

A flash-bulb inadvertently went off, and there came a muted apology. 'This is a right waste of time,' said Stella, but not angrily so: more because she felt pity for them being there. 'Look, let's cut out the formality bit,' she suggested. 'I'll sit with you and have a beer, and answer your questions in a nice 'n relaxed way.'

The ones who'd remained seated from the beginning sat up to make room for her as she strode over to join them. It made an incongruous sight to behold; the beautiful, almost diminutive, star, surrounded by a mixture of very ordinary-looking men, most of whom supported large beer-guts. 'Half a pint of best,' she shouted across to the bar.

The drink arrived; cameras flashed and a race started to see who could ask the most questions. Bertie glowed as he heard their laughter to her replies.

Forty minutes later they'd taken their pictures, asked their questions, and were now leaving. They told her what a good sport she was. The one female reporter remained behind. She went up to Stella and sat down beside her. Bertie tried to disguise a belch as he downed a neat Scotch that, in minutes, would be oozing out through his overworked pores. He bade a temporary farewell to Stella and the reporter, saying he had to meet up with the rest of the company. The two women were now alone; there was the barman; but, being a professional, he managed to blend in with the background furnishings. 'My name is Mary Holt, Miss Raven.'

'Oh, a double-barrelled name: "Mary Holt-Missraven."'

Mary Holt ignored the humour. 'I'm a freelance writer, and mostly use magazines as an outlet for my work. Would you answer a few more questions – the sort more suitable for the magazine reader?'

Stella gave an it-would-be-a-pleasure-to smile and said, 'It would be a pleasure to.'

'Lovely,' said Mary Holt, in a voice that didn't suppress her surprise. For some reason she had doubted Stella Raven was going to be so obliging. 'The sort of things these readers like to know about are the more intimate details of a star like yourself.'

'Oh yes,' said Stella, warily. 'How intimate?'

'I'll begin asking, and we'll see how we get along.'

That sounded fair enough to Stella. 'Okay, then.' Mary cleared her throat.

'Are you married?'

'No, I'm not.'

'Would you like to get married?'

'Yes. I love men – especially those of about thirty.'

'Would you mind telling me your age?'

'I'll tell you half of it, if you like. No, love, I'm twenty-three.'

'And how long have you been twenty-three, Miss Raven?'

Stella laughed. The girl had a sense of humour after all.

'Not long yet, but I hope to get another five years out of it.'

She wrote this out in long-hand, no doubt intending to use it as a complete and direct quote. Then she looked un-ashamedly at Stella's fur coat that she'd draped across a chair. 'It's beautiful. It's ermine, isn't it?'

140

'Yes.' Stella ruffled it with delicate fingers.

'Expensive, was it?'

'I've no idea,' she replied, truthfully. 'You see, it was a present.'

'From an admirer?' pressed the journalist.

'From someone who I represent ten per cent to,' she replied, spoiling Mary's next major quote.

'So there isn't a man in your life, currently?'

'No. There's no time. I'm too busy.'

'And what do you think of the men of Yorkshire?'

She hoped she'd trapped Stella into making a derogatory comment about the male species in this area. 'Rich,' she replied, thoughtfully.

'Eh?'

'When I think of the men from Yorkshire, I think of the rich ones.'

'Do you think you could marry one?' she asked.

'He'd have to be English, first.'

One of Mary's shoes fell off but she deftly turned it over with the other one and put it back on without once looking down. 'But they *are* English.'

'No, a Yorkshireman is a Yorkshireman, first, then he's English, then he's British. You see, you never ask a Yorkshireman if he's from Yorkshire. If he isn't, he won't mention it. If he is, he can't wait to tell you.'

Mary scratched her head with the blunt end of her pencil. It was a good moment to change the subject, she thought. 'How do you keep your skin looking so glorious?'

'Oh, thank you. It's Pears soap that does it.'

'Really?'

'Yes. I never use the stuff.'

'You're teasing me, Miss Raven,' she said, with a smile.

'Yes, I am, aren't I?'

Bertie wobbled in looking like he'd just stepped out of a Turkish bath. 'Oh, sorry, folks. I thought all the press bit was over.' However, he didn't then leave the room, but merely settled himself at the bar and had a large Scotch. He downed it before it had had a chance to become acquainted with the glass and then left without a further word.

'Thank you, Miss Raven,' said Mary, standing up and

141

drawing the interview to an end. 'You've been most co-operative.'

'That's quite all right. If you could send me a printed copy, I'd appreciate it.'

'Of the finished product when it appears?' she verified.

'That's right.'

'Certainly.'

Stella bumped into Bertie on the way out. He was loitering in the corridor with a self-satisfied grin stretched across his face. 'I've had a call from Cranbourn Mansions,' he gargled. 'They're thrilled with the advance, and . . .'

'So they bloody well should be,' snapped Stella. 'Look, Bertie, I'm not a front-of-house person. I never turn to complain to them if things go a bit wrong. I have no interest in them, just as they have no real personal interest in me. I'm glad the figures are good, just as I'm glad I'm getting paid, but after that I really wouldn't care if they all hung 'emselves.'

Bertie didn't know what to say. He slipped a soaking hand around her waist and it made her wince. He'd never before met such a no-messing female. 'So don't tell me every time they go making a phone call about the business,' she continued. 'Just tell me if they ring with a good idea for the panto, or that the advance is so good they can give the chorus girls an extra pound a week each.'

This short explosion was doing her good. She'd been feeling tense since arriving in Leeds. She'd needed to let off some steam, and the awful Bertie was the ideal target to let it off on. 'I've no need to know that business is good, because if it wasn't I would be out before you could say – before you could say I don't know what.'

Bertie felt as if he'd drown in his own perspiration. He stood hunched and immobile beside her, wearing a set grin that made him look as if he had lockjaw. All he knew was he mustn't offend the star. If he did, then he also knew that Moss Empires would crucify him. If her getting explosive with him maintained the smooth running of the show, who was he to take offence?

The advance was all that mattered, and that was the best it had ever been. 'And another thing,' she said, in summing up. 'If you carry on getting fresh with me I'll give you a firm kick

142

between your legs, and I'll make sure that you get your job here shoved up your arse.' He quickly released his grip on her waist. 'Is that plain enough speaking for you?'

He wiped his face as he watched her drift away. 'Wow, what a girl,' he told the empty corridor. He fell into the circle bar again. He needed another drink more than he'd ever needed another drink.

Still inside was Mary Holt. She was sitting by a window, re-reading her notes. 'Hi, Mary. Still working?'

'So it seems, Bertie. So it seems.'

'Want one for the road?' He tossed a glance at the bar.

'Not for me, thanks, Bertie,' she smiled. She held up her pad. 'I've deadlines to meet.' It didn't stop Bertie having one.

'And how did you get on with Lady Muck?'

Mary had met Bertie on several occasions, most of them in this very bar, and she'd always found him lacking in subtlety. 'Not bad,' she replied. 'I'm not sure I understood all she said. I believe she was pulling my leg for much of the time.'

'Bloody hard lady, that,' he said, from new-found experience. 'Anyway, the advance is good, and that's all I have to worry about, Mary.'

'Yes, I know, Bertie, I know.'

Slowly he rose from his chair, leaving a damp patch where he'd been sitting. Then quickly he poured another nip down his throat with about as much grace as a nervous sword-swallower. They left the room together.

Before making her entrance on-stage on the opening night Stella peered through a hole in the manager's prompt-corner. It was a small peep-hole that enabled artistes to view the audience without the audience knowing it. It was statutory in most theatres.

The view spanned all of the stalls and the boxes that flanked the left side of the auditorium. It was a packed house. Even every box was full – all, that is, except for one. Inside this particular box sat a very still figure. In the dimness she could make out he was extraordinarily well-dressed and very dignified-looking. 'How come there's only one bloke up there?' she asked Bertie in a low voice.

'No idea, my love. We're sold out and the box is fully paid for.'

He turned to the electrician. 'Stand by, Fred.' He turned back to Stella, who was now concentrating on the stage. 'Are you ready?'

'As I'll ever be.'

How odd that one man should take over a complete box, she kept thinking.

'Good luck.'

'Ooh, don't. It's bad luck to say good luck.'

She licked her lips as her entrance music started and, for the umpteenth time, straightened her tights. The midget, who was playing Tommy the cat, ran onto the stage ahead of her, rolled over onto his back, and, with his paw, waved Stella – the star of the show – on to greet her first audience.

She looked fantastic as Whittington, with her blonde hair cut extremely short to give her the appearance of being male. But it had a paradoxical effect: it accentuated her beauty – the perfect oval shape of her face; the long, slender gracefulness of her swan-like neck. Though diminutive in stature, she was woman personified.

Her ovation was tremendous. Two of the three circle lights hit her. She gave herself to the audience – the ever-demanding audience – through a radiant, professional smile. She knew they'd be walking back through the rain to the glum reality of their tiny, basic homes, which is why she'd conditioned herself to shine the best she could, every time she was on-stage. They'd paid to see her – to escape that reality for however brief a moment in time – and it was her duty, therefore, to send them home feeling they'd been entertained. It was no more than what she would have expected.

Surreptitiously, she tried to stare through the blanket of darkness to glimpse the mystery man in the box. The footlights were too powerful; she couldn't see a thing beyond the edge of the stage.

The young lady playing the role of Alice Fitzwarren, the principal girl, made her entrance and they went into their dialogue: 'Who are you, sir?'

'My name is Dick Whittington, and this is Tommy, my cat.'

After the thrill of her first entrance and opening lines it soon became a twice-daily job. The following week, the first full week, consisted of twelve performances – and the solitary

144

figure attended every one from the same position in the same box.

On the Monday of the second week she walked into her dressing-room after having a late breakfast. Annie was in the city doing some shopping for their tea, and so she decided to face the inevitable piles of fan-mail that lined her dresser in ever-increasing bundles. As she waded through them there came a knock at her door. A head popped in. It belonged to the doorkeeper. 'S'cuse me love,' he said. 'I've some flowers for you.'

'Oh, you shouldn't have done,' she joked, and his empty smile told he'd heard that one a million times before.

He left them on a table and disappeared. She saw that there was no note attached and so, with a shrug, persevered with her mail.

Two minutes later the doorkeeper was back. This time he'd brought with him a dozen red roses. 'More?' she gasped, placing them next to the others.

'Won't be a minute. I'll just go and fetch the others.'

'There's even more?'

'Yes, and there's no note attached to any of them, so I reckon they must be from the same source.'

'I think you could be right.'

Her delight at receiving such wonderful flowers turned slightly to irritation at not knowing who the kind sender could be. Was it possibly one of Mike's little gestures? He was the sort of person who would do such a thing and in a such mysterious manner. One thing for sure; it certainly wouldn't be Henry Charles – not unless he was on ten per cent.

'Good news,' announced the doorkeeper, returning. 'There's a card wedged deep inside with this lot.'

Eagerly, she put the glorious arrangement of flowers, supported in a wicker basket, to one side and pulled out the small, oblong card. 'What's it say?' She read it out:

'There may be none of beauty's daughters,
with a magic like thee,
And like music on the waters,
Is thy sweet voice to me.'

It was handwritten but, disappointingly, it was unsigned. 'No better off than at the beginning,' she said.

'At least we can be sure they came from a man,' he said, rather dumbly.

'I hardly thought they'd come from my mother.'

'I suppose not,' he said, slipping out the room.

Moments later Annie returned. 'My, aren't they lovely? Who sent 'em?'

'No-one seems to know. There was a card, but no name.'

'Oh, I see. Sent annonymally?'

'That's right, Annie.' Stella inwardly smiled.

'Must be rich,' declared Annie. 'Probably born with a silver fork in his mouth.'

There was no mystery man in the box for that afternoon's matinee performance. This made one of the cast joke, 'About time too. Last time anyone was in a box for so long they were buried.'

The box had apparently been paid for but it remained empty; well, almost empty. On the centre seat was placed a single red rose.

In a way this upset her. She thought it a shame that if the box had been paid for, children couldn't be allowed in to use it. She told Bertie as much.

'But it's paid for, my love,' was his defence. 'And anyway, I wouldn't be allowed to do such a thing without *his* permission.'

'So you know who he is?' she pounced. Bertie shrank away. He knew immediately he shouldn't have opened his mouth, and that now it would be interrogation-time.

'Well . . .'

'C'mon, who is he?' She kept a fixed stare on him.

'It's no good,' he said, bravely. 'I'm sworn to secrecy.' Stella was impressed. Whoever this man was, he had more power over Bertie than she had, and until then she'd have said that no-one could have more power over Bertie than she had.

Saturday evening, after the second show, Stella and Annie drove back to the Queen's Hotel by taxi. They went to the reception desk for the keys. The uniformed figure at the desk beamed when seeing who it was. He handed her a key with a rose attached.

For a dreadful moment Stella half-wondered if this receptionist was the mystery man. But then she realised that

146

that was ridiculous. No disrespect to the receptionist, but he would have had to put in a lot of overtime to afford all these flowers – either that or been left a florist's shop by a relation.

There was a note with the rose. It said: 'May I ring you at this late hour? If I may, then please hand the rose to your maid, at once.'

Quickly she looked around the foyer. There were three men. One was at least seventy, very tall and very bald. One was drunk and slumped untidily across a chair. The third was an insipid little man, who obediently followed a fat woman who could only be his wife. She glanced back at the note. It intrigued her. She gave it to Annie, who read it very slowly. Annie had to read it very slowly – she couldn't read quickly. She said, 'A rose from anybody smells as sweet.'

At eleven forty-five p.m. the phone rang in Stella's suite. She looked at it as if waiting for it to tell her who was ringing. The operator put the call through. 'Who is it?' she asked.

An American voice spoke to her. 'Miss Raven?'

'Speaking.'

'Thank you for allowing me into your room.'

'Are you phoning from the hotel?'

'Alas, no.'

Thank God for that, she thought.

'No, I'm ringing from a private home.'

'A home?' she queried. 'Are you sick?'

He laughed long and loudly at this, making her hold the phone away from her ear for a second. 'No, nothing like that. I'm at my brother's house.'

'So how did you know I would give the rose to my maid, then?'

She sensed the rise and fall of his shoulders. 'I didn't. I just took the gamble that you would.'

Cocky little bugger, she thought.

'You're not offended, are you?'

'No, I'm not. And thanks for the flowers – I'll set up my own florist business when the show's over.'

'Can we meet?' he asked, tentatively. 'My intentions are strictly honourable.'

Intentions, she wondered. I can't imagine what he means by that.

147

'I'm very busy,' she said, apologetically.

'So am I, but who works Sundays?'

She had overlooked that it was Sunday tomorrow. He'd obviously prepared himself very well for her excuses. He could match them one for one. 'Have you a favourite restaurant?' he asked.

'Yes.'

'Whereabouts?'

'In Paris.'

'Whereabouts in Paris?'

He was as sharp and persistent as she could be. But it was late, she was tired . . . 'Look, this is silly,' she said. 'I don't even know your name.'

'Let's just say it cost me a fortune getting that grey outfit to the Midland Hotel.'

Her heart accelerated as she recalled the extraordinarily attractive American. What was his name? Something Golding? 'The name's Bernard Goldman,' he reminded, in answer to her thoughts. 'I'm unmarried; I don't have a police record, either over here or in the States; I was educated in Washington; I like watching baseball and tennis; and I speak fluent German.'

He stopped talking but it was only to be a pause. '*Guter tee verdient es, gut gemacht zu werden.*'

She didn't believe this conversation was really happening. 'And what does that mean?'

'I don't know,' he replied, honestly. 'I'm reading it off a tin of Earl Grey tea.'

'Very well, Mr Goldman,' she sighed. 'I concede. We'll meet up. I mean, I owe you a date just for the suit, alone.'

'You owe me nothing, but I'd love a date.'

'What time will you come over?' she asked.

'Let's say mid-morning.'

'Sounds fine to me,' she said. 'As long as it's not before breakfast. I never get up before breakfast – I was twenty before I had a boiled egg, you know.'

'Well, I'll make sure it's after breakfast then,' he promised.

'Goodnight then, Mr Goldman.'

'Goodnight then, Miss Raven.'

They replaced receivers.

148

At midday on Sunday the phone rang. Annie answered it and the switchboard connected her. 'Hello,' said Bernard Goldman.

'Miss Raven's suite,' said Annie, with a forced, southern accent.

'Yeah, I know she is,' came the smooth reply.

'Eh?' Back to the usual Annie voice.

'May I speak to her?'

It was as much a command as a request, and to Annie it was delivered by a powerful voice, the sort not refused. 'Ooh, yes. It's you, isn't it?'

'I think it's me,' he said.

'Just a tick; I'll go and get her.'

In her excitement Annie put the receiver back in its cradle, so cutting them off from each other. She looked painfully at the dead phone for nearly half a minute, in the same way Stan Laurel looks at Oliver Hardy when he knows he's done wrong.

She ran from the lounge and into Stella's bedroom. Stella was in an easy chair, reading a paper. 'It's him, and he's been cut off,' she squeaked. Stella pricked up her ears.

'Could you re-phrase that, Annie?'

'Yer what, Miss Stella?' She didn't bother to explain the *double-entendre*.

'If he's keen enough, he will ring back within sixty seconds,' she said. Fifty seconds later the phone went again. She cut across Annie to ensure she reached it first.

'Hi there,' said a confused Bernard Goldman. 'Sorry about the delay; it seems I was cut off.'

'So I heard,' said Stella. 'And you so young too.'

'Don't worry, I know a good surgeon.'

'I hope he works Sundays.'

She could see the survival of a friendship between them being dependant on a continuous supply of one-liners.

He said, 'I'm downstairs – should I come up?'

She said, 'I'm upstairs – should I come down?'

'We could compromise. We can meet up in the lift.'

'I'll be down in the lobby –' she checked her watch '– in two minutes and thirty-three seconds.'

'Could you be a little more precise?'

Incorrigible man, she thought.

149

Bernard hung up and thanked the receptionist, then he gave a long sigh of relief. He wasn't used to maintaining this cool, comic approach. But it's what his brother, Vince, had suggested. 'Don't sound dull when you speak with her,' he had said. 'She's a comedienne: she won't have time for dull people.'

Stella wrapped her ermine across her slender shoulders and put on a pair of long white gloves. Her blonde hair was so short there was little she could do with it except make sure it was tidy.

The lift-gate grated open on the ground floor. A nervous, middle-aged man, who stood no higher than just below her bust, rolled out into the lobby, flushed and cheered. He'd never been so close to such beauty.

As she walked elegantly across the lobby's marble floor everyone in the vicinity seemed to take a deep breath and hold it.

The handsome American – six feet two inches tall; broad-chested; narrow-waisted; perfectly trimmed Ronald Coleman moustache, which rested beneath a perfect nose and above a mobile mouth which worked around a continuous smile – appeared to glide towards her in slow motion.

His suit was Savile Row and his shoes were hand-made. The hat, which he held so easily it could have been an extension of his hand, was made especially for him by the same makers to the Prince of Wales.

His gloves were the softest of brown leather, and she could believe they'd been measured individually for each finger. The cream-coloured scarf was, not surprisingly, made of cashmere. His narrow dark eyes were attractively wrinkled as though always laughing, and this fractionally unnerved the normally nerveless Stella Raven.

As she took a second to enjoy the mood of the moment she couldn't help but feel that all that was missing were the one hundred violins. But by his previous record she thought it best not to mention anything. He was just likely to arrange them for the next time – should there be a next time.

He put his arm out for her in a gallant, gentlemanly manner, and unquestioningly she took it. Together they stepped out into the cold, grey afternoon, but it could have been

Sunset Boulevard in the middle of a heatwave for all the attention they were paying it.

She swallowed apprehensively as a massive, white Rolls-Royce Silver Ghost pulled up at the front of the hotel. The engine purred like a satisfied cat as the 'perfect couple' approached it.

A chauffeur appeared and held open the nearest door. For a second she thought of Woody and Lester and it made her smile.

The car was so spacious they could have been at opposite ends of a room – a *big* room. 'Are you having a good time over there?' she asked, jokingly.

'The weather could be better,' he said. 'How about you?'

'It could be worse.'

She peered through the window onto the meagre activity of a Sunday afternoon. 'And where are you taking me, Mr Goldman?'

'Well, we could visit the Brontës' place – and the name's Bernard.'

His eyes flashed like diamonds on black velvet, and she tingled throughout her whole body. 'But are they expecting us?'

'Huh?' He was uncertain what to say. Maybe she was the one person in the world who hadn't heard of the Yorkshire Brontës. Then he saw, to his relief, humour at the corners of her lambent lips.

He pushed a hand through his short, sandy-brown hair and gave her his broadest smile, almost causing oncoming cars to flash their lights in response. 'Why don't we just go back to my brother's place? He'd love to meet you, I know. He has a cottage in the Dales.'

He studied her pale skin. 'We can get some colour back into those cheeks,' he said. He tried to reach across and casually pinch one of them, but the distance between them was too great, and he had to abandon the idea half-way and meekly return his arm to his side. 'To Bramble Cottage, please, James,' he instructed the driver. The driver somehow nodded without seeming to move his head.

'James?' she questioned, with some disbelief.

'No kidding; that's his name.'

151

They discarded the towns for the panoramic scenes of the undulating openness known as the Dales. Stella was now relaxing and enjoying herself. She had needed to get out. It reminded her of a school trip into the Pennines she'd once gone on.

The car slowed to no more than five miles per hour as a herd of cows were driven from one field to another and wobbled as they disrespectfully brushed against it. In the aftermath Bernard discovered that the gleaming Rolls-Royce was now two-tone.

He shouted to the farmer through his window. 'Hey, will you take a look at my car. It's covered in –' he remembered Stella's presence '– in mess. What are you going to do about it?'

'Don't rightly know,' grunted back the farmer. 'But leave it wit' me, and if it sez moo, I'll 'ave it.'

Stella started laughing, and Bernard felt a little crestfallen. 'Move on,' he told James, dejectedly. The farmer touched his cap as they accelerated away. Three or four cows gave what sounded like a splattering of applause. Stella laughed even more as she thought of the one hundred violins accompanying them at the hotel. Bernard folded his arms like a spoilt child and gritted his teeth.

An hour later, maybe a little less, they swung off to the right to follow an even narrower lane. Trees of varying shades of green lined the road, like soldiers in shabby uniform. It was dusk and they crossed a narrow bridge through a pretty hamlet, and the tyres grumbled on a gravel drive. 'This is it,' he told her, with the excitement of a schoolboy reaching home after enduring a long term away boarding.

She thought it a rather unusual set-up. Two brothers, Americans, living in England. One was apparently rolling in money but had no fixed address, the other lived a reclusive, very rural existence. Why was his brother so keen to meet her? she wondered. She imagined all would be explained to her quite shortly.

Chapter 13

In spite of their many differences – both physical and characteristic – the Goldman brothers shared the ready smile and easy vitality. 'So this is Miss Raven,' said Vince Goldman, in what Stella thought to be a voice tinged with disappointment. She took an immediate dislike to him. It was one of those chemical reactions, where a person can dislike another without having one specific reason.

Everything about Vince Goldman annoyed her: his plumpness, his shortness, his scruffiness, and his smugness. He had an active face that rested on several quavering chins, and even that annoyed her. The fat around his stomach rolled with every tiny movement he made, like a tidal wave threatening to crash down on a beach but never quite carrying it out. 'And you must be Vince,' she finally responded. He gave a dramatic bow – not dissimilar from a Milton Keens bow – and released an explosive, husky belly-laugh, as if he'd been saving it up all day, just for that moment.

'And I'm older than Bernie,' he told her, 'but don't let him kid you that I'm *that* much older.'

She gave a courteous laugh while thinking, I wouldn't trust you if you were the last person left walking the planet.

'Okay, you guys,' he said, a sudden blur of activity. 'Follow me, now.'

He was off down a dark, low-ceilinged corridor, with the two of them in hot pursuit.

153

She busily took in everything around her. She had never before seen so many paintings on so few walls. It sparked off a childhood memory. It was of her mother returning from Lancaster one day with an oil painting she'd picked up in a sale. It was entitled *Ship in Distress*, and appropriately it depicted a ship fighting for survival on rough waters. It was by a French artist with an unpronounceable name.

Everyone in the neighbourhood came to ceremoniously examine it in its, unsurprisingly, mounted position above the mantle-shelf. She would always remember her father's blank expression as he looked it up and down for the first time. 'What the flamin' hell's all this painting stuff got to do with you?' he had said to her mother. The next day the canvas was nowhere to be seen, and a part of the frame was being used to support an unsteady table-leg.

Vince pushed a bourbon into their hands. They had no choice on what they wanted to drink: *he* liked bourbon so *they'd* have to like bourbon too.

One thing she found that, when in the company of his elder brother, Bernard wasn't the dazzling, enchanting man of earlier. He became quiet, almost withdrawn. She didn't need to be a genius to tell that Vince dominated him, and had probably done so since they were children.

They ate a small dinner that was prepared by James, the driver. It was soon apparent that he was as all-purposeful as her Annie. He cooked; he drove; what else did he do for the Goldman brothers? Bring attractive female stars back to this cottage? That thought made her a bit scared – vulnerable. As she pushed away an empty plate she asked, 'Why is it I get the impression my coming here wasn't a spontaneous action?'

Bernard shuffled his feet uneasily beneath the table, while his top half – the visible part – tried its best to languish calmly in its seat. Vince became businesslike. 'You're a bright kid, so I won't mess you about,' he said. 'I'll come right to it.' Bernard nodded in thoughtful agreement, but remained silent. 'I'm in movies out in Hollywood – where else? I do a lotta directing, but I've been given this big break; a chance to produce my own movie. It's a low-budget deal, but it's still my own show.'

She tried hard not to appear impressed, but she was

154

impressed. The more she tried to disguise her interest, the more deformed her face appeared. 'It's a musical, and it's going to be called *The Last Springtime*. It needs an English girl of some talent to play the lead female role alongside the lead male role, to be played by Victor Clayton. You may have heard of him.'

She'd more than heard of him, she adored him. She'd kept his pictures when seeing them in a *Screenland* magazine in Henry's office. 'Louis B. Mayer doesn't give many second chances at MGM, so understandably I want this movie to work.'

'And where do I fit in?' she asked, directly.

'A few names have been suggested for the role,' he went on. 'Gracie Fields was a popular choice. She's had experience and she's not a total unknown. But then we decided she's too hard – too northern. The girl we want must have a soft edge as well as a hard one.'

'And presumably she has to sing, or you'd have gone for any number of talented actresses.'

'Exactly so.'

He watched her carefully, looking for any sign, any mannerism that would indicate what she was thinking. 'Well, what do you say?' he finally said. He was sure he'd won her over.

'But I'm northern,' she explained to him.

'Yeah, but not like the others. You have physical softness that makes you a suitable choice. I know Mayer will just love you.'

My God, she thought. I've spent my life dreaming about an opportunity like this, and now it's come I'm not certain I want it.

'So you're formally offering me this part, then?'

'Subject to events once we're over in Hollywood, yes, I am offering you the part in my film.'

She said, 'And what do you say, Bernard?' She was beginning to feel very angry with Bernard. His charm had all been an act to present her to his brother merely as a business proposition. 'I imagine you'll be pleased you won't have to bother sending any more flowers?' she said, cutting him down before he'd had a chance to respond to her question.

155

'Vince wanted someone fast,' he explained defensively. He didn't want her to misinterpret his involvement in the whole affair. 'The flowers I sent you I did because I wanted to.'

'Yes, of course,' she said as if it had been stupid of her not to have realised. 'And I supose it was a nice personal touch to help seduce me into coming here.'

'Now, that's not true,' he said, with remarkable firmness for Bernard. But how could he convince her he had genuinely been attracted to her since first setting eyes upon her in Oldham? Yes, of course – Oldham. 'When I sent you that grey suit,' he said softly, 'Vince wasn't even making his film, then.'

She didn't react for a moment, and then raised her head and stared at him in the eyes. He gave her a sincere and warm smile, and her anger, her hurt, evaporated into relief. 'And also, I'm not in the film business, I'm in real estate and development. I literally spent my share of an inherited family fortune on a more concrete career.' He opened his hands and tilted his head. 'I'm just here taking a holiday.'

Vince gazed on in bewilderment. The relationship between the two had nothing to do with the making of his film. 'Now then,' he continued, trying to re-establish some enthusiasm and authority, but as Bernard and Stella clasped hands he realised he'd lost his audience. Still, he tried. 'We'll be taking the *Queen Mary* on May seventeenth from Southampton to New York. From there we'll take the *Super Chief* – that's a train – right across country, east to west. And then we start on the preliminaries; screen-tests, and so on.'

He looked irritably at the two of them. They weren't listening to a word. 'Hey, you guys. Cut out the romantic looks, will ya? We've a trip to Hollywood to arrange.'

Bernard said, 'We won't be going to Hollywood, Vince. We've other plans.' It was the first time he'd ever stood up to his domineering brother.

The following few weeks glided by in sheer heaven for Stella. She spent a wonderful Christmas Day with Bernard at Bramble Cottage. What had made it all the lovelier was Vince's absence. He had had to go back to Hollywood early as he couldn't find a suitable female for the lead role. Mayer

156

had contacted him to tell him to give up looking – they'd have to use an American and dub an English voice on afterwards.

She had regrets about turning down the opportunity, and cursed her decision about twelve times a day, but Mike had cheered her by saying she was too needed in England to be allowed to go gallivanting over to America. And now, with Bernard by her side, she was sure she had everything she could ever possibly need.

He adored her; worshipped her. She was madly and passionately in love with him but also felt a need to protect him. She held the upper hand in their relationship, and he was weak enough to allow it to be that way.

Despite his large frame and outwardly confident manner she knew him to be a vulnerable person, and was sure that if she wasn't there to control him he'd only end up getting himself into trouble.

Already, he'd mentioned some difficulties he was having on a development in Santa Barbara, north of Hollywood, and that he might have to go over there and try to sort matters out. What mistakes had he made? Who was taking him for a ride over there, if anyone? Did he know what he was doing? His only previous success had been building small blocks of flats in Hollywood which had earned him considerable sums, but had that been luck? Had he just been in the right place at the right time? And if he had responsibilities in America, then wasn't it unprofessional of him to be romancing and holidaying in England? These were the questions that worried her, and he was evasive when it came to answering them.

Whatever was to come, she refused to allow it to spoil this moment in time together. On the first Saturday in March 1938, at a tiny village not a stone's-throw from Bramble Cottage, Stella Raven – legally, not in name – became Stella Goldman.

She had no intention of discarding her stage-name; it had taken her too long to bring it to the public's notice, and now it was there she was going to do her utmost to ensure it was going to stay there.

Out of all the people she loved and worked with, only Sadie and Tommy were not invited. This latest snub hurt Sadie more than any that had gone before, and her parents weren't left unaffected either. That apart, the Ravenscrofts were very fond of the dashing Bernard Goldman, and when Jack discovered how wealthy he was he rather overplayed his pleasure at the announcement of their wedding. He also got very drunk and maudlin at the reception held at the cottage.

Lilly cried with joy throughout the service, and later described Bernard to Stella as being 'the most handsome man I've ever set eyes on – since yer Dad'.

They went on to enjoy the briefest of honeymoons possible: a weekend – only staying Saturday night because of the show – at Bramble Cottage. It was hardly a honeymoon, as they spent most of their free time there, anyway.

Over the weekend Bernard revealed that he had to get out to Santa Barbara quickly. 'When I get back, I'll take you anywhere you want,' he promised.

Fumbling in his pockets he produced a crumpled piece of paper. 'I've got the name of some country inn here; it's apparently worth a visit.' He studied the piece of paper. 'Here we go; it's called "The Partridge".' He folded the paper badly and returned it to his pocket.

'Then let's spend the earlier part of our honeymoon night at "The Partridge", then,' she said.

She tried to put a brave face on for him. But it was difficult, knowing that his ship sailed the next Friday. He said, 'That's settled, then. We'll go and try it out. Who knows, it could be the high spot of the whole area.'

So they tried it out. And it was.

Chapter 14

Tommy cut through a piece of Sadie's home-baked fruit cake. It made as much impression as a spoon on a piece of solid oak. 'Think this cake'll have to be chucked,' he shouted to her from the kitchen. She came in.

'Don't waste it. Give it to the birds.'

'The poor sods'll never take off again if they eat this.'

'No swearing, Tommy Moran,' she scolded.

'Sorry,' he said, insincerely. He didn't mean to sound insincere, but it had grown that way because he was always apologising. 'I'll find something else we can nibble at with our cuppa.'

'I'm not hungry, pet,' she told him.

'You're never hungry, these days,' he commented. Tommy had been worried about her for some time, now. She hadn't been eating properly for months. At first, he thought it was due to her upset over Stella – the way she had virtually ignored them when they'd taken all the trouble and expense to go and see her in Manchester – but now he wasn't so sure. She was very thin, whatever the cause. Maybe it was his own fault. Most things were his fault, or so Sadie told him. Maybe he shouldn't have made such a big fuss over giving up the three-piece suite in choice of seeing Stella's show. Thinking back, he had gone on about it quite a bit, especially when it had turned into such a disappointing reunion.

As if hearing his thoughts, she said, 'I wish I was still working with Stella.'

How many times had he heard that recently? He'd lost count. 'Well, you're not, and that's the way it is. You're not even in showbusiness anymore.' His words were so firm he nearly made himself jump.

Sadie took a sip of her tea. She grimaced. Tommy had put too much sugar in it again. He was forever putting too much sugar in her tea. She turned towards him and said meaningfully, 'Sometimes I wish it really could be, you know.'

'You mean, us not married, and all?' he said, deflatedly.

'No, you know what I mean.'

'All I know,' said Tommy, 'is that she'll never forgive us for getting wed and breaking up the partnership. That partnership was her life at that time.'

'Of course she'll forgive us,' said Sadie, but she didn't sound too convinced by her own brave words. 'Maybe I should go and visit her. That could help sort things out with us. I mean, there has to be more to this life than the flamin' cake shop.'

'It's a good wage you earn at that cake shop, young lady . . .'

'Oh, shut up, Tommy. You sound more like Mam and Dad every day.'

He was dumbstruck. What was getting into her? She was changing all the time, and not just in the physical sense. 'She's a solo performer now, Sade,' he pointed out, less sympathetically than he otherwise would have. 'She's also a star and she doesn't need her sister following her about.'

Sadie gave him a piercing stare. 'You're cruel and you're a liar.' She threw a tea towel at him and stormed out into the garden.

When the season ended in April – a very long season, indeed – Stella forgot to give her routine sigh of relief. It was probably because she was so distracted by other things, such as how her husband was getting along in America.

As it happened, Bernard was getting on disastrously. He had got down to business the moment he arrived in Santa Barbara and called on all his various banking contacts to ensure that, at the very least, they would stand by him through to completion of his development project. He hadn't

160

anticipated spending so much on construction costs with the apartments and incurring so many small bills that, when pooled together, totalled a fair amount. His feasibility study hadn't shown the many pitfalls that had later been revealed.

Because of the excellent response he'd received from the banks when developing in Hollywood he'd expected an equal response to the Santa Barbara project. It didn't follow, and he should have known that it wouldn't. 'You've overreached yourself,' he was successively told. What's the old saying about banks? They give you an umbrella when the sun's out, then take it back in when it's raining. 'Hollywood's the draw of southern California. It was good business developing and speculating there. But Santa Barbara? Forget it. It won't overspill that far. You'll never shift the majority of those apartments at the right kind of price. You'll end up either lumbered with them or having to sell them for peanuts.'

That was how five consecutive meetings from five different banks had concluded. With each rejection he'd felt himself die a little bit more.

What do I do, and what do I tell Stella? That was all he could keep thinking.

It wasn't just the loss of money: there were the legalities of it all. How did he stand when he couldn't even pay off outstanding debts without making further loans? And that's to say nothing of completing the whole project. Several of the apartments had already been sold prior to completion. The money had been received and immediately ploughed straight back into his dwindling business.

Will this mean I'll get sued? he wondered. Of course I'll get goddamned sued.

Sitting over a quadruple bourbon his face was suddenly distorted with a spasm of despair and his hands tore at his hair. For a moment it was possible to glimpse the natural man, impulsive, keenly sensitive. The next, the mask of the calm cool American businessman was replaced.

I'll survive, somehow, he thought. And it was a brave thought – for someone on the verge of bankruptcy.

As it was to happen, Bernard was destined to be a fortunate man, although he wasn't to know this for a further eight anxious-filled days. They were days during which he con-

161

templated all the options that were open to him. Finding that suicide looked the most promising he felt even more depressed than before.

It was pride as much as anything that made him refrain from taking so drastic a measure: that, and the fact that he didn't like the sight of blood; especially his own, though, if dead, he wouldn't have been able to see too much, but Bernard didn't think like that.

While Santa Barbara would never make him a good, or even bad, profit, two men came to his rescue who could perhaps see the potential of being associated with a 'suit and tie' man of good standing: a man, that with their financial support at this awkward juncture, could benefit them in the future on more successful development projects.

Messrs Harper and Drewitt were informed of Bernard's plight through one of the banking executives who had initially given him little sympathy. Maybe this executive had time to reflect on Bernard Goldman as he drove home that night, and began to feel a little guilty for being so cold to the entrepreneurial American, and could only clear his conscience by giving him a small piece of indirect assistance. And he was genuinely sure that if anyone could or would help Goldman, it would be Harper and Drewitt. Both these men had professional backgrounds and knew when, where, and how in the speculative world of real estate.

Over an arranged lunch on the eighth day of Bernard's nightmare the two gentlemen offered him their support and full backing to see the Santa Barbara project through, though several times pointing out how careless it had been of him to take the success he'd found in Hollywood to an area relatively disconnected from that glamorous place. Bernard now knew better than anyone just how careless he'd been. These same two men would also one day be partly responsible for the building of Bernard's small empire.

Stella, meanwhile, was oblivious to all of this. She had returned to her London flat with the ever-faithful Annie. All that worried Annie was how, when Mr Goldman returned home, the three of them would cope with being squashed up together in the flat. It did threaten to be a shade over-cosy.

A dinner date with Mike Farrow informed Stella of her

possible future plans. He told her, while they sipped from balloons of brandy at the El Rico club, 'There's a strong possibility – nothing confirmed yet, mind – of Henry putting on one of the largest, most spectacular variety shows to hit London.'

'And?'

'And there could be a strong possibility – though again, nothing has been . . .'

'Oh, stop dawdling, Mike, and tell me,' she urged, impatiently. She hated waiting for exciting news.

'Well – he could want you to star in it.'

Unconsciously, she pulled at strands of hair while her mind raced ahead. 'But remember, you know nothing of it until he mentions it,' reminded Mike, who could see his minority shareholding in the company rapidly becoming an even smaller minority shareholding.

'What theatre is it going to be at?' she asked, in a dulcet voice. The club where they were at was renowned for its showbusiness clientele: it was very risky to talk secrets.

Mike looked either side of him then bent forward. 'The Windmill,' he whispered.

'But that's all nude women,' she said, and a passing waiter raised and dropped his eyebrows in one motion.

'Well, don't ask me. I'm only the agent, remember. I'm sure Henry will tell you all when he feels ready to.'

'I've made you go all secretive, haven't I?' she teased. Mike smiled, but he made no further comment.

The following morning they were both called into Henry's office to be told what they both already knew. 'I've got some grand news for you, Stella. That is, *we* think it's good news, don't we, Mike?'

'Yes, Henry.' Mike was standing bolt-upright beside Henry's chair. He looked like the headmaster's head prefect – Henry being the headmaster. 'Go on, Mike. Tell her all about it.' Henry enjoyed other people explaining his own ideas.

'We're putting on a big variety show; one of the biggest this country's seen,' he said.

'Really?' smiled Stella, and Mike had to smile back.

Henry said, 'We certainly are, my dear,' unaware that they were sharing a private joke.

163

'And anyway,' continued Mike, pulling himself together, 'it will be at the Windmill, date unknown, but likely to be around late August, early September. It will just run the week, and the opening night – Buck Palace willing – will be a Royal show.'

'A Royal show?' she queried.

'Yes,' said Henry, taking over. He loved talking about royalty when it involved him. 'We're hoping to have a member of the Royal Family attend the opening show. Apparently, you're quite a favourite there.' She was very flattered to hear that.

Henry lined her up along his smooth cigar. What was her reaction going to be? She said, 'Let me just get this right.' Henry's head nodded behind the smoke cloud. 'You want me to star in this huge show?'

'Correct,' confirmed Henry.

'Well,' she finally sighed. 'What can one say to such an offer, other than, do I get any comps?'

Henry roared with laughter, and Mike felt obliged to do the same thing. 'Only you, Stella Raven, could worry about such a minor point when considering such a major proposition.' He would have nudged Mike in the ribs if his colleague had been standing nearer. 'Isn't that right, Mike?'

'Yes, Henry.'

Their laughter was infectious, and she found herself joining in, though she didn't see what was so funny: all she wanted was a handful of comps. That sounded straightforward enough. 'The show does sound really great,' she admitted. 'Other than the nitty-gritty details –'

'– like comps?' interjected Henry.

'Yes, like comps,' she said. 'Other than all of that, you can count me in. I'd love to star in your show.'

By standing up, Henry was signifying the meeting was at a close. 'Very good, my child. Mike will remain here with you and go through the finer points. I, alas, have business elsewhere to contend with.'

Henry kissed her hand and marched out, grabbing his jacket from behind the door as he went. 'Just how many comps are you wanting?' asked Mike, after Henry had gone. Stella looked to the floor and delayed answering for a moment.

Then she said, 'Just four will do. Two for my parents and two for my sister and her Tommy.'

Mike had long known of the disassociation between the two sisters and his face couldn't conceal his surprise. 'I know what you're thinking,' she said, in answer to his looks. 'I've decided I've been stupid holding this grudge with Sadie. I was badly hurt by her once, that's all. I'd like to make up with her now, though, and I'm sure that's what she wants.'

'An excellent idea,' said Mike, cheerfully. He wished he and his wife could make up. They hadn't talked properly to each other for weeks, and all he could see ahead of him was divorce. How he wished he was married to Stella.

'Sadie saw me last in Manchester,' she went on. 'It would be nice if she could see me topping a big West End show. She could even stay on for a few days and meet Bernard, maybe.'

She stood up to leave. She felt it was unfair to prattle on too long to Mike all about her problems. 'When do you need me next?' she asked him.

Tonight, in my bed, he said, but only to himself. He knew for sure that there was no chance of it ever happening or he'd have said it aloud. 'There's a chorus being put together at the Camden Dance Hall,' he told her. 'They're going through the paces there tomorrow morning, if you'd like to pop in and take a look. Then we hope to commence rehearsals in three weeks from now.'

'Three weeks! That sounds a long way off from August.'

'The reason for that,' said Mike, 'is we intend giving it a trial fortnight at the Alhambra, Bradford. We stand to do well out of it, and it'll also give us the chance to iron out any unforeseen problems.'

'Bradford,' she sighed, miserably. 'I suppose I couldn't have expected all good news.' She didn't really mind too much. It was more done to let Mike know that in future she'd like to be told these things before they've been arranged. 'And when does Bradford happen?'

'Not long before London, so we can roll into town and straight into the big week.'

Mike held the door open for her as she moved towards it. 'The producer will be there, tomorrow,' he smiled, and she didn't know why.

165

'What producer?'

'Ever heard of Woody Woodville?'

'Oh, that's marvellous,' she said, with genuine delight.

The first person she set eyes on was the evergreen Lester. He was standing by the dance-room entrance, like a dark column supporting that part of the building. 'Back to work again, Lester,' she whispered, sneaking up behind him. He squinted at her.

'Why, Miss Raven,' he said, finally remembering who she was.

She glanced inside the room. The piano could be heard and she could see a group of girls tapping to the rhythm. 'Is he in there?' she asked. Loud, decisive clapping brought the piano to a halt and the girls with it. Woody emerged in front of them.

'Awful, girls; truly awful. Now, let's take it from the top, once more. And let's get it right, huh?'

Lester grinned a toothless grin. 'I guess you could say he's in, missy,' he chuckled.

Five minutes later Woody gave the girls a break and rushed up to greet Stella. 'Stella, Stella, Stella, honey,' he droned, and proceeded to give her a facial scrub with his strong, moist lips.

A couple of the chorus recognised who she was and asked her for autographs. Woody walked her away from the hall and into the outer room where they could have a little privacy. 'I'll be here all day,' he explained, 'but how about a little dinner tonight? We can talk about the show over lobster and some champagne.'

'Sounds good to me,' she said, and with a nod at the chorus, playfully added, 'if you can manage to tear yourself away.'

He grinned. He had been dying to remind her how perfect his teeth were. 'Hey, kid, I gave all that kind of thing up. People were having trouble telling me and Lester apart.' She didn't believe him for a moment.

'Now that's what I call lobster,' said Woody, pushing the pink shell and its remnants to one side. Stella wasn't as fast an eater. 'More champagne,' he ordered a waiter, who, with a short bow, disappeared to carry out the instruction.

Woody always ate at Rogues near Leicester Square when he was dining out in London. It had become his favourite fish restaurant and also the staff treated him very well, as they did all their generous-tipping regulars.

166

Stella didn't make any reference to Nola, though she was surprised how unaffected he seemed by the whole trauma. That is, it hadn't sent him prematurely grey or made him into a nervous person. He was just the same old Woody she had always known. It made her wonder if he'd been in similar dire situations before.

Woody was keen to hear more about Bernard and his business interests in the States. He thought he must have been a great man to have captured the heart of Stella Raven. She wasn't quite so keen to talk about Bernard, as she was greatly worried about him. Three weeks had gone, and she hadn't received news of any kind.

'He's a good husband, and I know he loves me very much,' she said. 'But he's very weak at times, and it worries me. I feel sure he's going to get himself into big trouble, if he hasn't done so already.'

'Can't you contact him?' he asked. She shook her head.

'He moves around a lot over there. I'd never be able to track him down to one place.'

Woody said, 'You're a strong-willed girl, Stella. I'm sure you'll keep it all together 'til he's home.'

'At times I'm not so strong as people think,' she said, looking distantly into her empty glass.

The champagne was brought to the table. It was Taittinger and, like the restaurant, was one of Woody's favourites. He filled their long, tulip glasses to the brim, and instantly the level dropped to just above the centre crest that depicted an armed knight astride a stallion.

'In fact, there are times I get very down and depressed. I suppose I miss being looked after by Bernard. He was always about to run around for me, and now at the moment, he, of course, isn't.' She looked up. 'My sister used to look after me before our big bust-up.'

'And do you miss your little sister?' he asked, knowing the answer before it had been delivered.

'Yes, I do,' she said, with much confidence.

Woody gave a long sigh and adjusted the cuffs on his double-breasted, double-vented blazer that bore the crest of Oxford University. He'd never studied there, but once, when driving through Oxford, had paid a student a large sum of money to have it. He enjoyed the traditional things of England – like Oxford University. 'Well, honey. I'm your man to lift those blues away.'

'Thanks, Woody,' she smiled. For a second, she half-expected him to burst into a musical routine right then and there.

He nearly did, as he added, 'Just a song, just a smile, can last as long, as a mile.' He smiled at her, full of self-pride. 'You like that?'

'I loved that.'

'It's my own composition, you know.'

'No, really?'

When they stood up to leave she found her legs were quavering. 'Come back and see my pad,' he suggested. 'It's sensational.' After being partly responsible for the consumption of two large gin martinis and two bottles of champagne she was agreeable to go back anywhere with almost anyone.

She managed to fall out on to the street without making it too obvious what condition she was in. All she knew was that she'd never felt so unco-ordinated in her life. 'Annie. I must ring Annie,' she told him, at least six times.

'No sweat. I've a phone in my apartment.' Woody waved down a cab.

'Are you all right, Miss Stella?' asked a concerned Annie down the line. 'You sound awful happy, like.'

'Is that such a bad thing, Annie?' she said, sleepily.

'Where are you?'

'At Mr Woodville's. We're working on the new show. I'm not sure when I'll be back. Don't bother waiting up.'

'Don't go drinking too much while you're working,' warned Annie. 'It's the devil's own water is alchy, alcho, alichy – drink.'

'Okay, Sadie – I mean, Annie. I'll see you in the morning. Bye.'

She attempted to hang up, missed, tried again and made it. Annie delayed for a moment before hanging up. Then, with a shake of the head, she finally did so. 'This is what showbusiness does to you,' she muttered, and went back to her knitting. She would be glad when Mr Goldman returned to look after his wife.

Calmly, Stella stripped off all her clothes and threw her naked body across Woody's double bed. Within seconds her breathing was slow and regular. She wouldn't be waking up for quite some time.

'I've poured you a brandy, honey. You like brandy . . .?' Woody had always considered himself to be the unshockable type, but just for a moment he was quite taken aback. He stepped closer and perched himself beside her.

It's sure as hell tempting, he thought. But he knew there were rules about that sort of thing. He couldn't resist, though, running a slow hand the length of her prone, slender body, bringing it to rest on her left breast. He knew it was unlikely he would have the opportunity again.

My, I can feel the girl's heart-beat. He couldn't see her breast, but he could feel the nipple becoming unconsciously erect. 'Now there's the miracle of human nature,' he said aloud, and with a long, heavy sigh, he pulled back one of the covers and put it over her as far as her shoulders. He kissed her back and said, 'You rest easy, honey.'

Throwing back her brandy, he knew that, come morning, he'd have as big a headache as she would.

When the lights went out, Lester, who had been watching through a crack in his door, whispered to himself, 'The man's improving.'

'So who do we go for, then?' said Henry Charles, as he paced his office, with a touch of irritation about him that morning. Mike licked an index finger and wiped away a dirty smear on his left, highly polished brogue.

'It's a big show,' he replied. 'We could use a big name. That would help give it a little glamour. It's all looking a little too English at the moment, I think.'

'What name?'

'An American, perhaps? Audiences love well-known Americans.'

'It's an idea,' said Henry, as though that was just about all it was. 'My own philosophy is to give the star what they want. If the star's happy, then the show is invariably right. In other words, we need to give Stella a name she would enjoy working with.'

Their dilemma was that the male singer – James Maitland – had had to withdraw from both the Bradford and London performances due to sudden unavailability: he was dead.

Henry gazed across the grey blur that was London as seen from his office window. 'How about that Shipton character?'

'Shipton? You mean, Milton Keens. That's who he became.'

'Can we get hold of him? Is he available?'

Mike stalled in answering. He had reservations. Keens was no big deal.

'Do you mean, you want me to get hold of him?'

'Yes, why not?' said Henry, with a loose flick of the hand. 'She likes him, and he does a fair act, as I recall.'

'But there's bigger fish who'd give their lives to be in the show,' he argued.

'I know all that, Mike,' he said, using the soft tone he always used when wanting to humour his junior partner. 'Thing is, though, we have quite a selection of names, so let's just watch the budget for a change, eh?'

'If you say so,' said Mike, with clear disagreement in his voice.

'I say so.'

Henry wheezed on his cigar as the smoke filtered down the wrong way. 'Jesus, these things are killing me. I've got to give it up.' Mike smiled.

'Sure, Henry.'

'And now, other business,' said Henry, as he picked up a blue folder off his desk. 'What's the latest on the Laurel and Hardy dates, then?'

'They're looking good,' said Mike. 'I think Stan and Ollie underestimate their own popularity. The fans will be swarming when the ship comes into Southampton, let alone outside the hotel and theatres.'

'You'd better organise something, then,' suggested Henry. 'You know the kind of thing – a decoy or something equally melodramatic. Maybe even a hotel-change.'

Mike gave a weak smile as he wondered how it was he always got landed with the best jobs. 'Leave it with me, Henry.'

170

Before Henry Charles had even left the land of dreams that morning the assumed realisation of the night just gone was dawning on Stella. Her throat was as dry as a sack of coke, and her head thumped like it had a heart of its own. She squinted as a bar of light caught her puffy face through a crack in the curtains. For a moment she couldn't remember where she was.

Am I in Hollywood? she thought.

She turned painfully on her side and leapt back when discovering a black, naked body beside her. 'Bernard?' she whispered, then told herself not to be so stupid.

Sitting up, she found her evening clothes scattered haphazardly across the floor and an empty brandy glass wedged into one of her shoes. Apprehensively, she raised the sheet that covered her. It was as she had dreaded: she was naked. 'What have I been doing?' she cried aloud, and Woody grunted in his 'hungover' sleep.

Memories continued to flood back, and with each one she felt a little more sickened with herself. You stupid, stupid girl. You've ruined everything; the show, your working relationship with Woody – and poor Bernard. My darling Bernard, I'm so, so sorry.

She dressed with silent control and, giving Woody a last, and slightly reproachful, look slipped out of the apartment and into the quiet morning street.

I can remember when I had morals, she told herself. When Sadie and me were working together, nothing like this would ever have happened. We hardly even talked to people in the show outside of working hours. What have I become?

Eventually finding a cab near Charing Cross Station, she told herself that she was no better than a prostitute. She was sure the driver thought the same thing, as his gaze lingered on her suspiciously dishevelled state.

When reaching her flat she found she hadn't got a key. It meant waking Annie up, who, in any case, had been awake half the night worrying about her.

'You're back, at last,' she said.

'Sorry, Annie. It was a long party and I got held up in heavy conversations.'

Why am I making excuses? It must be guilt.

171

She went to her bathroom. She hoped a long bath would cleanse her mind as well as her body. 'I'll make us a nice cuppa,' yawned Annie, still half-asleep.

Stella turned on the light and studied her features in the bathroom mirror. It took some bravado.

Twenty-three. My God, I look more like ninety-three. And my face. That high cheek-boned face, so perfectly oval, like a glorious pear. Now it looks more like a bruised apple.

After her bath and putting on some fresh clothes she sat down and tried to plan her day. When Annie nipped out to the shops she quickly went about tracking down Woody's telephone number. It was a slow process of trial and error, as she wasn't at all certain of his address – but she got through in the end.

'Hello, this is Woodville,' said Woody, sounding none too bright himself.

'Thank heavens,' she gasped. 'I didn't think I'd catch you in. I thought you might be at rehearsals.'

'With my hangover, honey, there ain't gonna be no rehearsals today – not for me, at least.'

He seems remarkably calm, she thought. Almost unconcerned with what has happened.

He said, 'Why did you sneak off without a goodbye? You had me worried.' There was a pause.

'I think we need to talk, Woody. About last night, and so on.'

'Don't you worry. I'll keep it a secret how much you drank.'

She gave an irritable little sigh. 'Look, don't make this harder for me than it is already.'

'I'm all ears, honey; but as yet your words aren't striking home base.'

'We slept together,' she blurted. Woody gave a short groan at something that never was.

'Ah, we sure did. Such a shame that that was all we did. But you're a married woman and I'm an honourable man.'

She fell into stunned silence while Woody went on to explain the true events of the previous night. When he finished she gave the biggest sigh of relief any living person could heave. It was more a moan of pure ecstasy. She hung up feeling reborn.

That evening, still feeling a little elated, she went to see a Gloria Swanson picture that was showing in Leicester Square. Deciding she needed some exercise – what with the show's rehearsals fast approaching – she took a cab only a short part of the way home after seeing the film.

It was a moonless night and the street-lighting was insufficient. This was a great source of infuriation to her, stumbling over a crooked paving-stone for the third time.

A hundred yards from her door, unbeknown to her, a figure moved out of the blackness and began trailing behind her at a short distance. The figure closed in on her, and when she was no more than fifty yards from her door Stella became aware of its presence.

She decided to play a game that she and Sadie always played with each other. One would speed up and the other would have to match the pace to try to maintain the exact same distance between them. The same applied if the leader then slowed down.

So Stella increased her pace and, to her surprise, the figure behind did likewise. It was eerie. She was relieved to reach the familiar steps that led to her door.

Home safely, she sighed inwardly, and began rummaging for her keys. The solid steps of the figure walked on by, and Stella told herself off for being so scared.

I'm getting too tensed up about everything these days, she said to herself.

As she twisted the key in its lock the figure sidestepped and lunged up at her with open hands that clamped around her throat with a vice-like grip. She choked as the air ejaculated from her windpipe. With head spinning, she fell to her knees, bruising them on the rough edge of the top step. Vainly, she struggled to free herself, but her attacker's determination was equal to her own. She was going to die, she was sure of it. 'I'll kill you for it!' cried the woman. Through a red haze Stella could see a pair of dark arms and a woman's face. Then she saw light.

Annie burst out onto the steps, brandishing a rolled umbrella. She began striking the woman across the head with it.

173

The attacker ran away, screaming back, 'Don't think this is an end of it.'

Stella saw Annie looking anxiously down on her. 'Oh, Miss Stella, Miss Stella,' she heard her cry. Then she passed out.

Chapter 15

Sadie continued to lose an alarming amount of weight, making Tommy quip that she more resembled an overworked knitting-needle than a person. But he couldn't make light of it for long. It was plain she was ill, and finally she gave in to his demands that a doctor be called out.

Doctor Atkins arrived with the kind of solemnity more commonly reserved for undertakers. Speaking slowly, he said, 'Show me to the patient, Mr Moran.' Tommy wasn't that fond of Doctor Atkins. He recalled how he loathed children, and how, as a five-year-old with whooping-cough, his mother had taken him to be treated by the doctor. He'd been most unsympathetic to Tommy's condition.

'She's upstairs in bed,' he said. 'Follow me.'

'In bed, you say?' queried Doctor Atkins. 'I was not informed of the gravity of her condition.' He wasn't expecting a reply from Tommy and he didn't get one.

Sadie was propped up against three feather-filled pillows, her face gaunt and pallid. In her spindly hands was a copy of the 'local'. It was opened at a feature article on Stella. 'Mrs Moran,' said the doctor curtly, so as to announce his appearance.

'Oh, hello, doctor,' she said weakly, her self-pride making her draw the blankets up to her neck so covering any exposed flesh. 'I'm so sorry to trouble you like this. I told my husband not to bother you.'

'It is no bother to me,' he told her, firmly.

His examination was brief. 'I should have been summoned sooner,' he said, with a reprimanding glance at Tommy. Oh, yes, he could remember that scruffy little boy with the whooping-cough.

'Er, well, we didn't really know what to do for the best, like,' stumbled Tommy. The doctor's glaring glance at him said more than if he'd spoken.

Within six hours of his call, Sadie had been admitted into the Lancaster General Hospital.

Individual run-throughs for the Bradford show began taking place on a daily basis at the Camden Dance Hall, come the end of June. Despite not hearing a word from Bernard in all that time, Stella managed – through sheer professionalism – to have her act sparkling. She had new material, new dance routines, new numbers – and she put in as a whole as much creative material to the show as Woody Woodville had. He kidded her that soon she would be sole producer, sole management, and star of all London shows.

Her work-rate was all the more remarkable considering the delay she suffered due to a 'throat infection' – as she had everyone know it. In fact, severe bruising to the throat and knees caused by a crazed attack upon her when walking home from the pictures was the genuine reason for the delay. And her attacker turned out to be none other than Woody Woodville's fiancée. He'd never told anybody he even had a fiancée. He believed it bad for his image, so he kept her locked away in his Long Island home. She'd apparently grown bored, and so had arranged a passage to England to surprise him. She'd surprised him, all right.

She tracked down his London address with little difficulty, very early in the morning of her arrival at Southampton, and arrived to see a young woman in ruffled evening dress closing his flat door and stepping out into the street. And that was how it had all come about; the attack was born from jealous anger. She followed the woman in evening dress in a cab – nearly losing her more than once – and then spent the rest of the day brooding on how she'd seek revenge.

Afterwards, when Stella was well enough, Woody called her

176

to his flat, and with his fiancée, Nancy, the truth of what had happened emerged. Understandably, Nancy needed some convincing, especially when seeing how beautiful Stella was and hearing how she and Woody had worked together before this show. But it concluded amicably enough – and thankfully remained a secret between just four people: Woody, Nancy, Stella, and Annie – and Nancy moved in with Woody.

Stella had to laugh about it afterwards. All that bruising she'd received and the trouble she'd gone to to explain her innocence, and she didn't even receive an apology. And Nancy was safe from the knowledge that Stella was hardly likely to press for assault charges, with the sort of bad publicity that would generate.

Stella's only reminders about the whole incident were the aches in her knees and around her throat, and, once they'd healed up fully, the whole matter slipped from her mind. And anyway, she had a far greater concern: Bernard.

Laden with luggage, Bernard pressed into the flat. It was soon evident he was alone there. 'Stella? Annie?' he called, as a token gesture. The walls and furnishings stared blankly back at him.

He had nearly finished unpacking when he heard the door crack open and Stella come whistling her way into the lounge. 'Is that you, darling?'

She must have jumped a foot off the ground from shock. 'Stone the crows, Bernard,' she gasped, half-angrily, half-delightedly while clutching at her pounding chest.

He rushed out to greet her, throwing his arms around her neck and holding her in a bear-hug. 'I've done it,' he told her. 'I've found backers.'

'That's wonderful, darling, but do you know the worry I've been going through? I've been worried sick about you.'

'There just wasn't the time to make contact,' he explained, hurriedly. He'd had a suspicion she'd be displeased with him about that. 'I was really up against it out there; life-and-death situation, and so on.'

They shared a long, warm kiss. Eventually she broke away, saying, 'Oh, Bernard. It's so good to see you again, and to hold you again. I've been lost without you.' She could feel the tears welling up in her eyes.

'Me too, angel,' he agreed, but more because he felt obliged to. The majority of his thoughts were still on the West coast of America. 'I found some private backers – some guys who back risky projects as a livelihood – and I've borrowed a whole load of money off of them. Now I just have to concentrate on selling the sonofabitch apartments.'

'As long as you know what you're doing,' she said, concernedly. 'I suppose you'll have to go back there soon?'

'In a short while, yes. But you must come with me.' He clutched her shoulders as his excitement raced away with him. 'We could make it that honeymoon we never really had.'

'I'll be working,' she told him, glumly. How she wished she'd never accepted to star in the show. She'd have to wise up to Henry's methods. Somehow he managed to make each proposition seem the best she'd ever have, and her hungry background had made her so easily cajolable to offers of work.

She told Bernard about the Bradford and London shows. He was understandably disappointed, but he didn't let her see that he was. He wanted, as much as she did, for the two of them to spend some time together. 'Well, if I go back there next month,' he said, thinking as he spoke, 'and get as much done as I can, I could return to London in time for your big show – the opening Royal Gala night.'

'And so you'd better,' she warned. 'I'll be counting on your support.'

'Ooh, hello, Mr Goldman,' said Annie, a little coyly as she stepped inside the room. 'We'd given you up as lost.' Stella laughed at this, and Bernard gently frowned.

'I get the message,' he said. 'Now, c'mon Annie. What's for lunch? I'm starving.'

'Before you eat,' said Stella, 'there's the little matter of the customary present.'

'A present? Why are you so sure I'd bring you back a present?'

'Do you honestly think you'd have dared come home if you hadn't of done?' He thought about that one for a moment, shook his head a couple of times and then went to the bedroom to fetch the sapphire ring he'd bought for her – and the gold watch he'd bought for Annie.

178

On August the third – twelve days before her twenty- fourth birthday – dressed in a pair of slacks and a pink blouse, Stella gazed proudly up at the theatre frontage of the Alhambra in Bradford.

The names of Flanagan and Allen were in the process of coming down and her own name going up in their place. Standing beneath a warming summer sun, watching this happen, somehow signified her arrival to stardom more than anything else that had gone before.

When the workmen had finished she asked them the time. They grinned that senseless grin of instant recognition, which Stella really didn't mind too much: it was better than not being recognised at all.

It was a bit later than she'd thought, but still she had time enough. She took a final look up. In tall, bright-red letters were the words, 'STELLA RAVEN AND FRIENDS'. Beneath that in smaller red letters were 'LONDON'S WINDMILL THEATRE SHOW'.

She liked the Alhambra with its attractive terra-cotta exterior. She could sense it was going to be a happy fortnight and to most artistes that mattered almost more than the success of the show itself.

Walking through the stage door she heard the music of The Freddie Banbury Sound – the orchestra for the Bradford and London shows – so she knew that band call had started.

It wasn't the most serious of band calls, but time was against them, and so Woody had suggested that everyone should appear in full costume. It wasn't such a bad idea, as it helped to avoid the last-minute struggle to find missing outfits on dress-rehearsal night.

She tapped her feet to the music for a while, then stared across the exceptionally large stage and proscenium opening that was capable of taking the largest touring productions. Somewhere amidst the eighteen hundred or so seats was stage manager, Tony Murray. She saw him. He was far back in the stalls, testing for sound quality and volume.

'How long have I got, Tony?' she asked, clambering up to him. Then she said, 'Hi, Woody,' to the producer, who was seated next to him. It wasn't easy to see Woody with the lights down – unless he smiled.

179

'Thirty minutes, love,' said Tony. 'Maybe a little longer.'

Yes, that would be time enough, she thought, as she skipped back to her dressing-room. Time enough to write a letter to her parents and then one to Sadie and Tommy. They wouldn't have to be long letters; it was only to invite them to the royal night at the Windmill Theatre.

That'll keep our mam happy, she smiled. Sadie and me back on talking terms. Haven't I been so childish?

Tony Murray nudged Woody. 'You been with her?' he asked, coarsely.

'Hey?'

'Been with her. Had her in bed?'

Woody said, 'No-one gets Stella in bed except her husband, so you can forget that one, Tony.'

'Just curious,' said Tony, though he immediately knew he'd have to settle for one of the chorus.

Due to another engagement, Milton Keens had had to delay making his appearance at rehearsals. Therefore when Stella turned in the corridor and walked into him it was the first they'd seen of each other. 'Milton,' she sang. Automatically, they hugged each other warmly. 'I like the flashy clothes,' she observed.

'A mere extension of my own flamboyant personality,' he explained. He was in sparkling tails and topper, and carried white gloves and an even whiter cane. She nodded at the cane.

'I didn't realise you were having trouble with your eyes.'

'Ha ha. I'm glad to see your sledge-hammer wit hasn't lost any of its bluntness.'

They stared at each other in silence for a moment, then she said, 'It's good to see you, Milton.'

'And you,' he returned. 'And I hear you're a married woman. Where is the lucky man?' He glanced over her shoulder as if expecting him to be there.

'In America. He's American.'

'Then it would seem appropriate that he's in America.'

She reversed the situation. She didn't want to talk about Bernard. He'd been away for a little while now, and she was missing him. 'And are you married to Jane, yet?'

'That I am,' he replied, and she thought it sounded a pained reply.

'And Adolf?'

'Oh, he's still keen to start a war in Europe.'

'Not that Adolf, silly,' she laughed, 'and you know it.'

'The other one's just as lethal.' He forced a smile. 'No; he's fine. And, too, the baby, whom I believe you know a little about.'

'Yes,' she said, taking a look at her wrist-watch. 'I have to rush now. I have a few things to get done before I go on.'

Am I deliberately avoiding this confrontation? she asked herself. No. I really *must* get a move on.

'I must rush, too,' he said, checking his pocket-watch. 'I believe I'm on just before your spot.'

He rushed one way and her another, and, she thought, a little bitterly, how that had been the story of their lives.

The curtain fell on tumultuous applause on the first night. Stella was compelled to take three encores. Her act was highly polished, and she could manipulate the audience with apparent ease. It was her cheeky northern humour that seemed to please them the most. She so understood her audience – what they liked and didn't like; where they lived; what sort of pubs they drank at – that she just couldn't fail with them.

Her routine was to do a gentle ballad; a robust comedy number; display her gift for dancing – all interspersed with comedy patter – and wind up suitably on a show-stopper. That's all it took. That's all it would ever take while there was a stage for her to perform on.

There were flaws in the show as a whole. One of them was Milton's act. He'd spent too long in Restoration comedy. He didn't look relaxed or natural in front of a variety-show audience. He also overran by four minutes, which would earn him a harsh word or two from either Woody or Tony – most probably both.

The dancing girls were splendid and didn't lose time once. As always, though, it was the unexpected that reared itself. Martino, the magician's assistant, broke a heel early on in their routine and had to finish in stockinged feet. The stage

181

was dangerously slippery, and noticeably so. After skating her way through the performance she took her bow to huge applause, but they didn't know if it was for the act itself or because she'd managed not to fall over.

The vent act – Bobby Perkins and Master – also met with a minor disaster. Master's mouth jammed closed. The last three minutes of the routine was completed with an inanimate dummy, so killing off the illusion of good ventriloquism – as well as killing off the audience's interest. Poor Bobby Perkins – or Booby Perkins, as he henceforth became known. He only received a courteous trickle of applause – hardly enough to stimulate attention in a small library.

The next night was near-perfection, and the third night *was* perfection. On the morning of the fifth performance two things happened to Stella. Firstly, she was sick, and then Henry Charles rang her at her hotel to inform her that the King of England – King George the Sixth – would, in person, be attending the Royal night at the Windmill.

Her sickness didn't last, and she was back on-stage that night to face another standing ovation. But the following morning, she was sick again, and most mornings until the end of the run there.

There was a small dressing-room party held on the last night. It had to be small, because the dressing-rooms were so small. Everyone seemed cheerful enough, especially Tony, who had found himself a regular bed-warmer.

Stella found herself feeling more morose than happy. When would she and Bernard be able to spend some time together, away from his projects and her work and fans?

'Here's to the Windmill, kids,' toasted Woody. It was met with many 'hear, hears'.

Woody clipped for Lester, who at once moped into the room. Probably to his surprise, his boss only wanted to give him a glass of champagne. Lester gratefully accepted, then, taking it outside with him, promptly poured it down the nearest toilet. Bubbles did strange things to his nose.

An hour before the London-bound train was due to depart, Mike Farrow went to the hotel to collect Stella. She was glad he hadn't come any earlier; she didn't like people seeing her being sick.

They slipped quickly across the city to the station. A group of kids – a large and a particularly boisterous group of kids – were waiting to catch a glimpse of her as she left. She smiled warmly as photographs of herself and autograph books were thrust under her nose for signing. 'Over here, Miss Raven.'

'Thank you, Miss Raven.'

'Give us a kiss, Miss Raven.'

'I was first.'

'No, I was.'

Stella firmly took them in hand. 'Now, calm yourself down a bit. I'll get round to all of you.' A little girl – no older than four – squeezed between the legs of her big sister. It made Stella laugh. She stopped signing to pick her up. Mike wasn't watching any of this. He was eager to get back to London. He had work to do. He stood by the door of their first-class compartment, waiting for her. 'What's your name, little girl?' asked Stella. The child became bashful and stuck a thumb in her mouth.

'It's Sarah,' said her older sister, as she nudged the girl as if telling her not to be afraid.

'That's nice,' said Stella. 'My sister's called Sarah. Well, we call her Sadie.'

'Why?' finally spoke the child.

'It's a sort of nickname.'

'What's a nickname?'

Stella laughed. 'You'd better get your big sister to explain that one, my little flower.'

'Why's your hair so short?'

Having found her tongue there seemed no stopping her. 'I had it cut for a pantomime. I got to like it this way, so I've kept it short.' The things kids pick up on, she thought.

As she bent to put the girl down she came over faint. Her hands went clammy and her forehead began beading with perspiration. Then her legs began quivering and she felt nauseous. 'Mike, Mike!' she shouted. He came bounding over, his awkward lanky legs making him a comical sight to behold. A porter was quick to clear a path through the kids, and she hobbled to the train on her agent's arm.

'Oh, I hate to disappoint them,' she said, as he sat her in a private compartment and loosened her collar.

'Sod 'em. You're the one who's unwell.' She managed a smile as she glanced up at him.

'I feel how you look,' she said.

'Why, thank you, Miss Raven. I do love a compliment.'

He touched her face, and in doing so experienced a buzz of affection for this frail, yet doggedly tough young star. 'You're as cold as a block of ice.'

'I'll be fine,' she said. 'Stop fussing.'

He shook his head despairingly. 'When we get back I'm seeing to it you see a doctor.' She groaned her disapproval, but she knew how determined Mike could be. As he went to fetch some coffee he couldn't help wishing he could exchange his wife for Bernard Goldman's.

With only ten days until the Royal opening night at the Windmill, Stella was informed by her doctor that she was to be a mother. Getting pregnant so soon after marriage, and with the promise of a long, full career ahead, had not been accounted for in any of her plans. She felt torn: she wanted to mother her child – their child – yet she wanted to stay at the top of the showbusiness tree; not take a long break to change nappies. And she knew that she was not the sort to neglect her child just for her own personal success.

Bernard came home five days later; but even before telling him the news, she had already made up her mind. After the Windmill week – the most prestigious week any artiste could wish to have – she would retire. Whether temporarily or permanently was yet to be decided.

Sitting up in bed on the night on his return, Bernard said to Stella, 'When you have the kid we'll move out to the country. We don't need the hustle and bustle of London, and I want for our kid to grow up in the English countryside.'

'I thought for a minute you were going to say the States,' she said, with relief. 'So whereabouts in the English countryside?' she asked.

He said, 'I was thinking Kent, maybe.' He shrugged. 'It's smart round there, and I've always liked it.'

She hadn't thought much about life outside of London. Living in the city had always been so practical for her. But now, with a child on the way . . . 'I suppose you're right,

184

love,' she said. 'Anyway, you're the fella in property: see what you can come up with.' He gave her a nothing-could-be-easier toss of the head, and said, 'Leave it with me. Nothing could be easier.'

Henry Charles went through the main doors of the Windmill Theatre; a theatre built on the site of a windmill that originally stood just a few yards from what is now known as Piccadilly Circus.

Vivian Van Damm – General Manager of the 'Mill' and affectionately known as VD – poured Henry a large Scotch over two ice cubes as soon as he saw the agent approaching his office.

Henry raised the glass and said, 'Here's to a great week, VD.' He took a biting sip of the Highland nectar, wincing in ironic pleasure as the golden liquid burnt his throat.

'We're only a three hundred-seater,' said VD, 'but, it goes without saying, we've sold out.'

'As was expected,' said Henry, 'though I know the news will please Stella.'

VD beckoned Henry to be seated. 'And how is your girl?' he asked him, through a serious expression.

'Stella's fine. I think she's just worried you'll have her doing a fan-dance or a can-can.' VD chuckled. 'No, I promise no nudity for that week.'

'I'll tell you what, though,' said Henry, his mind suddenly racing. 'Royal Gala night apart, I could see if Stella would do a spoof can-can with the girls. With Woodville at the helm they could come up with an amusing routine in time for the show.'

'Some of my girls scantily clad backing Stella Raven would add a certain spice to the week,' agreed VD.

'You fix it your end and I'll fix it my end,' said Henry, confidently. He knew how to handle artistes and producers. The secret was to make it look as though all the ideas had been theirs.

Van Damm said, 'Now, what about the Royal night? Do you want your girl presented before and after, or just after in a more convivial atmosphere?'

'I think just after.' They were back on Henry's favourite

185

subject. 'The thing is, it could be a bit chaotic just before the show goes on.'

His remark was destined to become the understatement of the year.

Chapter 16

Stella was at first upset, then worried. How many weeks was it since she wrote to her mother and sister? It must have been at least three, and still she hadn't heard a word. She wondered if they were holding a grudge against her: after all, it had taken her a long time to give in and make up with her sister. But then she knew her mother would still write even if just to tell her what a bad girl she had been. Sadie, understandably, might be holding a stronger grudge against her. But even so, she knew Sadie, too. She would write just to tell her she was not writing to her ever again. There was the fact that her mother hadn't written many letters before. Maybe she was scared to. Stella could remember the first letter she had written . . .

'Is this it, miss?' asked the driver.

'What? Oh, yes. Just drop me at the door there, please.'

She climbed out of the cab, paid the driver, tipped the driver, thanked the driver, then trotted into the Camden Dance Hall. The now-familiar sounds of tinkling piano and echoing taps caught her ears as Woody rehearsed the Windmill girls for a routine Henry Charles wanted them to do with her.

His suggestion had been met with fiery reaction from the contracted chorus who, through their agency, claimed could do as good a can-can as the Windmill dancers. Henry was quick to calm things down, but he had to promise them further work in the process. And how did Woody – the

187

choreographer, and therefore the one most in contact with the new girls – feel about it all?' 'If they've got no clothes on, baby, I'll train 'em day and night, whoever they are,' he'd told Henry.

Woody saw Stella come into the hall. 'Keep that pace going girls,' he ordered, and went to greet her. 'Hi, honey. Why not take somethin' off and join in?' She overrode the humour.

'I'd love to,' she said seriously and distractedly, 'but I've a few personal matters to sort out.' Woody sensed the tension in her voice. He decided not to push her.

'Okay. There's no big deal, anyway. We can go through the routine tomorrow if you like.'

'That's great, Woody,' she said. 'And thanks.'

'No trouble, honey. Just make sure you bring your feathers with you next time,' he teased. She wagged a finger at him.

'I believe, Mr Woodville, that you're loving all of this, aren't you?' He couldn't deny it.

'I'm in seventh heaven, baby.' He returned to work.

She went straight to Henry's office. He wasn't in. He was busy with a Laurel and Hardy tour, or so his secretary said. Stella wasn't that bothered. If he wasn't there, then he wasn't there. Mike Farrow *was* there. He, like Woody, could tell immediately when there were things on her mind. Her serious mood, her anxious mannerisms were two of the many telltale signs. 'I need a bit of help, Mike,' she finally built up to say.

He responded with 'Anything, my darling. You know me.'

'I've been trying unsuccessfully to get hold of my family for some time, just to let them know about the Windmill show. I've heard nothing back from them.' She told him of the two letters she had posted from Bradford. 'I could understand only one of them replying, but both of them not replying? Well, it's a little strange, wouldn't you say?'

Mike, who'd been standing until now, sat down and made a steeple with his hands and then rested his long, narrow chin on the spire. 'Yes, I see. It *is* a little strange.' He felt a bit like a doctor diagnosing an illness.

'I don't know what to do next,' she confessed, miserably. 'They're not on the phone, and I'm tied up with rehearsals, so I can't get up to see them. Have you any bright ideas?'

Come on, Mike. You must have an idea, he told himself. That's why Henry needs you so much.

188

One thing Mike didn't want, and any good agent would be the same, was his top artiste having domestic problems just prior to doing a major show. It needed dealing with. 'I do have an idea I can find out what's going on,' he said at length, lifting his head off the spire. 'I know someone I can contact up there. Someone who can check into things.'

'Oh, thanks, Mike,' she squeaked. The guilt she was feeling over Sadie was growing more each day. She had to make up with her before any more time passed by.

I should never have ignored her when she came to Manchester to see me. She made a big brave effort – but I just wouldn't let it drop. Oh, Stella, your stubbornness and selfishness will be the death of you, she said to herself. 'And you'll let me know as soon as you hear anything?' she said out loud. 'Oh, and tell your contact to tell my folks about the Windmill show. I'll keep them seats reserved for the opening night, and I'll arrange transport up here for them.'

'Will do.'

Nervously she toyed with her wedding ring. 'I hope they haven't all turned funny on me,' she remarked.

'If they have,' said Mike, 'I'll sign them up. We need new acts.'

Jean and I may have patched things up, he thought, *but what I'd do to be married to you, Stella Raven.*

'I'll see you later, Mike.'

'Yes. See you later, darling.'

Mike waited a full two minutes while a secretary traced Charlie Duncan. Finally, Charlie came to the phone. 'Hi, Mike, what is it?' said the cheerful northerner who was stage manager at the Winter Gardens, Morecambe. Mike told him about Stella.

'So if you can find out something we'd all be most grateful,' he concluded.

'Anything for our Stella,' he said. 'She's a local lass, yer know?'

'Yes. I know, Charlie.'

Stella awoke feeling decidedly jaded. *Stop thinking you're ill, and you'll feel better in no time,* she urged herself. So she did, and she felt worse.

189

She thought about the day ahead of her. The words 'Press Conference' sounded like the death-sentence to her. The things that have to be done in the name of publicity.

She checked her watch. Nine o'clock. She didn't have to be there until twelve. Mike was collecting her at eleven thirty. He arrived dead on time and they reached the Café Royal five minutes earlier than was necessary. There was a pleasant atmosphere there. One of anticipation and excitement. Stella was very popular with the press at this time. They'd designed many a good story around her. But even though she was a star, it took several minutes to pull the forty or so members of the press away from the bar where the free booze was.

She was led by Henry to a raised platform where she was seated to face the gathering. Behind her was an upright piano. It wasn't there for her benefit. It was there for the benefit of the Café Royal. However, when someone shouted out, 'What sort of songs will you be doing at the Windmill?' she couldn't resist singing a few bars, accompanied by Freddie Banbury at the keys. 'That's the sort of song I'll be doing,' she said, to big applause.

'Is it true you'll shortly be enjoying a happy event – that you are pregnant?' asked a young reporter. His shifty eyes shot from note-pad to Stella Raven. The room instantly hushed. Was this a story that no-one else but this young reporter had got hold of? Muffled conversation broke out and Stella flashed a look at Mike Farrow, who shuffled uneasily in his suit.

She didn't want to confirm she was pregnant just yet. It was bad for her image to be seen as a mum-to-be when she was launching a new show. It somehow looked wrong. She'd told Henry, Mike, and Bernard that she wouldn't announce it until after the show. She could only presume that this young reporter had heard a rumour through a friend of a friend of a friend of the doctor's. 'Where did you hear that?' she asked, as lightly as she could without looking guilty.

'Sorry, Miss Raven,' he smiled. 'I can't reveal my sources in front of my colleagues here.'

'Well, I'm afraid your sources have jumped the gun,' she said. 'I'm just enjoying practising.'

That was a bit close to the mark, she at once told herself. But at least it had the desired effect to shut them up – except for one more question on the subject. 'So we can print that you're *not* pregant, then?' asked another reporter.

'You can print nothing of the kind,' she replied, very calmly. 'If you print things like that you might as well print that I'm *not* a brunette or that I'm *not* a foreigner.'

They got the point. But it wouldn't stop one clever one – probably the young one who'd started it all – printing 'Stella Raven denies she's pregnant'.

The rest of the conference was far less exciting. It eventually petered out rather than concluded. But Henry was pleased with how it had gone. It would give her prominent coverage before the show went on.

From the conference she went back to her flat. Woody rang her there to let her know that a run-through with the Windmill girls would be at the Windmill Theatre itself. They were to be there no earlier than two and leave no later than four fifteen. She met him there at two. She was pleased with the routine. It was saucy without being offensive. She thought it one of Henry's better ideas. She also knew that whatever the chorus may have thought, there was no way they could have done it as well as the Windmill girls.

Mike spent the afternoon hovering in the background. When he heard about Windmill girls, semi-clad, Windmill Theatre, two p.m., he was first there. Afterwards, he swaggered across the stage under a hot collar and introduced himself to the girls – individually. Stella scowled at him, saying, 'Come on Casanova, it'll only send you blind.'

He trailed behind her to a dressing-room. She didn't take long. She just slipped a thick pullover and a pair of slacks on over her work-out costume.

As they went to leave they bumped into Woody, who hadn't exactly been hurrying to escape the predominantly female gathering. He'd been visiting a second floor to the building where there was virtually another complete stage. This was used by the incoming artistes to produce and rehearse their show while the current performances went on beneath it. But Stella's show wasn't allowed the use of it for rehearsing. Their one-week stay was considered a one-off type performance, not a major production. Ironically, of course, it was as big as any production the Windmill would see for some time, but apparently that didn't count: it was judged on a time-element basis only. 'Okay, kids,' said Woody. 'Lunch is on me today.' He wrapped a long arm around each of them and looked like a drunk being supported.

'It's four o'clock,' she pointed out. 'Lunch has gone by.'

He thought for a second. Nothing altered Woody Woodville's plans – least of all time. 'Okay, then. Tea's on me today.'

'That's better,' she said.

Stella led the way to the dilapidated staircase that would take them down to ground level. It made a useful short-cut to an emergency exit door that opened on to Great Windmill Street. Because of her long heels she was struggling with each downward step as if learning to walk for the first time. Without any warning one of them snapped and, with a yelp, she plummeted downwards.

It happened all so quickly that her stunned companions just stared at each other for a moment while she lay groaning at the foot of the staircase, her head wedged against the exit door. Then they sprinted down to her and reached her, simultaneously.

'So you can tell Stella that the message is, her sister's in hospital and her parents visit her daily so aren't at home very often. The feeling is they probably haven't had a chance to answer her letter and that Sadie, because of being indisposed, has been unable to. Charlie Duncan couldn't elaborate on that.' This was Mike on the phone to Bernard.

Bernard said, 'I see. Well, thanks for all your trouble, Mike. I'll pass on the message as soon as she's back.' He laughed ironically. 'It's crazy. I'm to tell her her sister's in hospital when she gets out of hospital herself.'

'That's life, Bernard,' said Mike, sharing the irony.

When Stella returned that evening – positively uneasy on her legs and pale-faced – Annie and Bernard presented her with a bouquet of flowers. 'It's like when we first met,' she remarked, through a faint smile, and her mind momentarily drifted back to a dashing young man seated self-assuredly in a box at the Empire Theatre, Leeds.

'You've only been gone two days,' said Annie, giving 'Miss Stella' a kiss, 'but I know what that hospital food's like. Yuk! I worked for a week in a hospital canteen once. I was filling in for a friend. Well, she weren't so much of a friend as someone I'd met when . . .'

Bernard dropped a firm but friendly hand on her shoulder. 'Er, yes. Okay, Annie. I think we'll take dinner now. I know you've been hard at it all afternoon, and I, for one, am ravenous.'

Mainly because of who she was, the hospital had arranged for an ambulance to drop her at the flat. She'd told them there was no need for special treatment but they'd insisted – for the sum of three personalised autographs.

This amused Bernard. 'An example that nothing's unobtainable to the rich or famous. Everyone has a price.'

Stella wasn't hungry, though she did her best so as not to disappoint Annie. Afterwards, she took Bernard into their bedroom. Seating him on the corner of the bed, she then leant against the wall, facing him in an attempt to find a relaxed posture. She didn't really succeed, and ended up standing upright with arms crossed, a little like how she'd seen Henry when dictating a letter to one of his secretaries. 'I'm afraid I lost it, Bernard,' she eventually said, in a level voice. He looked at her quizzically.

'Lost what, angel?'

'Our baby. I've had a miscarriage.'

Her eyes were puffy and tired. Not only was it torturing her to tell him this but it was taking her to the verge of breaking down and crying. She knew this because she could remember the last time she had broken down and cried. It was when Sadie had given up the partnership in preference to Tommy Moran. That all seemed a century ago to her now.

Bernard's chin fell the moment she told him. 'Oh, dear God,' he finally gasped, and pinched the bridge of his nose to restrain his own tears from falling.

'The doctors said it would have been the fall that caused it,' she explained in a whisper, though she didn't know why she was whispering. 'I'm sorry I've let you down,' she wept, as the first of the tears welled up in her eyes.

He jumped up and held her tighter than he'd ever held her before. 'There'll be other times,' he assured her, and assured himself. But he seriously began wondering if there would be.

Once the emotional aspect was over would she really take the risk of becoming pregnant again? Somehow he doubted it. He sensed a great burden being lowered on to their relationship. He prayed they would be strong enough to come through.

After a long, paralysed silence he suggested they went into the main room and told Annie. Later on, after Annie had taken herself to bed and he felt his wife was in slightly better spirits, he told her the piece of news Mike Farrow had given to him. 'In hospital?' she gasped with disbelief. 'But she's healthy. I wonder what's happened to her.'

'Well, your folks have been visiting her so I guess she must have busted a leg or something,' he said, trying to underplay the situation. His wife's nerves were tingling enough as it was. 'Maybe you should send her a postcard or something.' The idea appealed to her.

'Yes. I'll give Mike a ring and get the address of the hospital.'

She did so and also plied him with a dozen more questions, all of which he couldn't answer. It was impossible. He simply didn't know any more than what he had already told Bernard. 'I'm sure Charlie will get back if there's any further news,' he promised her.

She hung up. She no longer felt sorry for herself, concerned about her own problems. She was worried for her sister. Worried and frustrated. 'I'll never be able to go and visit her whilst I'm stuck with rehearsals,' she mumbled.

'Go up and see her then as soon as the show's over,' suggested Bernard. 'If Sadie's had an accident she won't be coming to London, anyway.'

'You're right.' She gave him a hopeful smile, and he answered the question before it was delivered.

'Yes. I'll come with you. I've yet to meet this gorgeous sister of yours.'

She kissed him on the mouth. He was glad she was perking up a bit. The glint had returned to her eyes. 'That's wonderful. I'll take Sadie a copy of the theatre programme to read whilst she's recovering.'

'I'm sure she'd like that.'

Then she said, through a blank expression, 'I just wish I knew what she *is* recovering from.'

Tommy Moran was as pale as the doctor's overcoat, which he was following up to the reception desk. 'There's a small parcel containing personal effects,' the doctor explained in a diplomatic tone. 'It would be best if you'd take it with you now. We wouldn't want to risk misplacing it and causing you any inconvenience.'

'Aye. Okay,' said Tommy, hoarsely.

The doctor moved uncomfortably from one foot to the other. He hated this part of his job. 'Is there anything I can do for you now? Anything at all? Perhaps something to steady the nerves?'

Tommy's vision was transfixed to the cream-coloured concrete floor. If asked what he was staring at he wouldn't have known. All he was aware of was bodily numbness, and the antiseptic aroma of the place that, paradoxically, put people – whether patients or visitors – off going to hospitals. 'No, ta. I need nothing now.'

The doctor glanced at his watch without taking in the time. 'I must be going,' he said. 'The mortician – Mr Webster – will be in touch with you regarding the, er, deceased.'

'Yes, I know. I was told that.'

'Then I shall say goodbye, Mr Moran. My deepest sympathy to you and your family. I'm so sorry there was nothing more we could do.'

'Aye!'

The doctor went away. He had other sick and dying patients with concerned relatives to cope with. Tommy outstretched his hands like he was sleepwalking. The girl at the reception put the parcel into them. 'There you go now, Mr Moran,' she said, with controlled cheerfulness as she tried to bring him back to the land of the conscious. She didn't want to send him home in too much of a daze. She'd seen all of this so often before. Strange how it never became any easier.

Without further word he turned and walked blindly along the corridor, and through the big swing-doors into the late summer sunshine. How could you die on such a lovely summer's day. You loved it warm like this, didn't you Sade? He marched mechanically for the bus stop, wondering what would become of him now his wife was dead.

Jack and Lilly Ravenscroft stared contemplatively at each

other over the rims of their tea cups. A clock ticked relentlessly on the mantle-shelf, surrounded by old mail. It had lived there so long that its sound had become a part of the silence. They would have been more aware of its presence had it stopped. 'Stella will have to be told,' said Jack, finally. One of them was due to mention Stella; it just happened to be him.

'Aye, I know. But not straight away. I've had letter come. It says she's to do a big London show very soon. She wanted us all to go.'

'We'll tell her afterwards then, eh? Give her a chance to get her show out the way.'

'Aye, okay. She may miss funeral though.'

'Oh, I don't know. These things take time to arrange,' he said. 'Got to get the priest an' everything.'

'Aye, but Stella and Sade weren't talking. I wonder how she'll take the news.'

Jack could only see her taking it one way. 'She'll be devastated. They were sisters, you know. And partners for some of the time. They just lost contact with each other when Stella became a big name.'

'I think *we* lost contact with Stella when she became a big name,' said Lilly, philosophically.

She began snivelling and pulled out a tissue from up a sleeve a little like a magician producing a silk hankie from supposedly nowhere. 'It's so sad,' she cried, and blew her nose very loudly. Jack began to slowly pace the room.

'Why, oh, why did you choose our Sade?' he said with eyes pointing accusingly up to Heaven.

He went to pour his wife another cup of tea but, for the first time that he could remember, she refused it.

196

Chapter 17

'Try cutting the tempo. The chorus can't keep up with you.'
This was Woody talking to Freddie Banbury, who were the
only vertical figures to be seen amidst the orchestra. Their
long, bored faces and rolled-up sleeves were evidence it had
been a hard morning. There'd be a few pints sunk during the
lunch break.

Stella breezed by them all mouthing a 'goodbye' as she left
the dance hall. Her body was responding well to the various
exercise routines she was putting it through.

Mustn't overdo it though, she thought as a cab swerved to
miss her and the driver made a suitable gesture to let her
know what he thought of her. I'll have to get through a week
of the real thing very soon.

Her next stop was Henry's office. She went there for her
now-weekly ritual of dealing with the wads of fan-mail that
poured in. Unless there was a specific or unusual request
within the mail Henry would have one of his secretaries type
standard replies and Stella would merely have to sign her
name to them. To a degree it could be considered cheating,
but at least she made some sort of effort. She knew of other
stars who didn't even bother to read the mail, let alone reply
to it.

As she sat cross-legged at a desk, getting on with it, Henry
attended to other business. A few yards away, in his own
office, sat Mike Farrow. He'd just answered the phone to

197

discover he was speaking to Charlie Duncan in Morecambe. Charlie came straight to the point. 'It's her sister,' he explained. 'She died a week or so ago.'

For a second Mike felt as though he'd lost an own next of kin. Ironic, as he'd never even met Sadie Ravenscroft. 'What did she die of?' he eventually asked. Charlie fleetingly thought of the old gag:

– What she die of?

– Shortness of breath.

He answered him. 'A stomach disease. Some sort of growth in her stomach. Bloody awful, in't it?'

'It certainly is, Charlie, it certainly is.' Mike took a deep breath. 'Okay, Charlie. I'll be in touch again. Thanks for getting back to me.' They replaced receivers.

I can't tell her about this with the show coming up, he thought. She'll go insane. But what right have I to withhold the information? I've got to. Henry would be furious if I upset her so close to the show. I'll drop in and see Bernard at the weekend, when he's back from looking at property in Kent. Yes, that's what I'll do. Then he can decide when she should be told, if her parents don't tell her first. He'll know the best moment.

He pulled out a rare cigarette from a gold-plated box on his desk. Subconsciously he took in the inscription.

'To Mike Farrow. A personal thanks for all your assistance in making it possible for me to break all existing box-office records during my summer season at the Queen's Theatre, Blackpool, 1936. Love, Max Miller.'

Yes. That's it. I'll leave it to Bernard to decide.

Mike was in need of a strong coffee. He slipped into Henry's office and made for the kitchen, hoping she wouldn't notice him. He couldn't face telling her about the phone call. 'Hi, Mike,' she said, cheerfully. 'Don't I get a good morning anymore?' She hardly looked up as she spoke, which was a good thing or she might have sensed there was something up.

'I'm sorry, my darling,' he said. 'I was miles away there for a moment. Lost in the world of thoughts.'

'Cheerful ones, I hope?'

'Yes.'

He diverted from the coffee to the hidden rotating bar. 'A bit early for that,' remarked Henry.

If he knew what I knew he wouldn't be saying that, thought Mike. But he made no reply – and still had a drink.

Mike didn't contact Bernard straight away. He kept putting it off for as long as possible, perhaps hoping the problem would go away. Two days before the night of the Royal Gala – with Stella still oblivious to her sister's death – he decided he must tell Bernard. He had delayed long enough. If he delayed any longer she would only end up hearing through her parents – or worse still, the press. How long before they would put two and two together?

He decided that his course of action would be to deliver a letter marked personal attention of Bernard Goldman. That way no-one would need to see him. He could slip it through the door-flap and then jog off down the street.

Annie brought a freshly baked cake into the room. 'It's not as solid as it looks,' she explained. 'I'm afraid I went a bit haywire with the ingredients. It'll be fine, though.'

'I'm sure it's lovely,' supported Stella.

Bernard reserved his judgement until the tasting of it. He reached forward with the water jug. As he poured, the click of the door-flap could be heard. 'Mail at this time of night?' commented Stella, as she delicately carved through a piece of cake. 'It's the latest post we've ever had delivered,' she joked.

Bernard scraped back his chair and went to investigate. 'It's addressed for my personal attention.'

'Better see what it is.'

'No need to, angel,' he said. 'It'll be more boring details from the estate agency. They said they'd send me some more. Guess they want to save the postage, the mean rats.' He tossed it onto a sideboard.

'They haven't come up with much of any interest yet, have they?' she said.

'These things take time, angel.'

He returned to his seat and tried a piece of the cake. 'I've got news for you, Annie. It *is* as solid as it looks.' She didn't argue with him.

Stella was helping Annie with the washing-up when Bernard picked up the hand-delivered letter again. He was grinning as he opened it. He remembered that the last details he'd been sent couldn't have been more unsuitable. He wondered what little delight they had for him this time.

His face lengthened as he read. When he'd finished he tucked it securely into his inner jacket pocket. Stella remarked upon its absence the moment she came back into the room.

Trust you to have such sharp eyes, he thought.

'Who was it from, then?'

'Just more property.'

'Any good?' she pressed.

'No. Lousy.'

He thanked God she didn't ask to take a look at it for herself.

When they'd undressed and were climbing into bed he smuggled the letter into his top drawer, beneath a batch of documents to do with property. She never looked in there, just as he never looked inside *her* personal drawer.

Thinking it a cunningly clever move to have made, he laid himself down and in the darkness concerned himself with how and when he was going to tell her about her sister. What would be the consequences of her knowing? He recalled how much she'd been talking about her recently: how she planned to patch things up once the show was over. What an emotional upheaval it would all be, and how guilty she would feel for having disowned her for so long.

All these thoughts, and more, flew furiously around his head, ensuring him a restless night's sleep.

There was an aura hanging over the Windmill Theatre that afternoon as Stella's cab pulled away from it in the direction of Trafalgar Square. She glanced back to witness the ever-increasing distance diminish her bold name that stood high above the *Revudeville* sign.

The West End's famous landmark always had an aura about it, but today it was extra-special – almost tangible. People were outside its doors, struggling vainly for any possible tickets before the show's commencement that very evening. Reports that King George would be there had quadrupled the interest, and Henry Charles was woefully regretting not hiring a larger theatre – one that could get more people in and, therefore, more money in the till.

Stella turned round once her name had been blotted out by a brown jumble of buildings. She had more than just butterflies today. She could hardly believe that in another five hours she would be appearing in front of her King. The grand honour had come around so quickly. But she knew that if she could get through tonight's show she could get through the whole week; that was a fact.

She paid the driver. 'And don't forget; pick me up here at four thirty – no later.'

'Yes, Miss Raven,' he smiled. He thought it was clever to show her he knew who she was.

She went inside the flat. Annie was out shopping and Bernard was out seeing Mike Farrow, though she had no idea why.

She drifted over to the largest pane of glass that kept vigil over the bustling streets. It was a miserable day, and as she stared out on to the grey afternoon she wiped a finger across the window, picking up a film of dirt. Doing this she found it wasn't as dull outside as she first thought, and she made a mental note to instruct Annie to wash down the windows.

She moved into her bedroom. The flat seemed deadly without Annie or Bernard there. She paused to examine herself in the dresser mirror. She thought her eyes were showing premature wrinkles at the corners, and so tutted. 'Your Royal Highness,' she said, holding her hand out and taking a short, delicate curtsey.

She turned sideways and, placing her fingers on her abdomen, checked her figure. She decided it wasn't too bad. Or as Bernard would say, 'Pretty hot stuff, angel.' She stopped her self-examination.

Now what will I be needing tonight? she asked herself. I think I've got everything at the theatre. Oh, wait a bit. What about earrings? The ones Bernard gave you for your birthday the other week? He'd appreciate you wearing them tonight – and they *do* look lovely.

She went on a massive earring hunt, but failed to find them. She was sure he wouldn't have put them in his own drawer – unless by mistake. It was worth checking. It was a simple enough error to have made if he'd been in a hurry to go somewhere.

She pulled back his drawer and rummaged inside. Within moments her attention was taken by the hand-delivered letter of the other night. She pulled it free from the other piles of papers and forms. As she opened it she sensed it had nothing to do with property. That was confirmed when she saw the Charles and Farrow Management heading.

The cab driver couldn't believe it. Five o'clock and not a sign of her. She'd been the one moaning about the time. No later than four thirty, she'd told him. He pressed once again on his car horn. Nothing. He tried the door-bell. A shabby-looking woman answered. 'What's to do with you, then?' asked Annie. He was a little startled that someone had come to the door. When he'd tried a short while back, no-one had been in.

'Is, er, Miss Raven ready?' He gave a single nod at the car to explain who he was.

'She's gone,' she said, and pulled the sort of face that said, are you sure you haven't lost your marbles?

'Bloody marvellous,' he cursed, but beneath his breath.

'She went out about four fifteen. She looked in a hurry. I presumed she was late for her show.'

'Four fifteen,' sighed the driver. 'Thanks, ma'am.' He doffed his flat cap and returned to his vehicle. 'Bloody stars. All the bloody same.' The car coughed into life, and he drove away in an angry mood.

Henry's gold-plated Swiss clock hammered out six rings from where it was stationed in the corner of his office. He looked at Mike, who returned the look. 'I think we appear quite dashing,' he considered, with a broad smile.

'Perfection,' exaggerated Mike. Henry gave his younger partner a hefty thwack across the back which nearly jarred his spine. Henry was always full of high spirits and generous comments on the night of a Royal Show. It was the cream-on-top-of-the-cake part of the business. He revelled in it.

'Fingers crossed the show will be a big success tonight,' said Henry.

'I'm sure it will be,' said Mike. 'After all, that's why we went to Bradford first.' Henry grunted his agreement. Mike wiped his hands on his trouser legs for the third time in as many minutes. 'We'd better get going,' he said. 'We don't want to keep the King waiting.'

'I think you're right,' said Henry, and then added, when seeing that Mike looked a little ashen, 'and you don't want to worry yourself too much. Tonight will be just wonderful.'

It wasn't 'tonight' that worried Mike. It was wondering if Bernard had decided to break the bad news to Stella before the show or after.

Henry took one last look at himself in the office mirror. He adjusted to the same pose he would adopt for any press or publicity photographers. No-one caught Henry's 'bad side'.

He straightened his bow-tie and, when satisfied, turned to face Mike. 'Come on then,' he beckoned. 'Let's get the wives and follow the road to the Windmill.'

Bernard watched at a gracious distance as King George was led through a line of theatre-management handshakes. He continued watching as he was then taken by Vivian Van Damm into a private room to be entertained until the commencement of the show. Henry and Mike plus their wives were also inside. Van Damm's wife, Natalie, joined them a minute later. The King was unaccompanied except for his equerry, who had the ability to be only a step behind him yet without seeming to intrude.

When the initial excitement of his arrival had quelled, Bernard rushed backstage to ask the performers if there had been any sign of Stella. There hadn't been. He grabbed a doorman who was whistling by him. 'I need a phone,' he demanded. The man pointed down the winding corridor.

'Second left, first right. Can't miss it.'

He ran up to it and clasped it as if it was the source of all life. He rang his home number for a full minute. Finally it was answered – by Annie. No. She wasn't there. She'd left hours ago.

Bernard told himself she'd probably turn up at any second, but failed to convince himself. He made in the direction of the private room where the King was being entertained. Naturally, being the husband to the star, he had been invited to join the private gathering.

He prayed that it was her cab that had broken down and caused this delay. He had the premonition that it wasn't that at all; that it was the news of her sister. But how had she found out? Only Mike knew. But there were her parents. Yet he hadn't seen any mail in from them. No. It had to be the letter.

My God, he thought, if she's found that then there's no telling what she could do. We must have been crazy not to have told her straightaway and got everything over and done with then and there. We acted cowardly. We were scared of what she would say and do.

By coincidence, Henry emerged from the room as Bernard went by it. 'Henry,' he called out. 'We've a problem with Stella. She hasn't turned up.'

'Hasn't turned up?' he repeated, in a loud whisper. 'She's due on in half an hour for the opening number.' Didn't he just know it.

Bernard swayed on his feet. The tension was driving him frantic. 'Well, she hasn't turned up and she was aiming to be here for five, would you believe?'

Henry tried not to reveal how panic-stricken he was. Dignity at all times, was his motto. 'Okay, now. I'll rescue Mike and the three of us will make a dash back to your place and see . . .'

'I've tried that. I rang. Annie said she's not there. She saw her leave.'

'Dammit!'

'But wait a bit.' Bernard's mind was racing as fast as the time until the curtain was due up. 'What if Annie was told to say she wasn't in?' Henry looked puzzled.

'What on earth would she do that for?' Obviously he hadn't been told about Sadie, thought Bernard.

'It's a long story. I'll tell you on the way there. Go and get Mike.'

'I'll do that now. And Van Damm can take care of things this end.'

He slipped back into the cordial atmosphere of Van Damm's private room. If only they all knew, he thought. He managed to disengage Van Damm from the King and left His Majesty talking to Mrs Charles. They were talking about shooting. She told him how Henry had once taken her to

Norfolk, but she'd been such an encumbrance he had banned her from any such further excursions. Having told Van Damm the problem, Henry said, 'Start without her.'

'But she comes out with the whole cast to sing, "Welcome to our merry little show."'

'It doesn't matter,' said Henry, emphatically. 'She's the star of the show. They don't necessarily expect to see her in the opening sequence.'

'I've just been talking to your wife about shooting, Mr Charles,' said the King.

'Er, yes, Sir. I took her along once: with dire consequences I'm afraid.'

Lord, don't trap me now, he said to himself.

The King gave him a knowing smile. 'I think one's wives are prone to excitement when on a shoot. Must be the heat of the moment. The thrill of the kill.'

'I think that must be it, Sir.'

Van Damm quickly intercepted with the champagne bottle, and Henry was able to excuse himself, saying he had to check up on various matters. His Majesty quite understood. 'Could you spare me a moment, please, Mike?' Mike put down his half-filled glass. He sensed things weren't running too smoothly by his partner's rare show of agitation.

'Tell me more about this Stella Raven, Mr Van Damm,' said the King. 'I've heard some splendid reports on her. She's done remarkably well for someone so young, wouldn't you say?' Van Damm told him everything he knew about Stella Raven – omitting, by choice, the fact she was perilously close to missing her first Royal Gala show.

As the curtain lifted to loud applause, Henry, Mike, and Bernard fell into the flat. Annie was shocked by all these men tumbling in on her. She recognised who they were, fortunately, or she may have started screaming rape. 'Ooh, Mr Goldman.'

'Hiya, Annie. Has Stella been back yet?' He was looking for flaws in her natural expression: signs perhaps that she was hiding her in one of the other rooms. But no. There wasn't even a hint that she was anything more than genuinely surprised by their bursting in.

205

'I told you when you rang. She left here at about four fifteen. I'm sure that was the time. You see, I had a cake in the oven and I had to . . .'

'Did she say where she was going?' interrupted Henry Charles. He was glad *his* wife didn't have a live-in help. Two women in one house was two women too many, in his mind.

'No. I thought she was going to the theatre.'

There was a frailty in her voice, and her face was starting to show the same concern that theirs were. 'Miss Stella. She's all right, in't she?'

'That we don't quite know as yet,' said Henry, discouragingly.

'Maybe she has a favourite haunt; somewhere she likes to escape to,' suggested Mike. A cool breeze filtered through the hallway, making them all shudder: all, that is, except for Henry. He never felt the cold. He put it down to being overweight.

'Not bad thinking,' congratulated Bernard, and he gave Annie a hopeful look. 'Do you know of anywhere she'd go if she were, say, a little down in the dumps?' Annie prodded her bottom lip as she thought.

'Nowhere special, like. If she's ever really upset or in a bad mood about something she goes to see a picture.'

There was a brief pause before all three men gave a sullen sigh. 'We'd never find her in a movie house,' said Bernard. 'Not even if we knew which one she was at.'

Mike said, 'Surely she wouldn't have gone to see a film with her own show starting and her sister dead. She may be devastated, but she wouldn't do that.'

Annie's eyes widened. 'Dead?' she whimpered.

Bernard rested an arm on her shoulder, but it wasn't a particularly affectionate one; more a dutiful arm. 'Let's get back to the theatre,' Henry said, resigning himself to the truth: his artiste had let him down and he'd have to make an announcement. He would probably say that she was ill. Audiences forgave illness. It's about the only excuse they do forgive: that and death. Van Damm would do the explaining to the King.

There was nothing else to be done. They went outside to the waiting cab. Annie closed the door and realised that she was

206

trembling. 'Oh, Miss Stella. Don't do anything silly,' she implored the empty room.

Stella sat down on a bench overlooking the river from the Chelsea Embankment. She stared as the sunset took the light from the water and left behind it a dark, ruffled blanket. As she watched, an old man in rags approached. His trousers were held up by a piece of rope and his hands were clasped lovingly around a bottle of label-less wine. His hair was long and uneven; evidence he didn't have too many barbers as friends. He sat down beside her.

'Hello. You on your own?' She nodded, but continued looking blankly out across the Thames. 'And me,' he said. 'Always on my own. Mind you, I like my own company.'

Now she glanced at him. She thought he seemed a sweet, gentle man and she felt sorry for him. His face was stained with ingrown dirt from a lifetime of rummaging through dustbins and sleeping in gutters, and his hands were covered in calluses for the same reason. 'Down on your luck, are you dear?' She nodded again.

Then she said, 'That's about the truth of it.' She found her voice didn't sound like it belonged to her. It was more like listening to one of her own recordings at the studios.

'Here you go, love,' he said, forcing the bottle into her hands. 'Have a swig. It'll warm you up.'

It tasted sour and unpleasant, but she was surprised at how soothing it was. She didn't dare ask him what it was – she was too afraid to know: or, perhaps, too afraid that he might not know. 'Thanks,' she said, and passed it back.

'That's okay.' He prodded his chest with it. 'I'm always down on my luck.' Then he added with a note of optimism, 'But I have big plans, though. *Big* plans. I'll get myself together one day.' He raised his head with dignity and pride. 'It wasn't always like this. Used to have a proper job, I did. Worked at Waterloo Station.'

'Did you?' She tried to sound interested, and in a strange sort of way she was; it was just that she was a little distracted at the moment. She had run away for some peace and quiet: to escape her problems – the reality. To consider her life.

He moved up closer to her, and began examining her face as

207

if she was a portrait on show in a gallery. 'I'm sure I've seen you somewhere's before,' he said, with a trace of suspicion in his voice. 'You're not on the run from the beat, are you?'

'No,' she said. 'I'm on the run from myself. I'm supposed to be on-stage in a minute.'

'Ah, that's it,' he said, excitedly. 'I've seen you in newspapers and on billboards and things.'

His mood suddenly changed. No longer was he hospitable. He felt cheated and now regretted having shown her kindness by giving her a drink of his all-too-precious wine. 'So you're not *that* much down on your luck, then?' he said, bitterly. She could feel his bitterness, and it upset her. She couldn't understand why he should have become nasty towards her just because it turned out she was well known. She'd taken him on face-value; couldn't he do the same?

She wondered if he really had had a proper job once, and by letting things slip he'd ended up in this sad and sorry state. She could see herself in his place, and sensed how easily it could happen. You become unpredictable, emotional, unreliable, argumentative. Then, perhaps, you begin to drink and your friends laugh at first. Then after a while, they don't like being associated with a drunk, so they desert you.

It was a terrifying thought, and one that seemed to propel her back into reality. 'I must go now,' she said. 'Thanks for the drink.' How silly that sounded.

She didn't expect a smile from her friend-turned-enemy, but she gave him one just the same. She thought about leaving him some money, but presumed he was too proud. With her hands dug deep into her pockets, she strode along the Embankment and took an eventual left turn towards Piccadilly.

It was nearing the end of Milton's act. One of his duties was to lead into Stella, who came on to close the first half. It was an idea Woody had had so as to give the audience a taster of what was to come later. Leave them wanting more. It was also good to close the first half on big applause. It was said to have a good affect on the critics who were watching. They'd be less inclined to make derogatory comments if the show was being received so well.

Milton made a meal out of taking his bow: first to King

George in his privileged singular position and then to the sea of anonymous faces. He received good applause; far better than he'd had in Bradford. He deserved it. His act was much tighter since Bradford.

The clapping subsided. He wished it could have gone on all night. 'Your Royal Highness, Ladies and Gentlemen. I now have great pleasure in giving you the star of our show: indeed, our country's most popular female star: Miss Stella Raven.'

Huge applause followed while Milton skipped off the stage, leaving it open for Stella to bounce out onto.

At the rear of the single-tier theatre, Henry, Mike and Bernard burst in. 'Christ! They've let them think she's here,' said Henry, through the machine-gun clapping of hands. 'They'll go beserk when they find out the truth.'

. . . and so Stella was standing in the wings, the applause sweeping over her like gentle summer rain.

I can see you now Sadie. No. I don't like this Mission Hall either. We'll never work here again. We'll tell Mam and Dad about it.

'Go on, Stella,' urged Milton. He saw the vague, distant look in her eyes. 'Are you feeling okay?' She gave a single nod, but wasn't really aware she had. Her enthusiastic reception was starting to wane, and in certain corners slow hand-clapping could be heard.

Sadie and Stella were watching Pop shelling shrimps and digging deep into his endless pockets for green arrows. And there was Mrs Bunting: what was she doing at the market? Probably shopping for her husband's tea.

The picture blurred and changed.

Stella, Sadie, and Tommy were climbing into a tram, cursing their luck at not winning the competition. Then they were hunched over a local paper, reading about themselves; broad smiles across their confident, young faces.

To London – a small, dingy flat.

Stop crying, Sadie. He'll wait for you. He'll always wait for you. Think of the act – of our partnership.

Billy Manners was right, poor little Sadie. SADIE DEATH. Why did you have to be right, Billy?

And now Stella could see her name towering above her in

209

bright lights but it was worthless. Sadie was lying cold on a slab in the mortuary, never again to smile, walk, run, sing, eat – oh, and how she could eat.

I'm going to marry him, you said. And you did. And now you're dead, Sadie Ravenscroft. You're dead. You're . . .

'Please get out there,' begged Milton. She fluttered her eyes as though awaking from a deep sleep. Milton saw she was coming round, though he hadn't a clue what from. 'Good girl,' he encouraged. 'Go on out there and shine for them.'

With a helpful shove from him she lunged forward. There was an explosion of pure joy from the audience. It was like a lull in a football match, broken by an unexpected goal by the home side.

'So how are you all doing, out there?' she bellowed, through a big, warm smile and authoritative stance. Loud cheers came back at her. 'That's nice to know. Sorry I was so late getting here, but the manager stopped me for wearing too many clothes.' Big laughter. 'I wouldn't have minded, but I was undressed at the time.' Bigger laughter.

Henry fumbled for a cigar and discovered that his hands were uncontrollably shaking. He took himself out into the corridor and enjoyed a quiet smoke while listening to muffled applause and laughter. Mike and Bernard remained, eyes transfixed to the stage.

Stella hadn't suddenly and miraculously recovered from the shock of losing her sister; she had simply, with Milton's help, found out just how professional an artiste she could be. She was scarred for life with wounds that would never really heal, but Stella, being Stella, would learn to cope and manage to make the most of her life.

She knew, already, that life was full of suffering; she just hadn't estimated receiving so much in such a short period of time.

The one-week run at the Windmill Theatre was a huge success, and after the opening night – the Royal Night – no-one asked her where she'd been hiding herself. It was no longer of any importance.

EPILOGUE

Supported by a gardening hoe, Stella held her face against the gentle August breeze. She loved her Jersey home and garden at this time of year, when nature had reached its potential and was ready to concede to the slumbers of approaching winter. It was grander, more idyllic than the home they'd had in Kent.

Her eyes caught dotted sailing boats, quivering carelessly on the shallow rocky waters beneath her cliffs. It was a tranquil, heavenly position to live in, overlooking St Peter's and beyond. How her weatherbeaten body thrived on the embracing walks and clean air this small but glorious island offered.

A seagull squawked its arrival just above her head. It was one she knew very well. She'd fed him with stale bread and, knowing he was on to a good thing, he made a point of returning every afternoon with uncanny punctuality.

She pulled a small crust from out of her garden apron and held it aloft for him. The bird swooped, collected it firmly in his beak, and, with a departing cry that could have been interpreted as being a thank-you, floated northwards to the secret place whence he always mysteriously came.

'Miss Stella,' said an elderly lady, hobbling down the garden path towards her.

'What's up, Annie?' she asked, loudly, as Annie's hearing wasn't very good these days.

'You've a telegram from Mr Bernard. I hope it's to say he's coming to your party tonight.'

'So do I,' she said, with feeling. 'It's not every year that I'm fifty.'

She opened it and read it aloud: ANGEL STOP WILL BE BACK IN LONDON ON BOAC FLIGHT BC 136A ARRIVAL 18.30 STOP HAVE ARRANGED CONNECTION STOP SEE YOU TONIGHT STOP B STOP

Bernard was getting too old to fly backwards and forwards to the United States to check on his property company. His manager – John Hammond – was more than capable of running things. But Bernard had had his fingers burnt so many times in the past that he considered any one younger than himself as untrustworthy, even poor John Hammond, who was probably the most trustworthy person he'd ever known.

A distant expression formed on Stella's face. It wasn't often that she thought about her dead sister – that is, not to the extent of dwelling upon the loss – but she did just at that moment. Maybe it was because she was fifty that day, and if Sadie was alive she'd have been at the party to celebrate the event. She would have been forty-eight, and would have teased her that she was old and past it now that she'd reached fifty.

But there would be no Sadie there nor, indeed, her mother and father, who had both passed away in recent years. She found it strange how capable the human mind was at dealing with the deaths of close ones. She loved and missed them – just as she did the late Henry Charles in a totally different way – yet now she even had trouble sometimes remembering certain features about them, and this frustrated and annoyed her and made her feel guilty, as if perhaps she didn't really care. But Bernard was quite right in saying, time plays strange tricks on the memory. But there was one memory that was crystal-clear. It was the day after Sadie's funeral, when her mother confessed to having been the one who broke up the sister's partnership. Stella had, at first, misunderstood her, saying, 'Don't blame yourself, Mam.' But then she went on to explain in full how it hadn't been Tommy pressurising Sadie – although, she couldn't deny, he did do a fair bit of that. And it

212

wasn't Sadie's own spontaneous decision when she'd reached London that fateful day to announce the split. Sadie deliberately blamed herself because she was a kind girl like that, not wanting others to suffer unnecessarily. But no, it had been Lilly Ravenscroft – their own mother – who had instructed her to finish it all with Stella and settle down in Lancaster with Tommy.

Sadie had refused point-blank, stating that Stella and she were inseparable. So her mother threatened to disown her, never to allow Tommy or her into the home again if she didn't do exactly as she said. She knew Sadie was softer and weaker than Stella, and that the threat wouldn't be received lightly. And she was right.

How Stella had cried when her mother had told her this, for it made their squabble all the more futile. 'If I'd known at the time, I would never have stopped loving her,' she told her mother. 'You realise you broke Sadie and I up as sisters as well as partners? Does that make you feel proud?' Stella had seen her mother cry for the first time.

With the passing of time, Stella found herself forgiving her mother for what she had done. On reflection, she considered it rather brave of her to confess to it all, for she must have known what her daughter's reaction was going to be.

Entertaining the troops with ENSA during the war years had played a big part in Stella's change of attitude to her mother. The war, and seeing the conditions that men lived and died in, made her mature as a person. And then there was Tommy Moran. How dashing and fine he looked in his uniform. And how ironic that after the war he should have married a wartime widow called Molly Chadwick – the girl who was reputed to have stolen a kiss off him by the tobacconist's on the corner of Penny Street.

But today was her birthday, and other than the thrill of now knowing that Bernard could make the party was that of knowing that their daughter, Emma, could also make it. It was over two months since they'd last seen her, but that was to be expected: the three of them had agreed that finishing school in Switzerland was by far the best thing for her – in spite of Emma's desire to get into acting school as soon as was feasibly possible.

She was tall and attractive, and with Stella pushing her every inch of the way, she would make it in the business – if, at the end of the day, that was what she was really seeking. There were times when her mother wasn't so sure; times when she behaved as whimsically as her father could. One minute a ball of total commitment and enthusiasm, the next a hesitant, uncertain shadow of their former selves. Stella couldn't understand it. What she'd ever wanted in life she'd driven herself to achieve. Perhaps there wasn't the motivation for kids these days. Perhaps life was too easy. One thing she hoped, was that her daughter wouldn't bring any of her Beatles' records home and spoil the island's tranquillity.

'How many will be coming, all told, Annie?' she asked. Annie screwed up her face.

'I've forgotten, exactly, but I think it's about forty-something.'

She put an arm around Annie's shoulder and smiled. 'Let's go and check the name tabs. It's good fun mixing them up and putting people together who you know don't get on very well.'

'Ooh, Miss Stella,' sniggered Annie behind her hand, really thinking it a wonderful idea.

As they drifted back to the house another seagull floated on to the lawn. She didn't see him as he looked blankly around for food. He would have to wait until tomorrow afternoon before having a free meal off Stella Raven.